# Sunsets Behind Us II —

# Somewhen

## PD MCNULTY

This novel is entirely a work of fiction. Names, characters, places, and incidents portrayed within it are products of the author's imagination or are used fictitiously and are not to be construed as real. Any resemblance to actual events, locales, organizations, or persons, living or dead, is entirely coincidental and not intended by the author.

SOMEWHEN

(SUNSETS BEHIND US, BOOK 2)

Published by GuideDaddy Enterprises, LLC

# Dedication

To Momma, for every memory you gave and give me. For raising me exactly the way I needed to be raised. And again, for promising never to read my books. Any of them. Not even a page. Not a sentence. Okay, you can read the titles but don't ask any questions. I love you forever, Momma.

To Dad, for being my engineer, building most of who I am today. My Marine Corps Senior Drill Instructor told me I was perfect raw material for the Corps, and to me it was a given that you mined every ounce of that raw material and built me from it. I love you forever, and I miss you, Dad.

To my sister, Kathy, for never flinching in the face of hardship and showing me how to fight. I wouldn't still be here today without your example. I love and miss you, Sis.

To my brother, Tim, for taking this Marine and making me a better, stronger man. Your influence was important to me. I love and miss you, Bro.

To my brother, Kevin, for being my childhood idol. I wanted to be like you so bad that falling short actually made me better, stronger. I love you, Bro.

To my sister, Joan, for being so resilient in the face of hardship. You carry great weight like a beast, and I admire the mind that refuses to bend under pressure. I love you, Sis.

To my Little Bro-Man, Tony, for choosing me. I sometimes feel as though we're intertwined in ways we don't even understand, and I can't thank you and Sanny enough for the support you've always offered. I love you, Bro.

To my boys. For, for, for, for. For being my most precious memories of the past and my most desperate hopes for the future. I'm sorry. I love you both more than absolutely anything in this life.

And I dedicate this second book to the Readers. You validate my craft and me. Thank you for the confidence you give me. It is an honor to create art that resonates with you.

And again, to my Publishing Team, all of you. From editing to cover art to layout to *every* team, thank you for working with me so hard and so well. It is a pleasure and an honor working with you. Look at this... *we* did this. And there's much more to this story after book two, one step at a time. Left foot, right foot...

# PLAYLIST

- Chapter Six: *Brujeria* – "Things That Make You Go Hmmmm…." by C+C Music Factory

- Chapter Thirteen: Mission Accomplished – "No Ordinary Love" by Sade

- Chapter Thirteen: Mission Accomplished – "Justify My Love" by Madonna

- Chapter Twelve: Mission Accomplished – "Realize" by Colbie Caillat

- Chapter Thirteen: Mission Accomplished – "Fallin' for You" by Colbie Caillat

- Chapter Nineteen: Stomping Grounds – "Steal Away" by Robbie Duprie

- Chapter Nineteen: Stomping Grounds – "Today Was a Fairytale" by Taylor Swift

- Chapter Twenty-One: Same Story, Different Decade – "I Don't Want to Know" by Mario Winans, feat. P. Diddy

- Chapter Twenty-Two: Odyssey – "When a Man Loves a Woman" by Percy Sledge

- Chapter Thirty-One: Juice Boxes and Shoe Boxes – "The Lazy Song" by Bruno Mars

- Chapter Thirty-One: Juice Boxes and Shoe Boxes – "I Love Rock 'n' Roll" by Joan Jett and the Blackhearts

- Chapter Thirty-Five: Galaxy S II – "Just a Dream" by Nellie
- Chapter Forty-Three: The Heist – "Back to the Hotel" by N2Deep
- Chapter Forty-Three: The Heist – "Birthday Cake" by Rhianna
- Chapter Forty-Four: Birthday Cake – "Birthday Sex" by Jeremih
- Chapter Forty-Four: Birthday Cake – "In Da Club" by 50 Cent
- Chapter Forty-Nine: Invitation Only – "Rumor Has It" by Adele
- Chapter Fifty-Four: Impasse – "Diary" by Alicia Keys
- Chapter Fifty-Five: Bend – "Iron Man" by Black Sabbath

# Contents


Dedication .................................................................iii

PLAYLIST ...................................................................v

Preface ......................................................................x

PART I: MACROCOSM .....................................................1

Chapter One: Shots Fired ...............................................2

Chapter Two: Reflection ................................................8

Chapter Three: Kay .....................................................12

Chapter Four: Echoes...................................................21

Chapter Five: Bizarre..................................................24

Chapter Six: *Brujeria* ................................................33

Chapter Seven: Lee .....................................................40

Chapter Eight: Ronny ..................................................48

Chapter Nine: The Inevitable Tiptoe Toward Paranoia ...............57

Chapter Ten: Backtrack ................................................66

Chapter Eleven: Jailbreak .............................................72

Chapter Twelve: My Mistake ..........................................78

Chapter Thirteen: Mission Accomplished..........................84

Chapter Fourteen: The Drunken Barn Dance, Revisited.............91

Chapter Fifteen: Intel Collection ....................................97

Chapter Sixteen: Logan-Gate ........................................101

Chapter Seventeen: The Secret ......................................107

Chapter Eighteen: The Region Beta Paradox.......................112

Chapter Nineteen: Stomping Grounds .............................119

Chapter Twenty: Study Buddies.....................................124

Chapter Twenty-One: Same Story, Different Decade................131

Chapter Twenty-Two: Odyssey ......................................133

Chapter Twenty-Three: The First Casualty .........................143

Chapter Twenty-Four: Week Two....................................148

Chapter Twenty-Five: Little Boys and Their Daddies................154

Chapter Twenty-Six: *El Quiere Taco Bell* ..........................163

Chapter Twenty-Seven: Claddagh....................................168

Chapter Twenty-Eight: Thanksgiving ...............................173

Chapter Twenty-Nine: *Xenia* ........................................181

Chapter Thirty: Telepathy ...................................................... 188
Chapter Thirty-One: Juice Boxes and Shoe Boxes ...................... 191
Chapter Thirty-Two: Little-Man Mantra ................................... 198
Chapter Thirty-Three: *Muy Mal* ........................................... 205
Chapter Thirty-Four: Lesson Learned ..................................... 210
Chapter Thirty-Five: Galaxy S II ........................................... 215
PART II: MICROCOSM ........................................................ 222
Chapter Thirty-Six: Q&A .................................................... 223
Chapter Thirty-Seven: Sonar ............................................... 225
Chapter Thirty-Eight: Walter ............................................... 229
Chapter Thirty-Nine: ROBIN I .............................................. 234
Chapter Forty: Operation 40 Candles ..................................... 243
Chapter Forty-One: The Pledge ........................................... 250
Chapter Forty-Two: Spoiler Alert .......................................... 257
Chapter Forty-Three: Heist ................................................. 261
Chapter Forty-Four: Birthday Cake ........................................ 266
Chapter Forty-Five: Mrs. Osorio ........................................... 271
Chapter Forty-Six: Doublespeak ........................................... 278
Chapter Forty-Seven: You Two ............................................. 283
Chapter Forty-Eight: Challenges ........................................... 289
Chapter Forty-Nine: Invitation Only ....................................... 297
Chapter Fifty: Games ........................................................ 302
Chapter Fifty-One: Rumors .................................................. 309
Chapter Fifty-Two: A Blessing and A Curse .............................. 313
Chapter Fifty-Three: Damage Control ..................................... 316
Chapter Fifty-Four: Impasse ................................................ 322
Chapter Fifty-Five: Bend .................................................... 328
Chapter Fifty-Six: The Assumptive Close ................................. 331
Chapter Fifty-Seven: My Way ............................................... 338
Chapter Fifty-Eight: Seeing Red ........................................... 345
Chapter Fifty-Nine: Howl at the Moon .................................... 352
Chapter Sixty: Steal Away .................................................. 358
Chapter Sixty-One: To Boldly Go........................................... 362
Chapter Sixty-Two: A Different Kind of Ring.............................. 368

Chapter Sixty-Three: No Easy Way Out ........................................ 372
Epilogue: The Dani Project, Revisited ........................................ 379
About The Author ........................................ 383
Author Contacts ........................................ 384

# Preface

Well, Cal and I are at it again. He's not bad at this story-telling stuff, huh? And when we started writing this book, he told me that anyone who comes back for *Sunsets Behind Us*, Book Two: *Somewhen* must have enjoyed Book One: *The Taboo Prophecy*. That thought had never occurred to me before, but when he pointed it out, I found comfort in it.

Cal's doing the storytelling... but *I'm* doing the writing. It's his name in the story... but it's *my* name on the spine of the book. I'm just the writer, but publishing a book series can make a new author feel very exposed and vulnerable. I mean, sure, people have seemed to enjoy my writing from the time I was a kid, and yes, I had college professors who thought they'd see my books in bookstores someday (there was no *Amazon* back then, and one creative writing professor even said she was sure I'd be on the Best-Seller wall someday). But publishing Book One still felt risky for me.

Now, though, with Cal's insightful thought that anyone reading Book Two must have enjoyed Book One... well, it's empowering. Since he said it, I don't feel so self-conscious or *tight* with my writing, and so I think you'll agree that Book Two is the better book of the first two in this trilogy. It is freer. I feel like I can just trust my instinct at the keyboard, now, and I'm less haunted by the spirit of the Jaded Reader who only reads books to tear them apart, chapter-by-chapter, character-by-character, plot-point-by-plot-point, phrase-by-phrase, punctuation-by-punctuation. That probably comes across as kind of extreme, but it is a real thing... at least in the minds of some writers (like me).

I can recall many times when I was in the middle of writing or revising a chapter of Book One and feeling like I was really getting after it, *really nailing it*... until that image of the Jaded Reader would flash in my head. Then I would slow down. Then I'd pause. And then, sometimes, out of being intimidated, I would leave my laptop and find something to distract myself. Because the insecurities many newly published writers harbor start small and then grow and grow exponentially as they feast upon the writer's self-doubt.

So I have to thank you, Reader. You came back. You trusted us to pick you up where we left you at the end of *The Taboo Prophecy* and set you back down in a comfortable spot with *Somewhen* in your hand or on your device. And by coming back, you give me confidence and strength to revise Book Three: *Chaos & the Garden* with what Cal would call supreme confidence. I know now that the spirit of the Jaded Reader does not exist and, therefore, cannot shred my writing. And just as I know you trust me, now *I* trust me.

I wouldn't be deserving of your trust, though, if I didn't share with you the list of potential triggers that Cal and I came up with. These potential triggers are not new since *The Taboo Prophecy*, but we might just spare someone distress if we share the concerning terms again. So here you go: foul language, divorce, assault, death, age-gap, taboo, rumors, cheating, adultery, grooming, child abuse, statutory rape, and maybe even murder. I say "maybe," not because it's not in Cal's story, but because we'll have to see if Cal wants to tell us about it when we get there. Or will he say nothing, let it go, let us just coast right past it, and let it be forgotten?

Not all of these potential triggers are found in every book, but across the series, all of these elements will probably arise. If these are elements that might cause you any concern, Reader, we encourage you to use your best judgment about reading further.

So you've already taken a bite of that apple, huh? *What apple?* You know exactly *what* apple. The apple you're not supposed to take a bite from. The one from that tree. You know, the *forbidden* tree? You took a bite of that apple, and now you know everything Cal had to tell in Book One. You've had a taste of how dicey things will get. You know about the extreme language, about the taboo, the cheating, the barely 'R' rating that some scenes have had, and some will yet have. Well, if you liked that first bite – and I know you did because you're back, lol – then you're going to *love* this next bite. There is a great deal to digest in the following pages. So I'm driving, you're riding shotgun and fastening your seatbelt, and Cal is in the backseat telling me where to go and how to drive. Let's get back on the road. This is gonna be a trip.

# PART I:

# MACROCOSM

*"The macrocosm is in its entirety in the body. The body is in its entirety in the heart. Therefore, heart is the summarized form of all the macrocosm."*

– Ramana Maharshi, Guru

# Chapter One:
# Shots Fired

*March 15, 2012*

*Welles County Courthouse*

*Danverston, Illinois*

"*Okay*, I'm sorry to interrupt the two of you," Hathcock sarcastically interjected. She wasn't sorry to interrupt us. "Before we go any further, Mr. Callahan, we have some basic business to attend to. With your permission, we'll be audio recording the meeting from this point on. Do you have any objections to the Illinois State Police and Welles County State's Attorney's office audio recording this meeting, Mr. Callahan?"

I shook my head no.

"Good. Then we'll proceed. I'm going to start the recording and ask you again if you are okay with being recorded for the record. From this point on, *right this moment*, please do not simply nod or shake your head as part of our discussion – we will need to *hear* your statements on the recording. *Every* answer, *every* word." I nodded. She gave me a stern look, pressed "Record" on the audio device, and the reels began turning.

As I had been small-talking with Cruz and as Hathcock had been informing me of the general procedure of the interrogation, I was taking inventory of these two. Hathcock looked several years younger than her actual age of 35-years-old, which says a lot for a state police detective. She was pretty, fair-skinned, and upon meeting her outside the conference room, the very first thing I noticed was that she had eyes the exact same color as mine, a very light green.

For just a moment, it had caught me off-guard, as I'd never seen my eye color on someone else before, other than my boy, Lee.

Hathcock stood about my height – 5'10" – and had a lean, athletic frame. She wore black slacks, a light green blouse, an evergreen sports jacket, and comfortable-looking black leather shoes. I supposed she often wore green, as I did, because it made those eyes *pop*. I caught myself wondering what other colors she might be wearing in the coming weeks, with spring just around the corner.

As I was wearing long sleeves, I pinched the hairless side of my right forearm, hard... a trick I use whenever I catch my mind wandering off track. It almost always snaps me right back into focus. I never pinch my left forearm, of course, because I wouldn't feel it – my left side is permanently nerve-damaged from a training accident in the Marines. No sensation of pain, no tickles, no extreme heat or cold. Just numb.

Hathcock had autumn red hair pulled back tightly into a Marine Corps-style bun, and I mused that her hair color probably did a better job of bringing out her eyes than my own dark brown hair did. She had probably assumed that the hair bun was what gave away her Marine Corps background, though that would be an incorrect assumption. It also wasn't the surname she shared with U.S. Marine Carlos Hathcock, one of the deadliest snipers in history. What Hathcock couldn't have known was that I had a friend named Rocky McGinty who used to manage the marketing department of my brother Ron's businesses. Remember him? The man who could get whatever you needed, as fast as you needed, for the right price, Black Friday or Black Market?

*Information*, for example. Rocky was the one who had acquired the personal information on the bartender/pick-up artist Lilith fucked around with in Miami Beach. After speaking with Detective Hathcock on the phone the day before, there was no way I was going to walk into this interrogation blind. I had called Rocky to enlist his services and expertise. I spoke with Rocky again an hour before this interrogation, and he told me all about Illinois State Police Special Investigator Detective Janine Hathcock.

I hadn't mentioned to Selena that I was contacting Rocky, mostly just because I wanted to keep my mind focused on this interrogation, on what I had to do. I didn't want to get caught up in the full explanation of who Rocky was and why I was contacting him. Whether or not Selena remembered, she already knew a little about Rocky from the story about his involvement in Lilith's Florida Fling, but it was just simpler not to bring it up until after the interrogation. I hoped she wouldn't be upset when I'd tell her about it later.

I hadn't asked Rocky anything about Cruz, though, as

Hathcock hadn't mentioned him the day before on the phone. Didn't matter... it seemed I had already learned everything I needed to know about him. Hathcock would be running this interrogation, and Cruz would follow her lead, adding in his two cents here or there, wherever he could. He was probably ten years younger than me, about six feet tall, and athletically built in what I'd now call a CrossFit kind of way (which was impressive). He dressed and groomed like a pretty boy: dark brown slacks, a powder blue button shirt, a Navy blue sports jacket, dark brown silk tie, and expensive but uncomfortable-looking brown leather dress shoes. I guessed his clothes were name-brand, but if they were, I'd never know it. My brand knowledge stopped with my Puma cross-trainers.

Cruz's hair was almost black, gelled and neatly slicked back. He sported smiling, dark brown eyes and a squared jawline. He was an attractive dude. I thought the ladies probably found him to be a sharp-looking motherfucker until they got a taste of his energy. I couldn't decide if he was a touch awkward or just not quite the stud he appeared to be. I sensed that I had already made him somewhat self-conscious, recognizing that I knew too much about his partner and probably wondering what I knew about *him*. Once the tape recorder had started, Hathcock hit me with a curve ball.

"Mr. Liam Connell Callahan, we must inform you of your Miranda rights here today. As I'm sure you are aware, this is an investigation into a suspected crime or crimes, and as such, this recording *could* be admissible in court, *should* we find ourselves there. Please be assured you are *not* under arrest at this time. You're familiar with your Miranda rights, correct?"

"I am," I nodded, completely masking my surprise at being Mirandized. It meant that I was *officially a suspect* in a crime or crimes. This was indeed about to be a court-admissible interrogation, and it occurred to me for the first and only time that I was without a lawyer. Once I talked to Hathcock on the phone the day before and slipped into supreme confidence mode, I was prepared to take on all challengers and challenges, and seeking outside help had never entered my mind. Now, though I knew I still had time to halt all this, to protect myself by retaining an attorney, the thought slipped out of my mind as quickly as it had entered. It was just them and me, now, facing off, and the bell to round one had rung the moment I saw my neighbor exit the conference room. Shots fired, rounds coming down range.

"Good. Mr. Callahan, you have the right to remain silent. Anything you say can and will be used against you in a court of law. You have the right to speak to an attorney and to have an attorney present during any questioning. If you cannot afford an attorney, one will be appointed to you at government expense. Do you understand these rights as I have explained them to you?"

"Yes, I do."

"Excellent. So, then, let's recap some of what we talked

about before the recording began..." and they went on to officially pose the questions they'd already asked, and I answered exactly as I had already answered. That brought us into new territory – the interrogation, proper.

# Chapter Two:
# Reflection

*Present Day - Chicagoland, Illinois*

Well, welcome back, Reader. I must admit – I wasn't one hundred percent convinced that I'd *be* back after Book One. It took me quite a lot of soul-searching before I could convince myself to sit down here and continue what we've begun. This psychological project of writing about my past has already helped me to identify issues and valuable lessons that I didn't know I needed to uncover. It took some time, but eventually, I realized that these discoveries are worth the hardship of revisiting my past here. And so I now plan to continue on this journey until it is complete, wherever it takes us, despite whatever doubts or fears confront me along the way. Thank you in advance for choosing to join me again. It helps to have someone along with me for the ride. Dani says hi, by the way.

As I tend to do from time to time, I'm reflecting on all I've already shared, everything you already know about my life through the 1990s, 2000s, and especially November 2011. You've met people... Dani, my current Department of Veterans Affairs mental health therapist, who prescribed this exercise of writing out my past in order to identify the hidden issues and lessons that might help bring me Peace. My wife of almost 12 years, Lily. My young boys, Lee and Ronny. The likable but somewhat mysterious Mr. Mirai. The confident, demanding 18-year-old former student of mine,

Selena Osorio (yeah, I thought that description of her might make you smile). And you know some of my memories, too... the years I spent running my brother Ron's businesses. CSI: Miami Beach. The Drunken Barn Dance. The loss of my father. Q+0, the night of the Question. And, of course, the inevitable minor heartbreak that concluded what I can now call Book One.

I suppose that, since I'm doing my best to be completely honest with this, I must admit that I didn't conclude the last book where I did simply because it was a convenient place to stop. I wasn't thinking about the story structure, or about stopping with any kind of cliffhanger, or really about anything at all. No, I didn't have that kind of luxury. I ended it exactly where I did because it hurt too much to keep going. Let me briefly explain, but I don't want to make too much of this.

Reader, you've probably already figured this out, but you're dealing with two different guys narrating this story. First, you're seeing the story through 39-year-old Cal's mind in the moment, back in 2011. You're in *his* head, the me that I was *then*. You're reading *his* perception of what was going on. In the case of Selena Osorio, I had only been aware of my feelings for her for like five days, Sunday through Thursday, Q+0 through Q+4. So for *that* me, my own sexual failure and the end of our little arrangement wasn't a monumental blow, but it hurt. It wasn't a serious heartbreak, but it was one.

Keep in mind, though, that you're also hearing this story

from 52-year-old me today, which includes the dozen-plus years since November 2011. So for *me*, today, reliving the loss of Selena Osorio on Q+4 packs a fucking wallop. It set a long, wild sequence of events into motion that changed my life forever, and now, looking back... eh, it's difficult to think about all this. So anyway, I finished the last book where I did because reliving that experience for the first time since 2011, breath-by-breath, hurt enough to make me end the book right there. That's all I want to say about that.

Writing what is now Book One, revisiting all those people and places and memories... it just wore my ass out, cut-and-dry. But Dani recently texted me. She said it was time to get back to work, time to go in and talk with her again and pick up where we left off, time to continue the labor of writing out the story of my life in 2011-2012. She knows how difficult this task is for me and what it means for me to pick up this burden again and shoulder it. But she also knows the value of it, and she's right, we have work to do. I've never backed down from what needs to be done, and I'm blessed with the shoulders to carry any load.

For as long as I can remember in my adult life when I would call to talk to my parents, my dad would pick up the phone and say the same thing, the same way, every time: "How's she cuttin', me boy?" It was just a routine we'd somehow developed over the years, a make-believe conversation between two Irishmen out in the bog, cutting the turf for fuel or to sell on the streets of Castleisland,

County Kerry, Ireland.

"How's she cuttin', me boy?" he'd call over the phone line.

"Oh, she's cuttin' away," was my line in my bullshit excuse for an Irish brogue. We'd both laugh like it was the first time we'd ever had that exchange, and then we'd talk away for an hour or so about football, boxing, and everything mixed martial arts.

My father didn't build me to be a Narrowback. My father witnessed what I've survived in recent years, and if that man was still alive today – and if he knew how I'm trying to heal myself from the past – he would tell me to get off my arse and get to cutting away. And I would get off my arse and get to cutting away. So that's what I'm doing.

# Chapter Three:
## Kay

On Q+4, that all-important night that ended what had barely begun with Selena Osorio, my attempt at coping reminded me of something that happened with a girl over the summer of 1990, after I had graduated high school on June 2, and before I left for Marine Corps Boot Camp on October 1.

The girl's name was Kacey, but I called her Kay. You might want to remember the name because she wasn't just some girl, and I'm pretty sure she'll come up again somewhere down the road here. She was tall, athletic and beautiful, seasonally bronze-tanned, with golden blonde hair and deep blue eyes. Kay and I met at a graduation party for a common friend after my junior year, and she quickly became my female best friend during my senior year of high school (her junior year). We went to my senior Homecoming together as friends and sang together in the fall Variety Show '89.

One summer night in June 1990, she and I went to get ice cream, and afterward, as we sat in her parents' driveway in the full-size luxury van I typically drove (it technically belonged to my parents), she turned the topic of conversation from plans for our respective futures to feelings. She was single at the time, but she knew that I was in two totally uncommitted, non-exclusive, summer-fun relationships... one with a beautiful, little strawberry-blonde girl named Lori from Buffalo Grove, and one with a beautiful brunette who was in the same class as Kay, named Emma, who I had dated for a few months my senior year. And then, I guess I was also talking to my long-time high school girlfriend Julie again, and it seemed like that might be fun for the summer (and who knew where *that* might go?). I can't really say that I was over Jules at the time, but-...

"Cal, can I talk to you? I mean, not about Life and the future and everything, like we do, but I mean, really *talk* to you?"

She seemed nervous, and I hoped everything was alright. She was the sweetest, most innocent person I'd ever met – still is to this day – and I never wanted anyone or anything to cause her any harm or hardship. I already loved her, in my own way, though I'd never have admitted it to anyone.

"Yeah, of course."

"Do you ever get lonely?" she asked. I was totally taken off-guard by this, and I asked what she meant. "Like, when you're by yourself, and you're not in a relationship, do you ever just wish, like, someone was *there*? Like, that you had someone to just be *with*, someone you could *trust*, but *not* someone who was your girlfriend?"

Funny enough, I knew *exactly* what she meant, and I thought about joking that *that* was why I was seeing those two girls, but she was serious, and it seemed like a bad time to be a smartass. On a deeper level, though, I really *did* know what she meant. I *did* get that kind of lonely from time to time, even with the other two girls and flirting around with the third.

"Yeah, I do," I replied. "I know what you mean. When you're an emotional person, like you and me, someone who kind of lives in your own heart, it gets really hard when you have no one to be close to, to share a little of it with." I knew Kay hadn't been talking about sex... she was truly innocent, and I knew it. But she was emotional and a lover, like me.

"Do you ever... like, *think* about me?" she asked. I didn't see that coming, either.

She and I had been extremely close friends for a year, and capital 'T' Truth be told, I *had* even had feelings for her. I'd had feelings for her when we had gone to Homecoming together, and I was on Homecoming Court. There was a dance where the Court all danced with our Court partners, and that's when it hit me that I'd rather be dancing with my date, Kay. Then I realized I had feelings for her. But I never felt like she had any feelings for me.

"Yes, I've thought about you... like... about *us*."

The next thing we knew, my female best friend and I were kissing in my front seat in her parents' driveway. But that was where it stopped with Kay, and I knew it. We wouldn't be making any trips to the fold-out bed in the back of Cal's party van. She liked kissing, holding hands, and holding each other, but there was no sexual touching or anything else with her. She and I had never talked about that – I had heard all about this from other guys who had dated her and tried to score. They all tried to hit me up for the playbook on how to get with her, but I'd honestly maintain that she and I weren't like that... or, rather, that *she* wasn't like that. Everybody knew *I* was like that.

She would be going into her senior year after that summer, and she was as pure as it gets. But kissing was nice on this runaway pre-Marine Corps summer. Spending *any* kind of time doing *anything* with Kay was nice on that runaway pre-Marine Corps summer. But kissing was best. I mean... that was as far as I was going to get with Kay, so yeah, kissing was best.

We talked about it... about *us*, that is. We agreed that we were not exclusive; we were just there for each other when we got lonely, and no one needed to know. We could talk, cuddle, and kiss whenever we felt like it – *but* – if either of us started a committed relationship, we would end it, no questions asked, no hurt feelings.

Which was cool for a couple of weeks. Until there was a small gathering at a mutual friend's house where we were watching *Bloodsport* with Jean-Claude Van Damme. She and I were sitting on opposite ends of the room, and *I assumed* it was to make sure no one caught-on to anything out of the ordinary between us. Then, from across the room, she started making a big deal about how hot

Van Damme was and how built he was. And she was overdoing it, as though she was trying to make sure I could hear her, as though she was trying to make me jealous. At least, that was my perception.

I kind of thought it was funny, except that I didn't. In those days, I was unaware that my upbringing had left me with a severe self-confidence issue that showed up just about everywhere except on athletic fields.

Then I heard her loudly start telling the other girls about this guy that she had just started dating exclusively, some guy a couple of years older who drove a red Corvette. I couldn't believe what I was hearing. She hadn't honored our agreement and told *me* about this new boyfriend, and I had been thinking maybe we would end the night enjoying a little time together. Self-confidence bruised, I took my leave from the party in pretty short order, escaping out the back door, kind of in a huff. But she followed and caught me in the backyard, by the driveway.

"Cal, slow down. Are you okay?" she asked.

"Of course, Kay... I'm always good. Why wouldn't I be?"

"Well, you just rushed out so quickly. You didn't say goodbye to me, and you seem like something is wrong."

I wasn't really mad that our little thing was over. I was upset that my best friend – who had initiated our *arrangement* in the first place – had chosen to tell me it was over the way she just had. She could have and should have just told me what was up. She shouldn't have made it hurt. I was so upset, I could barely contain myself, and I couldn't articulate it, so I just raised an open palm and left her there. I knew we both knew, and that was enough for me.

There was a massive 24-hour lifestyle/workout center one town over from us, in Mt. Prospect, called The Charlie Club. It's long gone these days. I had a pass there that summer, as that was the place where I did all of my pre-Marine Boot Camp workouts, playing racquetball and running (on stormy days). I was in very good shape, more than ready for Boot. But after that happened with Kay, I immediately began two-a-days with a vengeance. Sometimes, *three*-a-days. In my mind at that time, girls could be unreliable and inconsistent, but in the brilliant words of Henry Rollins, "Two-hundred pounds is always two-hundred pounds."

I would typically work out in the early afternoon, go to work in the evenings at Little Caesars Pizza, and then work out again in the middle of the night. I remember thinking about Jean-Claude Van Damme and some built dude in a red Corvette. I made up my mind to go full tilt with my physical training for the rest of that summer, and it was probably the best thing that could have happened to me before the Marines. I lifted heavy weight hard and with intensity because I wanted to show Kay what a built, shredded body looked like. I ran three to five miles every morning, sun or storm, sleep or insomnia. Sometimes, I pushed a buddy's car around the block while he applied a bit of pressure to the brakes from time to time.

Very quickly, I started putting on more shredded muscle mass than I already had. I had always been a lean, strong, athletic kid with solid musculature from working construction sites and high school weightlifting, but by the end of that summer, I was in the best shape of my life. I became a muscular, shredded cardio machine going into Boot Camp, doing 48 clean Marine Corps pull-ups with no kip and no cheat, and running three road miles in under 18 minutes. As a freshman in high school, I was benching 220 pounds. By the end of high school, 245 pounds. By the end of that summer of 1990, 275 pounds, weighing-in at 175 pounds. I was jacked and in great cardiovascular health, literally a machine. I couldn't buy a Corvette, so I turned my body into one.

I don't think I saw Kay much or at all for those two months while I beasted-out. When she called to ask if I wanted to join her family at their property up in northern Wisconsin for ten days, I took the opportunity. I still really cared about her, I still considered her my best friend, and over those two months I had leveraged how upset I'd been for the specimen I had turned myself into. I was friends with her older brother, I had grown close with her younger sister, and I had grown very close with her parents over the past year.

So I went to their land in northern Wisconsin, and Kay

wasn't seeing that guy anymore. She made many comments about my new build, and though I wouldn't know it until much later, when I'd view the video of the trip, she started zooming the video camera in on my arms, shoulders, back, and abs. By about day two of the trip, we were lying together on the hammock. It wasn't romance – especially since her younger sister joined us on the hammock sometimes – just friendly snuggling when we were alone.

Her family later threw me a surprise going away party before I left for Boot Camp a month later, and at that party, her parents were kind enough to present me with fake adoption papers, signed by all of them (even their dog, Scout), adopting me into the family.

It probably would have meant a lot for most guys my age, going away to the Marines with the Gulf War amping up. But for me and the childhood I'd come from, well, hell, I don't think I can even *try* to explain how much it meant to me, so I won't.

I didn't know it yet, but I would pair that new body with a brain that I would only come to realize for the first time in my life in Marine Corps Boot Camp, and I would graduate as Guide, Platoon Honorman, second of 540 or so Marines. How does a kid with confidence issues go through grammar school in special education classes – watching filmstrips and playing the Memory card game part of every school day with the other so-called *dummies* – how does *that* kid become a shit hot Marine with exceptional confidence, cunning, and top intelligence test scores? That is a question we might very well consider another time.

Funny enough, Kay and I would become boyfriend/girlfriend when I graduated Boot that December, and she became the love of my life for the next five years, through the Marines, through the year-long recovery from my botched skull surgery (problems which are ongoing today, 30-plus years later), and through most of college. I considered her my soulmate, and yep, she was my girlfriend when I started studying with Lily. Kay was the relationship that ended right before my future wife knocked on my college apartment door for the first time.

Kay and I still communicate from time to time today, mostly on social media. And she's still an angel, probably the sweetest, best person I've ever known. And I still call her parents Mom and Dad, mostly on social media, even if we don't know each other the way we once did.

# Chapter Four:
# Echoes

Okay, now, back to Selena and I – November 2011. After I'd been unable to perform sexually with Selena... then her reaction, the radio silence that followed, the certainty of the fact that it was over, and the hurt I felt... after *all* that, the middle-of-the-night workout at Danverston Fitness reminded me of that summer of 1990... back when Kay hurt my feelings and my pride... except this thing with Selena had hurt my heart.

It hurt more than I would admit to myself, and I even *knew* I was distracting myself with the gym so I wouldn't have to face it. It was the old Smeagol/Gollum thing that shows up in me from time to time and that I think most of us have, whether we recognize it or not. *One pill is Trixy, one's the Trixier pill, and which is which is Trixier still.*

But I couldn't be tricked when it came to losing Selena. There was no distracting myself from the capital 'T' Truth and the hurt. And so, likewise, I needed to do something about it to help cope with what I was feeling.

Selena and I were of the past, and I was all too aware of that fact. It fucking hurt. But 200 pounds is always 200 pounds, so I went to the gym that night and tried to hurt myself *more* – a distraction, kind of like the old forearm-pinching trick, but on steroids. In a small way, I was grieving and striking out at the situation at the same time. *Picking a fight with the iron,* as I call it to this day. Still, I kept my phone close so I wouldn't miss a text, just in case Selena might happen to send one.

She *didn't* happen to send one. *All night.* Right now, as I write this, I remember how alone that felt.

In my experience, it is only when one feels *completely* alone that one comes closest to feeling how impossibly infinite and empty the universe is. At those times, simply looking up at the vast cosmos doesn't do it... looking inside at the depths of one's own heart does. And I couldn't help feeling like I was calling out echoes into those depths for a chance... a chance... a CHANCE... *a CHANCE! Goddammit, Cal! Say you'll give us a chance!*

Sorry. Rant over. I'm not even gonna lie. That did feel kind of good to let go of. Whew. That felt as though I just dropped some weight off of my shoulders. I feel lighter. Anyway...

Oddly enough, I slept well that night, if only for a couple hours. It was undoubtedly due to the energy I had burned off at the gym, but it was probably equally due to the situation surrounding my whole visit with Selena the night before, as well as the energy I had burned mulling over the whole thing. And when I laid down to sleep that night, I resolved in my mind that it was over, that the drama was done, that the silly puppy love bullshit had been fun but was finished, and that there was no more risk with which to worry myself. I would just continue to look for a divorce attorney, and eventually, that inevitable move would all work itself out, too.

Still, the next morning, I couldn't ignore that I was hurt by it all. The troubling realization that I had feelings for her, the impossible knowledge that she had had feelings for me, the building of it all inside me to the point of just starting to believe in I don't know what... to the loss of it all. It was heavier than the iron, it hurt more than my body, and I would continue to feel every inch of the depth of my solitude. So I tried to set my sights on some future love I'd find somehow, somewhere, in somewhen.

# Chapter Five:
# Bizarre

As I was walking out the door that next morning – Friday morning – I recall thinking that I must finally be getting old, as I had murdered my workout in the early morning hours, and I was already feeling the deep creep of delayed-onset muscle soreness from maybe a handful of hours earlier.

*Delayed-onset, my ass*, I thought, knowing this was going to be a painful weekend, *More like instant-onset muscle soreness*. And I had a busy weekend planned that I hoped might help distract me.

When the flip-phone buzzed in my pocket, I figured it was just Lily telling me that she was going out with some friends for drinks that evening or something regarding our plans for the weekend, as was normal for a Friday. Then, it occurred to me that it *could* be Selena. I tried to ignore that possibility, as all hope could do at that point was hurt me, and I didn't need any more of that.

*Don't start doing that to yourself, Smeagol... or Gollum, whichever you are...*

I finished some instruction at the head of the class, fielded some questions, made clarifications, held a little large-group discussion, and then walked to the back of the class to sit at my desk while students gathered their thoughts and reexamined the text for further discussion.

My desk faced the front of the class from all the way in the back, behind the students, as they faced the whiteboard at the front, opposite all those windows. It was a huge classroom and one of only two classrooms on the third floor, south exposure of the high school building. My classroom had a wall of 13 huge single-hung windows behind my desk, looking out over the attached, one-story elementary/middle school building and farmland far off into the horizon. By that time of year, those fields were all long-harvested and tilled for winter for as far as I could see. I looked around the classroom to make certain no one was creeping into my business, and then I took a quick look at my flip phone.

It was a text from Selena: *I want to see you tonight.*

My emotions went swishing around in my head for a moment, almost like dizziness, and I remember looking at the text, then looking away, taking a deep breath, and looking back at it. Yep. Still there.

*She wants to see me? She's not through with me? What is she thinking? We can't possibly keep this up! I can't see her tonight!*

But I *wanted* to, and not to rectify my shortcomings from the night before. I just wanted to see her, be together with her in whatever space we could find to make our own with whatever time we could scrap together.

*Okay, slow down, Cal. I'm getting ahead of myself.*

Of course, I *couldn't* see her that night. I had seen her Sunday night when she popped the question, Monday night when she made her argument that we should give *us* a chance, Tuesday night when we kissed, Wednesday night with the Caramel Mocha Frappe Macchiato Choco Latta Thingy, Thursday night was, well, the fucking disaster... there was no way I could make another night work.

Although I had only told Selena about it in casual conversation on Sunday before our talk, the fam and I were headed to a University of Illinois football game in Champaign/Urbana on Saturday morning. And then I would be headed straight from there up to Chicagoland to watch a UFC fight card with my little brother, Pip, at my best friend Cass's house. Reluctantly, concerned about how to respond without changing the energy, I texted to let her know I couldn't see her that night.

*Besides,* I texted, *why would you want to see me again after last night?*

*I'm sorry I didn't text or call last night,* she replied.

*I'm not talking about you not texting me,* I replied. *You know what I'm talking about.*

*Oh, LOL! Sorry! I was just really frustrated, and I was sooooo tired after all the stress of it I just went home and fell asleep after I dropped you off but the thought of not seeing you this weekend is killing me.*

She was rambling. She was usually much better at punctuation with her texts, so I could tell she was excited, and I couldn't believe it. Then, after a pause, she added: *Wait. Do you think I just wanna fuck you?*

I thought about how to answer that.

*Did you?* she texted before I could reply. *Did you think I just wanted to fuck you?*

*No,* I replied. *It's just like, who wants a guy who can't take care of business, you know? I just figured I blew it.*

*Seriously Cal! It's not like that with us. We're fine,* she texted back. *You were right. There was a lot of pressure on you, and we have time for all that. But I need to see you. I don't mean for THAT. Tonight? Please? Pretty please?*

I could see her playful smile and tilted face, batting her eyelashes. I could also see that she had calmed down, stopped rambling, and started using punctuation. This determination of hers to see me meant more to me than I probably even remember today. I guess it took me too long to reply, so another text buzzed in:

*I'll buy you a drinky-drink.*

She was talking about that crack cocaine beverage from McDonald's.

*Baby,* I replied, *Let me call you on my lunch. I'm in class right now. We can talk then, okay?*

*Okay. Fine*, she texted, *But think of a way for us to see each other, even just for a little bit. Promise?*

*I promise*, I texted, though I knew there was really no thinking to be done.

I *couldn't* see her that night or that weekend. But the thought that she wasn't done with me... *what the fuck?!* I was so happy after those texts. As I sit here typing this story, it makes me happy right now for that 2011, 39-year-old me. Though I would never have admitted this to Selena, and I never did, I must admit that on my way to the gym the night before, the thought had started whispering through my mind that maybe she really *had* just wanted to fuck me.

Maybe she had read me like an open book and decided that approaching me from an emotional angle was the most strategic move to get what she wanted. It would make sense. Maybe she had never even had feelings for me at all, instead just looking for a notch on her bedpost, like Torch and Sully.

Now, though, after these texts, I was a little ashamed that I had thought so little of her intentions. She *did* want us to have sex, of course, and so did I, but now, her texts had taken some of the pressure off. I was sure we'd work out all the physical stuff sooner rather than later. In a very strange way, though, I was almost glad things had worked out the way they did, or rather, the way they didn't.

I saw a few students side-eyeing me as I looked at my phone, and I would have bet money that the class noticed a considerably heightened energy when we began our final discussion of the text moments later. Weird situation.

Had the fight between Selena and Letty never happened... had Selena's mom never moved them out of town... had her mom never contacted me that summer to discuss the Marine Corps with Selena... had her mom never invited me to Selena's birthday party... had Lily actually woken me up on time for that party... if all of those things and others had never happened exactly the way they had happened, then this little arrangement with Selena would never have happened, either. Selena would be a student at my school, in my class, and... just wow, all the little what-ifs that *had* to happen just as they happened for *this* to be happening. It reminded me of that 1990 tune by C+C Music Factory called "Things That Make You Go Hmmmm…."

After that class was my lunch break, and although I was being observed directly after lunch by my principal, Rick Lincoln, and although I should have been preparing for that no matter how confident I was of my teaching, I instead texted Selena to see if she was available to talk. It was one of many, many times that my ability to prioritize would falter when Selena was in the mix.

*Can you talk now, Baby?* I texted, and my phone rang immediately.

"*You called me baby!*" she said happily as soon as I picked up. "*Twice!*"

"*Heeeeey, Babyyyy,*" I whispered, though I was alone and had closed my classroom door. "How did you call me so quickly? Don't you have class right now?"

"*Duh!*" she exclaimed. "Don't you think I know when your lunch period is? I used to have that lunch period, remember? I skipped class so I could hear your voice."

I found it *exceedingly weird* that I was on my lunch break from teaching at a high school she had attended the year before, 25 or so minutes away and almost across the Illinois River from a high school where she was skipping class to talk to me. *And* that the night before, she and I had been crazy close to fucking.

What. The. *Fuck.*

Just bizarre. I think every time my brain recognized weird shit like that, it just automatically clicked over to the fact that she was 18, an adult who had signed on the dotted line to offer her life to the U.S. Marine Corps, and finishing her senior year was little more than a technicality before she could hit real life. So, in that way, my brain never really focused on the high school thing... shit, in November of *my* senior year of high school, I wasn't even 18 and hadn't committed to signing for the Marines yet. She was quite a bit ahead of where I was at that same stage, and I had my shit together back then.

She wasted no time, asking directly when and where we could meet that night. My heart literally ached hearing her ask, knowing what I had to say.

I explained that I wanted to see her, too, but I absolutely *had* to stay home that night, reminding her that it was only Q+5 and detailing everything we had already crammed into that week. There was no way I could come up with another reason to give my wife about why I'd be gone from the house. It wouldn't be safe to test that.

*Why don't you tell her you're going to work out in Danverston?* she asked.

I had to end this talk quickly and put it away because there was no way I was going to risk going out to see her for another night. Besides, Lily would have known that I wasn't going to work out because I'd been complaining about my full-body muscle soreness that morning.

I explained that I had been so distraught about how things had gone the night before and how I thought we were through, so I hit the gym hard pretty late. Lily would have some serious questions if I went back to the gym after complaining about being sore that morning and telling her how hard I had hit it. I went further and reminded Selena that the next day, Saturday, November 19, I had the U of I football game with the fam and a trip to Chicago on my own. There was just a lot going on, but I'd be back in town early afternoon on Sunday, we could talk on my way up to and back from Chicago, and maybe we could work something out for Sunday evening.

"*Take me with yooouuu,*" she purred like a kitten.

I felt a slightly warm, intoxicating black magic tingle in her words, like it might feel when a *bruja* slips a little sumthin'-sumthin' into your drink and whispers just the right words to get what she wants from you.

"*Ha!* Yeah, take *you* with me to Chicago, to my *best friend's* house? Girl, you are too much," I joked back. Except Selena wasn't joking.

"Take me *with* you, Cal," she repeated. "If you *really* wanted to spend the weekend with me, you could figure out a way. Think about what it'd be like."

# Chapter Six:
## *Brujeria*

Something happened in my head just then. The potion in my drink and her spiced bit of black magic mixed with my blood and did indeed get me thinking the way she wanted me to think. Instead of arguing with Selena about this ridiculous idea of taking her to Chicago for the weekend, my brain started working out the logistics. Again, my ability to prioritize faltered because Selena was in the mix.

"Selena..." I said. "*Baby-...*"

"You're thinking about it... You *could* make it happen, couldn't you? You can make *anything* you want happen, Cal... I know that about you..."

"Baby... How could I take you? I'm headed over to Champaign-Urbana for the U of I vs. Wisconsin game. So that's like two hours east of Kent. Afterward, the fam and I are splitting up... I'm heading straight up north on I-57 to Chicagoland, and they're headed home here. There's no way to make that work."

"Yes, there is," she said, seemingly working it out in her head in real time. "Instead of going straight north on I-57, backtrack almost all the way to Danverston, instead. I could park my car out at Grand Valley High School, East of Danverston, where no one knows my car and anyone who does know it won't see it all the way out there over the weekend.

"You'll come all the way back west on Hwy. 136, but east

of the river, shoot up I-25 North. Then just shoot across Route 11 to pick me up at Grand Valley High School, and we'll head up to Chicago from there. *Together*. What would it take us, like three hours or so, to get up there?"

I was thinking about it.

"*You're thinking about iiiiit*," she sang in a sweet falsetto that really said, *I'm winning*. She had a sweet little voice on her.

"No, Baby, I'm not. It can't work," I said, still thinking it through. "I can't drive west almost all the way back to Danverston because that's the route my *wife* will be taking. Even if I kill some time in a gas station or something, Lilith and I would be traveling along the same stretch of road for almost two hours, and I'd have no idea where she would be. If they happened to see me, I'd have no way to talk myself out of why I was on that route, going totally the wrong direction. It simply can't work. I'm really sorry, Baby."

"So find a reason to leave the game early... then you'll be way ahead of them. When they get close, they'll get off I-25 on Route 10 and take it into Kent, but you'll already have exited on Route 11 to take it toward Danverston and Grand Valley High School," she said. "See? *Easy-peazy*."

She sounded so proud of herself, but I remember thinking that *nothing* was going to be easy anymore. The days of easy were gone now, and though I sensed that to be capital 'T' True, I didn't even have a clue yet what the fuck that meant. I would learn, in time.

*Damn*, I thought. *There are a couple of minor details to figure out, but that part could work. What about up in Chicagoland, though? Does she expect me to introduce her to Pip and Cass? That can't work.*

"Baby, even if we could make that part work, once we got up into Chicagoland, what're you going to do, hide out in the van? You can't meet my brother and best friend."

"Well... I've got birthday money, so we can check into a room with my cash, and I can stay there while you go watch the fights. Then just come back to the room, and we'll have the night and next day together." I thought about that. "You're thinking about iiiiiit..."

*I swear... this girl... her fearless ideas, her knowing what I'm thinking, and her honey-sweet voodoo are all going to be the end of me*, I thought. *Part* bruja *curse, part* curandera *cure...*

***

A little over an hour later, my principal's formal observation of my teaching was over. I knew I had aced it, as I had never worried about any of my professional observations. Rick asked if I wanted to stop in after school and knock out the post-observation meeting, so we did.

At the post-observation meeting, Rick praised everything about the class period, which meant a lot coming from my principal, but it meant a lot more coming from a parent with a daughter in my class for the third straight year. The admin was always very supportive of me – Principal Rick Lincoln and Superintendent Brant

Beckett (who had a son in my senior class, as well). I seriously appreciated these two men and the support they'd showered upon me from the moment they had interviewed me. When we were wrapping up our post-observation meeting, Rick had some personal remarks to share off the record.

"I gotta just say it, Cal, you seem in the highest of high spirits this week, and that's great to see. Not that you weren't before; you always have been, but this week, *wow!* Amy has even mentioned it at home. Last night at dinner, she asked if there had been a big Illinois State Lottery winning ticket left unclaimed. I asked why, and Amy goes, 'Mmmm... I dunno. If there *is*, I think Mr. C has the winning ticket. He's got something going on because he's even more enthusiastic and funny than usual.'"

Amy was Rick's daughter, my student, and Class of 2012 President. That was the same Class of 2012 for which I was the advisor, with whom I had fundraised and hosted prom as juniors and who were now seniors. It was the same Class of 2012 that Selena had been a member of when she went to my school. Amy and Selena had grown up together, and their families had known each other for probably around twenty years.

Rick didn't ask directly why I was so chipper lately, but *I* knew very well who had spiked my Kool-Aid. I just told him that I was feeling healthy. I was hitting the gym heavy again, getting stronger, taking longer and faster power walks, losing some weight, and gaining muscle. And life was good, of course. My boys made life an absolute joy. Rick said he and Amy had noticed me looking trimmer, and he was glad to hear how well things were going.

*** 

When I got out to my minivan after school, I called Selena, who had been texting me all afternoon, though my phone had been muted since my observation period. She picked up immediately.

*"I'm going with you, aren't I,"* she asked, or rather said. "You're going to make it work! You *want* to be with me. I *knew* it!"

"Of course, I *want* to see you, Baby," I assured her, as if there was any real question about that. "But I don't know about all this."

There was radio silence on the other end of the phone. I could hear her moving around a little. She shushed someone and then addressed me.

"What-... what do you mean? What do you *mean*, Cal? You're *not* taking me with you?"

I couldn't let it continue, so I busted up laughing and told her, of course, I was taking her with me. I just didn't know about all of this time we'd spent away from one another that day. She pretended like she knew I was joking, but I had heard some real panic in her voice at first.

"You aren't around other people when we talk, right?" I asked.

"Huh? *No*. No, some people just walked past. I'm alone."

"Just had to make sure we're keeping this... you know, to *ourselves*," I said.

"Don't worry about that. I got this end of it."

"I know you do," I affirmed, then changed gears. "So, not to kill the mood, but where has Homeboy been all week? Where does he think *you've* been? What are you going to tell him about tomorrow and Sunday?"

"*Don't worry about him,*" she told me bluntly, all business, and I got the sense that she had been anticipating some questions to arise about Homeboy sooner than later. Then she switched gears back on me.

"Don't think about *him*," her now high, sing-songy, playful voice insisted. "I told you. Now listen to my words... *This is about us, nobody else*. It's not about your wife, and it's not about him. No one will know, and no one will get hurt. This is *just* about us, nobody else."

*Damn*, I thought. *Her words sound hypnotic, almost like lyrics to a song. Or... words to a spell.*

I knew she was right about my wife. She wouldn't get hurt – she *couldn't* get hurt – because she didn't really give two shits about me, anyway. If she ever caught on to what we were doing, she'd just be fucking furious like nothing I'd ever seen.

I doubted the same would be true for Homeboy. That dude

might get hurt. I understood what she *really* meant, though. I got it. She meant for me to worry about my wife and for Selena to worry about Homeboy. Not that I really cared one way or another about that guy. But it seemed strange that he wasn't giving her a bitch of a time about this past week. But whatever, if she said not to worry about it, I wasn't going to. We had a ridiculous weekend planned.

The next morning, the fam and I headed to the University of Illinois vs. the University of Wisconsin football game. Since I was going to Chicagoland directly after the game, I drove my minivan and Lily drove her little gray Toyota Corolla. Lee wanted to drive with Daddy and Ronny with Mommy. It was just the way it had always been. In fact, this is probably a good time to explain how Lee came to be Daddy's boy and Ronny came to be Mommy's boy.

# Chapter Seven:
## Lee

Lee was born in 2004, and I knew he was my son from the moment my wife surprised me on video camera (yes, a big-ass, hand-held *video camera*, not a cell phone) in late 2003 to tell me we were pregnant.

All I could do was lay back sideways on the couch, rolling left and right, holding my belly, laughing and laughing out loud. It must have continued non-stop for at least ten minutes. I think it was the purest outpouring of joy I have ever had in my life, a totally blissful meltdown. It got to a point of mania where, for a moment, I was worried that I couldn't stop laughing and I couldn't breathe. The first time one has the realization that he made a person is life-changing and can never be duplicated.

All those wives' tales and other methods for discerning the sex of an unborn child throughout pregnancy flagged ours as a girl, according to every female who offered an opinion (*all* of them) ... but, alas, *Wrong answer, chicas!* My own method proved to be singularly effective: I had simply *willed* him to be my son.

I never for one breath doubted that Lee was a boy, and it was somewhat a matter of spirituality for me. If God or the Universe gave me a son, He knew what He was doing; but if the Universe gave me a daughter, either there was no Great Entity, or He had no fucking clue what He was doing. Because I only knew how to raise men. I'm not built to raise ladies. A sane God would never build *me* and then give me daughters. So I *knew* Lee was a boy. If I were a betting man, I would have gone all in on this one, and we would have been rich.

It was the happiest time ever for Lilith and me. We had spared no effort or expense to create the perfect baby's room in our new northwest suburban home. We bought a new white maple bassinet and changing table and had light beige carpet installed. I had installed a natural pine chair rail around the large, six-walled room, painting the walls white above the chair rail and beige below. I had hung new natural pine closet doors and baseboards. I had installed new vinyl thermal pane windows into the large, framed bay window that looked out on the front yard of our home, framed in natural pine.

To top it off, I had searched for, selected, and installed a pine, frosted glass door etched with a large, cartoonish stegosaurus playing with alphabet building blocks, as our theme was Baby Dinosaur. I think Lily had picked out the theme, which was light brown and sky blue, boy colors, as Lily fully trusted me that Lee was a boy. In our minds, the nursery was perfect.

It was a baby boy's room, even though we chose not to be informed of Lee's sex until he was born. Why ask when I already knew? I always gave my wife a great deal of credit for the faith and trust she placed in my intuition when it came to major decisions like the baby's room, buying and selling our homes, etc., as she allowed me to lead our mostly balanced, mildly patriarchal marriage.

As I'm being frank, my wife was involved with and loved everything about baby Lee's room, but it was mostly my influence and hard work that created it. She would dispute that fact today, but when it comes to me these days, she disputes just about everything I say for the sake of disputing me. I say it all plainly, clearly, and honestly, right or wrong, good or bad, and she'll always be the only one of the two of us with an agenda that doesn't allow for capital 'T' Truth. I hope I'm wrong about that someday.

Back to the point, the baby's room was perfect, but Lee would almost never sleep in that room. As he was born while I was running the family businesses, my wife left for work far earlier than I did every morning. And I admit that Lee had slept in our bed with me from the time he was born until about the age of two, just after we had moved down south to Kent.

I know, I know... as a responsible parent, you're not supposed to have a baby regularly sleeping in *your* bed. But... as you're probably aware by now, I'm not good with rules, and it wasn't like there was any activity in that bed between Lily and I, anyway. My wife and I had discussed all of the expert opinions about how Lee sleeping with me/us every night was not a good idea, and after Lee was about one-year-old, she applied gentle pressure for me to let him sleep in his own room.

But I never did. *Fight me*, LOL.

I'd take Lee to daycare every morning, and it was common for me to take lunch breaks from work and go look in on Lee playing with his little daycare friends for an hour. I remember pulling into the parking lot on lunch one rainy day; the sky was dark, and the lights were turning on and off again and again in Lee's daycare room. I was concerned, and when I ran to the window, I looked in to see Lee holding a hula-hoop, turning on and off the light switch, and showing the other toddlers how to do it. The childcare workers were standing together, watching and laughing hard. Lee was about eighteen-months-old. I know this because, around Lee's second birthday, we moved down south.

After work each day, I got back to town long before my wife, and I picked up Lee from daycare, took him home, and kept him within a few feet of me while I made dinner every evening. First, I kept him in a highchair. Then I kept him standing up on a chair, holding onto the backrest next to me. Then he'd sit on the counter next to me. And eventually, he'd stand next to me, waiting for me to ask him to grab this or that from the pantry. Those were some of the best days... just little man and me, joking and laughing non-stop. I can still hear his little laugh. He had stridor that first year, and it gave him a faint, kind of rough-whispery-sounding laugh and cry that you couldn't even hear from the backseat of a car.

I remember I'd be fast asleep in the morning, and when I'd

open my eyes, many, many times, there would be tiny Lee, holding himself up with a hand on either side of my head and his face maybe six or so inches from my face, eye-to-eye. He'd be holding himself up, waiting there for me to awaken, and I never knew how long he'd been waiting... minutes, hours? And when my eyes would open, I'd see my own green eyes and that adorable little face smiling into mine with mischief clear, and then he'd just start cracking up with his light, airy little stridor laugh. He was a joker from birth. God, what memories.

They tell you to cherish your children when they are little because they grow up so fucking fast. But they don't tell you that no matter how much you cherish every second of it, every little laugh, every breath, every blink, no matter how many snapshots and video clips you pack away in your heart... it won't be enough. As they grow up, you'll love every new version of them, but you'll miss those little tykes terribly for the rest of your life. You'll never see them again, except in the little moments of glints and glances that reflect those days past. Trust me, I'm a leading expert on the subject. And I'm getting choked up right now just thinking about it.

You can never go back. There are no time machines.

Perhaps a perfect example of how close Lee and I were occurred when Lee was probably around five-years-old, and Ronny was around three. By this time, we were living down south in Kent, of course. Lily and I had been checking the mail every day to see if the educational kiddie magazines had arrived that she had ordered for Lee. We were all very excited about them.

Finally, the morning came when Lee's magazines were delivered. He was jumping up and down in the playroom, right next to the front door, and Mommy was there in the doorway with us, checking the mailbox. She handed them to me, and I showed them to Lee, one at a time, telling him, "I know you can't read yet, buddy. But looking at these pictures will be fun, and then Mommy or Daddy can read the words to you and Ronny later. Maybe you can figure out the words by looking at the pictures... "You know, that whole thing.

Later that morning, I was working in my den for some time, maybe an hour or so. I realized that Lee hadn't come in to ask about any of the pictures in his magazines. He wasn't in the playroom, right across the front door from my den. I found Lily and Ronny watching TV in the sunroom, but Lily hadn't heard a peep out of Lee since those magazines had arrived. Ronny said he'd gone looking for Lee earlier, and he couldn't find him: *I think he's hiding, and I don't care.*

So, I started my own hunt for my firstborn. After checking every single *other* place on the property – including downstairs, the garage, and all around the outside of our house – I found him. He was sitting on my toilet in the master bathroom, pants down to his knees, "reading" his magazines. The toilet in the master bath had its own nook behind a privacy wall, so I had missed him on my first pass-through. I asked him why he was in *my* bathroom, on *my* toilet. He smiled as though waiting for me to ask him that.

"Look, Daddy, now I can sit on the toilet and read magazines just like you," he said, emphasizing the similarity by pointing to the magazine rack across from him.

My magazines were *Time*, *The Week*, and *Entertainment*, all of which were light reading for current events and what was happening in Pop Culture, as *Instagram and TikTok* weren't around yet, and *Facebook* – the new social media platform quickly replacing *Myspace* – wasn't nearly as diverse as it is today. I read those magazines to be well-informed as a teacher of high school students.

"I do *everything* you do," Lee said.

My heart still warms when his little voice echoes those words in my mind. I can't remember and don't care what I had for breakfast yesterday, but when I think about a million little times *just* like that with my boys, even over a dozen years ago... I'm transported *back there*. It's very much like my own little time machine. I can *see* them, *hear* them, and *be* there with them. Partially living in the past with my boys... well, it's what keeps me carrying the load in life these days, left foot, right foot, repeat. It's quite literally the single greatest reason why I've overcome so much and why I'm still alive today. But that is another story, and perhaps someday I'll find the strength to write about that, too.

Given dozens of little stories like this, it was only natural that this little boy gravitated toward his daddy. Aside from the fact that he had brown hair, very light green eyes, looked like me and that we had developed what my wife called a "telepathic" connection (*Liam, I swear you two are telepathic!*), we also just spent a great deal of one-on-one time together.

At the dinner table, it was not uncommon for us to look at each other and just burst out laughing for no reason anyone else could see, from the time he was tiny, in a highchair. My wife would get so frustrated with Lee and I being so close, but then later that same day, she'd go and say it: "Oh, he is *sooooooo* YOU." Or, "Of course he just did that... he's *you!*"

Lee was a total daddy's boy, and there was nothing that would ever change that.

# Chapter Eight:
# Ronny

Ronny was born in July 2006, just weeks before I began clinical school two days a week for a year, up in Chicago. As we had moved to Kent just a couple of months before all this, Lily's immediate and extended family members were a new, welcome, significant presence. Lily and I decided to find out our second child's sex in advance, though, in order to prepare.

But I didn't need an ultrasound to tell *me*; I knew he would be my second son. There was no question in me. Told you, I simply *willed* it.

In Ronny's first year of life, my second boy and I had very little chance to bond, as I was seldom around or available. Wednesday evenings, I tended bar at the supper club. Wednesday nights through Saturdays, I was in Chicago. Saturday nights and Sundays, I tended bar. Mondays and Tuesdays, I took my studies very seriously, locked away in our basement. With a handful of tests taken weekly in a handful of classes, by the end of the school year, I had only missed one test question total. Anatomy, physiology, kinesiology, pathology, biology, etc... they had become my passion.

Once I graduated in September 2007, a year had gone by with little interaction between Ronny and me. I always figured Ronny and I would just have to catch up after I graduated. I *so* wish

I could go back and talk to that younger me. I would never let that Cal make *that* mistake. I'd smack the sense into him if need be, but he would not make *that* mistake. *My* mistake.

Along with sharing his mom's crystal blue eyes and light auburn hair, it all makes a lot of sense that Ronny gravitated toward his mom. When I was around on a regular basis after graduating school, it was glaringly apparent that I had made a grave mistake in going to school for that year; one-year-old Ronny didn't know me and didn't want to. I had already missed much of the necessary bonding and had hurt much of the potential for our relationship.

So it wouldn't be incorrect to say that Lee and I were always tighter than Ronny and me. Parents always say they don't love one child more than another, that they don't have a favorite child, and that they're not closer to one child than another. Those are the virtuous, safe, socially correct things to say. I can't speak for other parents, and I don't pander to social correctness, but I've *never* had a favorite child, and I've *never* loved Lee more than Ronny; however, I was always admittedly closer to Lee. *Fact.* It's just the way it always was, and it would have been foolish of me to ever deny that.

After my schooling was completed, whenever I held Ronny, he just cried and cried until I put him down or Mommy – or *anybody else* – came to the rescue. If I could take back that year of school and hold it off until later, give Ronny and I a chance to bond, I would take that opportunity in a blink, no matter the consequences. Although it was the single most valuable, greatest formal education of my life, I'd go back and give it up entirely, if I could, simply to gain back that bonding time with Ronny. We never recovered from it.

And yeah, I know you know: there are no time machines.

Here's just one prime example of what I'm talking about. In August of 2011 (just a few months before Selena posed the question and made the argument that would change my life forever), I traveled to Ireland for the twelfth time in my life, very much looking forward to a visit with my parents. Just the prior December, Lily and the boys had joined me for a two-week trip to visit my Ps in Ireland, but having my parents living so far away never seemed to get any easier, so this was a trip I needed to take annually.

Several times the prior week, Lily had pulled me aside to remind me how badly the boys would probably react to my departure and absence. At the O'Hare International Departures food court, we found a place to sit and grabbed some dinner. The closer it got to time for me to part with them and go through customs, the more I noticed a difference in how my two boys were handling it.

Ronny seemed content to sit quietly by his mom and eat, but Lee... Lee became quieter as time passed, moving physically closer and closer to me until we were chair-to-chair. I had to ask him several times to give me just a little room, but I knew what was happening.

He started asking questions about *where* I was going (again), *why* I was going (again), *how long* I'd be gone (again), *why* they couldn't go with me (you get the idea), why *he* couldn't go with me, *who* was going to coach flag practice, *Who is gonna cook our food?!*

### *Facebook* Post August 1, 2011

Today, Lee wears the silver Celtic Cross that I've worn since buying it in 2003 in the tiny Ireland town where my folks live. Ronny wears the military dog tags I haven't taken off in years. My wife wears the dog tags I wore during my Marine Corps enlistment. I get them all back in 10 days.

It had been a last-minute decision before we left for the airport to give them each something to hold onto. Though it was really about helping Lee cope with my departure and absence, I knew I couldn't leave the other two out, even though they'd have a much easier time without me than Lee would. But my Celtic cross sure didn't help Lee when it was time for me to go through customs.

He began to whimper to himself a little at first, his chin beginning to quiver, and then I saw the beginning of panic in his eyes, as if he was realizing for the first time that he really couldn't stop it, that he couldn't slow this *leaving*-thing down, that it was all happening too fast. Ronny, on the other hand, just watched his older brother going through the advancing stages of near-despair. No matter how much I hugged and held seven-year-old Lee, he started to cry and pull on my hand as if to stop me. He didn't want to hear that it was going to be okay (*"No, it won't!"*) or that I'd be back soon (*"Just STAY with us, don't GO!"*).

Airport security saw how troubled Lee was, and they permitted us a little latitude, allowing him to hold my hand in the customs line for a short bit longer than they should have. But eventually, they motioned that he could go no further, and as Lily led him away by the hand and as the customs line swept me slowly away, Lee went into full-out crying, calling, *"DAAAADDYYY!"* over and over. I felt bad for my wife's job over the next eleven days.

By this time, I was tearing up considerably, too. I kept waving back to Lily and the boys, much the way my parents had done for me over the past decade, every time they'd left to return home to Ireland from this same airport, same terminal. Once cleared through security, instead of taking a right to go to my departure gate, I took a left and met the fam at the spot that Lily and I had arranged earlier. It was about a ten-foot-wide wall of glass where I could say a final farewell to my boys – Lee bawling away, *"Daddy, don't gooooo!"* with his hand held up to mine on the glass, palm-to-palm, and Ronny watching him go through it.

Inevitably, the time came for me to go to my gate and for Mommy to get the boys home, as they still had a three-hour drive back to Kent. As I boarded my plane, Lil called to let me know that Ronny was doing okay, but Lee was a mess. And she called one last time, too, with what I now see as a perfect example of the two different relationships I had with my two boys.

### *Facebook* post August 1, 2011

As I just boarded the plane and took my seat, Lil called. I heard Lee wailing away in the background. Lee: "Ronny, you're not crying very much!" I'd expect no less from Lee. Ronny: "Lee, Daddy is going to see HIS parents!" I'd expect no more from Ronny.

Though my schooling had taken place over the course of Ronny's first year of life, it had detrimentally influenced the trajectory of my relationship with him, as we would always be more distant from one another than Lee was with his mommy. And, of course, it didn't help that my wife reinforced the distance between my second boy and me by vocally pointing out every chance she got that I coached Lee in sports but never Ronny, that Lee and I were "telepathic," and that "Lee is aaaaalllll you," but Ronny was left out. She absolutely hand-crafted the wedge that her words drove home between my second boy and me. On at least two occasions with Ronny in the room, Lily had actually *said* that I loved Lee more than Ronny. *Why don't you love Ronny the way you love Lee?*

I saw Ronny's face at those times... I saw his *eyes*. If she was going to say these things, she should have done so only when we were alone, as she did all the other times. But no, she selfishly used her bullshit opinions and comments to drive that wedge between Ronny and I. She knew what she was doing, and I considered it to be parental malpractice. It's the same kind of nonsense she's been pulling ever since: creating self-serving narratives, convincing the people around her to believe and perpetuate them, and then sometimes even convincing herself to believe that her self-serving lies were capital 'T' True.

But, I mean, it wasn't like there was *nothing* loving between Ronny and me. There was *lots* of laughter and love between us, even if his mom wouldn't acknowledge it. There were occasional instances when he would just walk over and sit on my lap in the sunroom, or come visit me for a hug in my den, or come show me a picture he drew, or take my hand while walking through a store.

I recall one Saturday morning when Lily and the boys were fast asleep at 7 am. I had walked into the kitchen from my den for some reason, and a few minutes later, out danced Ronny from his and Lee's bedroom, still half-asleep.

"What are you doing up, kid?" I laughed. "It's only 7... you should still be sleeping."

Without saying a word to me, he spun and simply danced his way back into his bedroom. I immediately went into my den and posted the cute little story to *Facebook*, commenting on how every moment with kids is a joy. Just as I clicked the "post" button, back came Ronny, dancing his way around the corner and into my den. He was mostly awake now.

"Daddy, I'm hungry," is all he had to say.

"I can fix that, Little Man," I replied. Then I woke up his brother to come cook with me, and Mommy received her normal Saturday breakfast-in-bed early that morning.

Later that day, I posted the following to *Facebook*:

"Daddy, I'm hungry," are the best first words to hear first thing in the morning.

I remember another time when I was working in my den, and Ronny walked in to show me something. I was in the middle of a thought that I just had to finish writing on a student paper, but Ronny couldn't have known that, so he just climbed up onto my lap and went straight into talking about whatever it was he wanted to show me. I guess I was so focused that he felt the need to say, "Daddy, why aren't you responding?" That snapped me out of it.

"*Responding?* Ronny, did you just ask me why I wasn't *responding?* That's a pretty big word, kid. Where did you learn the word *responding?*"

"From you, silly," he replied, looking at me as if I should have known that. "I learn all my words from you." I almost squeezed the goo out of that little kid, and I posted it to *Facebook*, like I used to do with all those little stories about the boys.

And there were times when I would try to include Ronny with something Lee and I were doing (like grocery shopping or cooking dinner), or I'd sit on his bedside to talk a little after tucking him in like a taco, or I'd join him playing his favorite game on our Wii system. There were lots of little times like that.

So, yeah, Ronny and I always had our own little chemistry going – it was just very, very different from the chemistry between Lee and me. But still to this day, I can't help but think about how much Ronny and me could have been more like Lee and me, if I had just known how important it was to be present for that first year of Ronny's life. But once that first year had been lost, compounded by Lilith's claim that I loved Lee more than Ronny, there should have been no wonder why my relationship with my two boys was so different. I could never play catch-up enough to get as close to Ronny as I was to Lee.

Ronny and I just never had much of a chance.

# Chapter Nine:
# The Inevitable Tiptoe Toward Paranoia

So, off the fam went to the U of I game in Champaign/Urbana, Lee with Daddy and Ronny with Mommy. I had texted Selena early that morning to let her know that there would be no phone calls unless I found a time and place to call her, but under no circumstances was she to call me. Along the way, Selena texted several times.

Let me take a time-out to briefly reflect on the general situation on that Saturday. The prior evening had afforded me some time to consider everything from the previous week. It pulled out of me a spectrum of emotions.

I felt a very strong friendship with Selena, similar to what I've heard called kindred spirits. We found that we shared a common sense of humor – laughing at each other's jokes and appreciating each other's sarcasm. We enjoyed talking with one another about anything, down to the most minute details, for as long as possible. We enjoyed agreeing with or debating each other's perspectives. And we had a sense of mutual protection... we would go to bat for one another, as you will see. I had growing romantic feelings for her, the way our eyes examined one another with what seemed to me to be a scale of potential that kept growing in promise and sensing that in time, maybe there could be a chance for... well, we'd have to see. But every time our eyes met... I don't know. There was just *more* there with every glance.

I wasn't certain yet that a legitimized relationship was what either of us was or would ever be interested in, but I felt the needle slowly starting to point in that direction, that there could be a chance for a real relationship somewhere far ahead at magnetic north. And I noticed that I had a great deal of respect for this young lady who saw something in me and went for it despite her fears. Despite the taboo of it. Despite my middle age. Despite the damage she risked to her reputation if we were discovered.

She seemed to have little fear of anything now that I had reciprocated her feelings. Her lack of fear scared me a little at times, which only made me respect her more for it. The way she decided that I should take her to Chicago on a forbidden runaway trip... and then – on the fly, in real time – she amazingly figured out the logistics to make it work. I had learned that she was an extremely unique young lady, to say the least.

I also respected the fact that she had feelings for *me*. I had to wonder what she saw when she looked at me, because she sure didn't seem to see middle-age. She knew she could find a shredded young buck any day of the week, and yet she went *far* out of her way to choose me, a man around the same age as her parents. She wasn't looking for commitment or security, as I was married and couldn't offer her those things. She wasn't looking for money, as I was not wealthy. She wasn't looking for just sex, or she would no longer be interested in me. So, I recognized she must have been interested in something *more*, something *bigger* and more *genuine* than all of those things. Like the ladies I'd been with before her, she saw in me a genuinely good, friendly, intelligent, capable partner and she found *that* attractive. I had to respect her for all of this when most of the world was comparatively shallow – myself included, in a lot of ways.

And, of course, I'm sure she enjoyed the thrill of what we were doing, the danger of potentially getting caught. She liked my daring and that I was willing to risk quite a lot for her. She liked that I treated her as the adult she was instead of the minor student she had once been. And now that I *did* have feelings of lust for her, I knew *that* part of us would develop over time, too, sooner than later. So now you know as much as I did *or more* about where my head was on that Saturday morning, headed to U of I. But it doesn't mean that this wasn't still a crazy plan we were about to put in motion.

So, anyway, back to the text messages...

Since this was 2011, and keeping in mind that smartphones didn't start becoming mainstream until about 2012, the vast majority of cellular phones did not have keyboards on the screen. Rather, texting keyboards were tiny, physical, push-button, difficult things to use, and the entire alphabet was on nine physical keys. That meant you had to push a key several times to get a single letter you wanted – for example, you'd have to press the '7' key four times just to get an 's' – making it particularly dangerous to do while driving.

But in 2011, we didn't think it was any more dangerous than taking a bite of a McDonald's cheeseburger or taking a pull off your Starbucks Iced Caramel Mocha Frappe Macchiato Choco Latta Thingy (yeah, I bet *they* have those, too). The first Illinois law enacted regarding the use of a cellphone while driving, mandating a hands-free device, wasn't until 2014.

So if it wasn't difficult and dangerous enough to text and drive without a hands-free device, with only a flip-phone physical nine-key keyboard, it was even more dangerous if photos were involved. With these primitive flip phones being the technological norm of the time, the camera option was also fairly new and very primitive. But we didn't know anything different, so we thought they were awesome.

You may also recall from earlier in this story that the first time I ever even saw a digital camera was in 2003. I literally couldn't believe what I was seeing – there was no film cartridge, the image popped up on a screen, and you could take and delete as many photos as you wanted... it was like wizardry, lol. It was my brother Pip's new digital camera that he took with us in 2003 on an Ireland trip. Camera phones didn't become mainstream until 2004.

And even now, in our story of 2011, camera phone pictures were still very primitive in quality. We thought they were great, of course, but I still have some pics that I've kept over the years from 2011, and the quality is even surprisingly bad to me, making it difficult to decipher what's in the pic. And I was *there*.

So it didn't make it any easier to text Selena and drive when she sent me a provocative pic. It was just a single photo that is still very clear in my memory today. Know why? Because I recently saw it. I was looking through some old flash drives recently, and somehow, a huge folder of pics from past cell phones included the picture that she sent me the morning I was driving to U of I. That day I received it, the image was kind of hard to see, with the poor camera phone quality, the bouncing around on the road, the glare shining in, and the reflection of the daylight on the screen. But when I saw it, the photo had the full effect that she had intended. I was instantly hard as a fucking rock.

Although the word "selfie" was coined as early as 2002, here nine years later I don't think I knew the term. I knew people were taking them, but I'm not sure if I knew the term "selfie" yet. Selena had apparently taken a selfie in a mirror, from neck to thigh, with her shirt pulled up to reveal a neon green and pink bra and her jeans unbuttoned and pulled down to show black and purple panther print string bikini panties (say that ten times fast), her tan lines from months earlier still visible, and a message of simply six words:

*All yours. Come and get it.*

It was when I was holding up the phone to reduce the reflection on the screen that I thought I noticed my wife, directly ahead of me on the highway, hitting the brakes, slowing down a bit, repositioning her rearview mirror, and beginning to look back at me with more frequency. I was almost certain she had noticed me checking texts along the drive, which, by rule, I almost never did. I put my phone away for the duration of the drive after that. When we got to the stadium, our vehicles were directed into two different lanes to park. I took note of where her car was in relation to mine in case it might come in handy later when employing my exit strategy.

"Who were you talking to on the drive?" Lily asked after we parked, with more than a touch of suspicion.

*Is she possibly on to us? She can't be, can she?*

"Nobody. I wasn't talking on my phone. (pause) I was talking to Lee... and we were singing some songs." That wasn't a lie.

Then Lee chimed in because children are always listening, "Yeah, Mommy. Me and Daddy were singing Bruno Mars and-... "

"Well, *texting*, then. Whatever. *Who* was it?" *That* didn't sound good. She wasn't assuming it was Pip or Cass. She was onto something.

*Can she be on to us, really?*

And then it occurred to me that just as Rick Lincoln and his daughter had noticed that I'd been even happier than usual lately, perhaps my wife had noticed, too. More likely, though, someone else noticed and said something to her, as I could get a fucking Mike Tyson-style face tattoo, and she wouldn't notice.

"Just the guys... they were blowing up my phone about tonight. Mostly about the fight matchups on tonight's UFC card." That *was* a lie. Tip... toe.

Then, I had a great real-time idea. "They were also kind of pushing to see if there's any way I could get up there sooner. About halfway here, I told them no more texting, and I put the phone away. Had to." Yeah, that was *all* a lie. *Tip...* toe.

Though she looked away and didn't ask about it again, she looked unconvinced. But I was unsure if she *really* looked unconvinced or if I was *imagining* it. Perhaps I was beginning the inevitable tiptoe toward paranoia that often carries a cheater down the road of deception. *Tip... toe.*

The football game was a trainwreck for Illinois. I could literally sportscast the game right now for you, almost play-by-play, offensive drive-by-drive, but I won't. So here it is: Illinois was up by ten points at the half, 17-7, then gave away *four turnovers*, and Wisconsin scored 21 unanswered points in the third quarter. Toward the end of that quarter, I took my shot. Basically, I had cheered hard the whole first half, trying to make my wife think I was really invested in Illinois winning. After all, I am a football coach. All the turnovers in the third quarter served my cause as I turned my cheering to yelling. So I tried to use my outrage at the game to get out of there and on my way.

"I'm not wasting any more of my afternoon on this, Lil. Remember the guys were pushing for me to get up there early? With this score, I'm just gonna get outta here and head up to Cass's early. The way this is going, the Illini have already quit... I bet they won't even score again."

"Are you leaving, Daddy?" Lee asked me. His voice melted my heart a little, and just then, I wanted to stay with him. But I pushed through that.

"Yeah, kid. You know I'm going to see Uncle Pip and Uncle Cass today, remember? But I'll be home tomorrow sometime."

"Awwww," was his response, which still melts me away to this day. It's literally choking me up right now. I can almost hear him in my head, as I do every day of my life.

I have no doubt that there will be a lot in my telling of this entire story that will have me from choked-up to outright crying, so please bear with me. I will never see those two little boys again, as Lee is an adult, and Ronny is finishing up high school. The two little tykes I had dedicated my life to back then are now found only in old

2'x2' photographs that almost wallpaper my living room walls today. There are no time machines.

# Chapter Ten:
# Backtrack

My wife was not taking kindly to my exit strategy, and it confirmed for me that she was onto something.

"What's your hurry? The fights don't really start until 9," she spat, and then, "Well, we're just going to leave now, *too*, then. Boys, grab your stuff, we're leaving." I felt like that was really her way of following me on my way out of town.

She knew *something* was not right, but she couldn't have known anything like what it really was. If she had known *that* or even sensed something close to it, she would have addressed it and found a way to stop it. I think it was as early as this day that she had secret cameras set up in the house and garage while I was gone up north. I never *saw* those cameras, so I don't actually *know* that they ever existed. They didn't play a part this particular weekend, but down the road in this story, you'll see why I'm fairly certain they were there. And I'm pretty sure they were installed this weekend.

So, Lily and the kids headed out with me, which completely blew the whole idea of my leaving early to get ahead of them on the road. We were parked in separate rows of vehicles, so after all of the hugs and kisses with the boys at my vehicle, the three of them headed to her car.

I jumped in my van, given the only small head-start that

might help my cause. With getting to their car, getting in, buckling up car seats (we adults still did that for them, ourselves, to be perfectly safe), and getting out to the street, I had an opportunity to be long gone by the time they were pulling out of their parking spot. I did notice, though, that Lily was hurrying the boys along. She couldn't have known my intent, though, and even if she thought there was something sneaky going on with me going up north, what was she going to do... *follow* me there?

I pulled out, cruised around my short row of cars, and *dammit!* An elderly couple wearing Illini orange and driving an old, rusty Oldsmobile with a *"IT'S WEIRD BEING THE SAME AGE AS OLD PEOPLE!"* bumper sticker had apparently lost faith in the team, and the old man backed out of his parking space right in front of me. And then he sat there, yelling at his wife while she flailed her arms and shook her head.

I could see Lily's brakes light up further down the row. Now the man was crawling forward, still straightening out his car. By the time I got to the main road, Lily and the boys had pulled right in front of me.

I had to find a way to buy time, because if I got on that highway headed back toward home and Lily stuck with me, I would be forced to actually get on I-57 North toward Chicago. If that happened, I did not know how far out of the way it would take me or how much time it would burn before I could reverse course and head back toward Grand Valley High School where Selena would be waiting. Vehicles and flip-phones didn't have GPS yet, in 2011. At least *mine* didn't.

So, at the last moment before we both got onto I-74 West, I turned into a gas station. Lily had no choice but to continue onto I-74 West, so that was good. I called to let her know I had to get gas before the trek up north, but she didn't pick up, so I left a message while I filled my fuel tank.

She had seemed suspicious – *of what* I couldn't exactly tell – but in the message, I asked her how she was set for gas. I was trying to find out if they would be making any fuel, food, or anticipated potty stops. If they were, we might bump into each other on the road, as now I would have to trail them at a distance, and it could get messy. If they pulled back onto the highway toward home after a potty stop only to see me cruising along... what could I say? Lil never returned my call.

And so began the long, slow backtrack toward Selena, on the same roads my wife would be driving somewhere up ahead of me. It was agonizingly slow. I knew she tended to drive around 70-75 mph, so when I decided I had wasted as much time as possible getting gas in Champaign/Urbana, I got on I-74 and cruise-controlled at 65 mph so I wouldn't catch her. And then it occurred to me that if Lilith got off at an exit, then I passed them, and they got back on behind me, they would catch me from behind. There were too many variables for there to be any best course of action, though, so I had to choose one and stick with it. I would drive 65 mph and keep my fingers crossed.

Every exit that had a store or gas station had to be surveilled as I passed in case I might see her pulled off of the route for fuel or a potty break. Every entrance ramp joining the highway had to be examined to make sure she wasn't getting back on the highway after a stop. It was a torturous drive, and it lasted about two hours.

I called Selena to let her know I was on my way to see her. She had stopped and picked up snacks and beverages for the drive up toward Chicago, and she was soon heading over to Grand Valley High School to wait for me. I explained what had happened with the escape plan and that we couldn't communicate much while I was on my way to get her because I had to pay attention to the exit and on ramps and every other goddamn place I could cross paths with them.

When I was finally exiting from I-25 North just a mile or so after my wife's exit, about ten minutes out from reaching the high school where we were leaving Selena's car for the night, Selena called me to say that she could have sworn Lily and the boys had just cruised past her spot at the high school. The timing was about right for that to be possible... *if Lily was going to Danverston*. But that made absolutely no sense. Why would she go to *Danverston*? Could she have somehow found out about our plan? Was she going past the school to see if Selena's car was there? But none of that made any sense. Still...

"Are you certain it was her?" I asked, and Selena said no, she couldn't be sure, but it really looked like Lily's car with the two boys in the back.

"If it *was* her, could she have seen your car where you're parked?" I asked.

Selena said yes, there were no other cars in the lot and nowhere else to park it. I didn't think my wife knew what Selena's car looked like, though. There had never been a time I could recall where she was around Selena's car. I wouldn't have even known what it looked like until that past week.

I got off the phone and made a call to my best friend, Cass. I had to ask if he'd talked to Lily at all. Of course, Cass didn't know anything about Selena any more than my little brother Pip did. I just hoped that if Lily *had* called Cass, she hadn't asked him about all the texts to me earlier in the day and about pushing for me to get up there to his place earlier than planned. That would be a problem. Things had been so much simpler and easier a week earlier when I told my wife the Truth about everything (everything except for being checked out of the marriage before this whole thing had begun with Selena, that is).

When Cass picked up, I gave him my ETA, which was behind schedule for me but not too far off from what I'd originally told him because I had left the game after the third quarter. I asked if he had talked to Lily at all lately, and he said no. That was good.

"Why do you ask?" Cass wondered, and I told him I had left her a message quite a while ago that she hadn't returned, and I'd just thought to check with him.

So that made me feel better. Cass hadn't heard from Lily. The only two who could have known about the plan for me to double back and pick up Selena were her and me. *There's no way Lily knows*, I concluded. But there had been so many indicators pointing to Lily being onto me. It seemed my inevitable tiptoe toward paranoia was beginning to speed up into a trot.

# Chapter Eleven:
# Jailbreak

So I picked up Selena. I was ridiculously happy to see her when I pulled up, and she looked very excited to see me. She grabbed her snacks and overnight bag, along with a favorite pillow, hopped into my van, kicked off her shoes, and laid an extra heavy kiss on me. We kissed for a minute or two or three. She looked so happy just then, as happy as I'd ever seen her, and I remember almost getting choked up at the thought of anyone other than Lee being *that* happy to see me.

After some small talk, Selena and I recapped how our days had gone. We were both remarkably relaxed once we really settled in, and that was when I heard on the radio that the Illini had indeed not scored again in the game after I had left, and Wisconsin went on to win 28-17. Selena asked about the game, and I filled her in.

With that out of the way, I quickly steered our conversation to Selena's belief that she had seen Lily and the boys while waiting for me in the Grand Valley High School parking lot. After she talked me through it and after I had asked for minor clarifying details, I was pretty sure that it had been Lily. I just didn't know *why*.

On one hand, Lily would have no reason to take that route, as it was totally out of the way. On the other hand, even if she could somehow have known about our plans – and I was pretty sure no one could – why didn't she pull into the school and confront Selena, wait for me to arrive, and put the kibosh on the whole weekend? It just didn't make sense. But she hadn't, so there was little sense in worrying about it.

***

Not only is this next episode difficult to communicate to you, Reader, it is also difficult for me to understand myself, even today, over a dozen years later.

Something kind of important happened on that three-hour drive up north. Whatever voodoo Selena had woven into her *brujeria* to somehow make me agree to take her with me, it was powerful, and it was still working. I think a major part of it was that Selena and I were really making a genuine jailbreak.

Sure, we had stolen a kiss and done some holding each other one night on the down low. *Ooooohhhh, sneaky-sneaky*. We had taken some time together to just talk and flirt at McDonald's that Wednesday afternoon. *Big deal*. We had executed a considerably serious plan to be physically together, and that didn't work out as we'd hoped, though we had made it through a very dangerous attempt without detection. We had been truly alone together that night, and we had been pretty fucking intimate in that effort.

But now, with this, we had executed a much more delicate plan with far greater risk and a much greater payoff: two days and a night together and a hotel room in a town where no one knew us, where we could be ourselves. Now *that* was something, and these little victories began to galvanize us together in the belief that we could make this thing work, whatever it had to be, however short- or long-term, however playful or serious. And this trip also brought something wonderful and unexpected. We really got to *know* one another on a level that would potentially have taken us months of sneaking around to achieve otherwise.

Selena and I settled in for our three-hour drive. We talked. We laughed. We talked. We sang. We talked. We snacked. We talked. We laughed. It was during that drive that I fell in love with her laugh, genuine, loud, full, and unreserved. It got to the point that we turned the music off, and we just amused ourselves with conversation, laughter, one sad story, a few tears, and a warmth in our bellies that intensified a little every time we caught eyes.

Something was happening. It wasn't the anticipation of a hotel room and the fun that would surely be had. No. It wasn't the excitement inherent in breaking the rules. No. It was something newborn, and it was right there in the van, fully clothed and not even physically touching. It was *us*.

We talked about anything and everything. We talked about dogs, the joys they'd brought to our lives, and the inevitable hardship they brought in saying goodbye. We talked about our families with little bits and pieces of history to help the other better understand the often difficult subject that is family. We talked about our younger school years and sports. We even accidentally fell upon talking a little about significant others, but neither of us seemed thrilled to wade into those waters, and we laughingly agreed to change the topic. I even generally filled her in a little about Lily's transgressions in our marriage over the years.

We imagined what would happen in hypothetical scenarios where certain people from my school found out about us – who *this* student would tell, how *that* teacher would react – and though we didn't shy away from it, we didn't dwell there long, either. I did take that opportunity to ask how she had gotten away for the weekend. What had she told her mom?

"I just told her one of my new friends at school invited me to go up to Chicago with her family to see relatives. Like, for the weekend. That I'd be back Sunday."

"Wow. That seems legit enough," I replied. "Where does she think your car is?"

"Ummmm... at my *friend's* house," she answered sarcastically, rolling her eyes. "My mom doesn't know anyone in Delphia, so it's not a problem."

"Cool, cool," I replied. "I know you've thought of everything. I'm not questioning your ability to handle this, but I just have to ask... have you considered how you would handle a phone call from your mom right now asking why someone from Bigtimber or Firedance, or anywhere really... if someone contacted her to say they saw your car parked out at Grand Valley High School?" Her focus shifted from out at the road down to the dashboard. Then she looked over at me.

"Just... don't even say that, Cal. I mean, let's not... *everything* is taken care of. Let's not take away from our time together to re-think the *what ifs*." But she was looking at the dashboard again.

"Yeah," she continued after a moment, "Sorry. You're right. I didn't think of that. But I know what I'd say if she *did* call. I got it. Thanks for asking that. I probably would have handled a call like that fine, but if you hadn't brought it up, and if that call *did* come... it could have been bad."

"How do you think she would react... if she somehow found out about us, I mean?"

"*Cal!* Enough! Let's turn the radio back on, or change the subject, or *both*, just something else." Again, she was staring at the dashboard, until she caught herself, then she looked back over at me. "If she finds out about us, it'll be bad. Like, *really* bad. THE bad. And if my dad finds out..." Her hand shot out to turn on the radio, but not before I saw the answer in her eyes.

We talked about the Marine Corps, about her expectations,

questions, and a little about my experience in that realm. In fact, only now do I realize that our discussion never once stepped foot into our future, be it a week or a month, or several months. I wonder if somewhere deep down, or maybe not so deep, one or both of us might have been afraid to talk about tomorrows, as though it might shatter the illusion that we really were as free as we felt on that little getaway. The only guarantee of time together was those two days.

# Chapter Twelve:
# My Mistake

By the time we reached the Chicagoland area, I felt more drawn to, more connected to this young lady that I was getting to know on a level I hadn't seen coming... that neither of us had seen coming. Before that drive, it had all seemed kind of wispy, kind of fairytale-ish, as we both wanted to do what we were doing, but it lacked anything of real substance.

All we had really been doing up to that point was stealing little puzzle pieces of the bigger picture under what would undoubtedly be the hostile gaze of society if we were found out. And that's probably why we didn't talk much about any possible or impossible future for us. Because to talk about it meant potentially talking about an *end* to it. Maybe we just weren't ready to step out of the fairytale yet.

When we passed Joliet, I let Selena know that we were getting close... we'd be at the hotel in around 20 minutes. She asked what the plan was, suggesting that she'd be staying at the hotel while I went to visit with my little bro and Cass, who was practically an adopted brother of Pip's and mine. Then, she supposed, after the UFC fights, maybe around midnight, I'd head back to the hotel to her.

Reader, it is right here in particular that I have no explanation for what I did next. Black magic? Voodoo?

I told her that I'd check in to the hotel, and she mentioned that she could check us in... she was eighteen and had brought cash for the room. I declined, insisting that I'd get the room. So I'd check us in, then we'd go get her something to eat for dinner, and if she wanted a little something alcoholic to drink, nothing to get drunk with, I'd get that. Then I told her I was going to take her to Cass's with me. Yup. I did. I know, I know. What the *fuck* was I thinking?

For the first time ever, a look of almost fear crossed Selena's features. She asked if I thought that was a good idea, taking her to Cass's house. Would Pip and Cass keep it quiet? I told her that I'd tell them she and I were strictly platonic friends, but I imagined they'd both know that I was just telling them "The Story," and they'd know what was really up. I was giving them an out... in case anyone ever found out anything, Pip and Cass could always fall back on not being told the Truth, that they were told it was platonic. But that really was a thin layer of insulation I was offering them. I also told her that those two were my brothers, that I could trust those two with anything, and that they would have my back no matter what.

Again, she asked if that was smart. I said something like, *Well, it's not the safest way to play it, but I'm no stranger to taking risks, and I'm not really feeling like playing it 100% safe tonight... it will be fine.*

Spoiler Alert: it wasn't going to be fine.

I asked if I was really supposed to work as hard as I had worked to get her up in Chicago with me just so she could sit at the hotel until I was available? No. She would come with me to Cass's. So, I checked us into the hotel, and when I got back out to the van, she made a comment that she liked the swagger I was walking with. It occurred to me that, yes, I had walked in and out with the touch of a drop step and a little stalking sway in my shoulders. It was a happy, if slightly aggressive, gait. It was the way Lily probably saw me walking into our first class together at WIU, how I used to walk when I was a young buck, once upon a time, before the Florida Fiasco and the Drunken Barn Dance.

We parked, went up to the room, and hung out for a while before heading to Cass's. Of course, we fooled around a little, but I let her know... *Easy, Babe, there's no hurry – we've got all night.*

I stopped to get a couple of wine coolers for her to sip on, and we picked up some dinner for her at a burger joint I always enjoyed when visiting Cass's. And then we moved forward with my new plan. I could feel how nervous she was.

I called Cass to tell him I was almost there. When I pulled into the driveway, I could see Cass looking out his front window, seemingly waiting for me, which was odd. I came walking up to the front door by myself, and I told my brothers that I'd brought someone with me, that she was a former student of mine and close friend, and that I wouldn't be spending the night there at Cass's. After the fights, I had to get my friend back home down south.

I could see that Cass and Pip understood perfectly well what was going on here, but again, at least they had been told this was just a friend of mine. I caught a concerned look on Cass's face as he looked at Pip. I mean shit, who could blame him for being concerned? She and I were almost 22 years apart in age, I told them that she was a former student of mine, they hadn't known anything about me and her, and they did not know I was bringing anyone with me. They both knew I'd been planning for years to eventually divorce Lily, but this? I knew Cass would be able to roll with it, though – he was a big boy. Pip was already rolling with it. He trusted me. And I definitely wouldn't have brought Selena to the house if I didn't trust those two.

As we walked in, the preliminary fights (or undercard) had already begun. Tonight was Ultimate Fighting Championship (UFC) #139, with the main event being a contest for the 205 lb. Light Heavyweight title belt between Shogun Rua and Dan Henderson, two legends of the sport. Two other legends of the sport made up the co-Main Event, as Wanderlei Silva took on Cung Le for the 185 lb. Middleweight title. Selena sat and ate quietly with me at the dining room table, which was really part of the living room. Cass showed us some of the bells and whistles of his new 3D television, and other than the noticeable but minor sense of caution from Cass, the four of us settled in and enjoyed a night of fights.

After Brazilian Muay Thai artist and PRIDE Fighting Championship multi-champ Wanderlei "The Axe Murderer" Silva secured a technical knockout over highly decorated Vietnamese Sanshu/Kickboxing champ Cung Le in the second round, American MMA champ Dan Henderson wound up winning a five-round decision against Mauricio "Shogun" Rua. Soon, our nervous energy from the fights subsided, as it was already after midnight, and as Cass and Pip were having some drinks, things seemed to get kind of slow and tired. I told the guys it was time for Selena and I to head back down south, not mentioning that we had secured a nearby hotel room. Nobody needed to know about that.

"Cass and your brother are really nice," Selena said as we backed out of the driveway. I thanked her and agreed that *Yes, they are nice; they're my brothers*. "Well, I'd bet your brothers are in there right now talking about you, about *us*..." I thought about it, then shrugged in agreement. Of course, they were. I had shown up without first letting them know about Selena. Why would I do that?

Of course, I know that it was because I wanted to spend time with Selena, but I was so set on doing it that I admittedly handled the whole thing all wrong. I should never have put those guys in a position to keep secrets from my wife (not that either of them would normally be talking to her anytime soon, anyway) or Pip to keep it from his wife (not that it would come up in passing conversation, anyway). I clearly wasn't thinking straight, and that night, I knew I hadn't been a good brother.

I made a note to myself that I owed them both an apology for the way I handled the whole thing. If I could go back and do it over, I would have stuck with Selena's plan and left her at the hotel, and I wouldn't have even mentioned her to the guys. But, as you know, Reader, there are no time machines.

# Chapter Thirteen:
# Mission Accomplished

When we got to the room, she gave me the eyes. I knew the look. *You* know the look. I had anticipated this, of course, so I was prepared to slow us down. She was anxious, and I was too, but as I told her, "We have all night, Baby. We don't have to rush like we're in your mom's basement."

Laying on the bed with her, I felt a happiness I hadn't felt in many years save with my boys. It was more than the feelings flying wildly around inside me... this had just as much to do with the feelings flying around inside her... her *wanting* me.

We undressed each other slowly, no reckless abandon. Like before, I had every intention of warming her up right, but when I began moving slowly down toward her hips, she stopped me. She just wanted to rinse off in the shower after the long evening in the car and at Cass's. True to her word, she was in and out of the shower, and I asked her not to dry off, to just come lay down.

We progressed in much the same way as we had at her house two nights earlier. I took good care of her to start, but I failed to help her achieve more than a single climax. And when it was time, my body just wouldn't respond... yes, *again*. It was almost a perfect duplicate of two nights prior; except this time we knew we weren't in a hurry... we literally had all night. I had no excuses.

She assumed top position, as she had ultimately done the

other night, and again, it was apparent that she wasn't comfortable warming me up with oral, nor with her hand, which was kind of odd but fine. Then, as she lay atop me, clearly very, very frustrated, she growled the magic words.

"I just want you inside me *right now*, ERRRRRHH," and she *literally* growled out loud in my ear, and then she bit down on my right shoulder. *Hard.* I have never really been one particularly turned on by dirty talk or violence, but hearing what she wanted, cut-and-fucking-dry, and that frustrated primal growl, the bite, the heat of my fight-or-flight response firing... *that* shit lit me up.

We fucked fast and furious, loud and lewd, and although I was able to hold off my climax, it became apparent that she would not climax again, and I allowed myself to release. She rode it out like a champ, and I had a climax that, for a few moments, I thought was going to kill me. After a shower together, we fell asleep holding each other, talking, giggling, and pleased.

In the morning, we did not fuck. We made love, soft and slow, the way the very young almost never do and those long-married never do again.

By then, Selena had music playing on the bedside alarm/radio, so there was a soundtrack to our lovemaking. I remember this exactly: two songs played while *we* played. They're kind of longer tunes, but don't make any assumptions about that,

Reader. I'm quite sure I didn't last through both songs, beginning to end. But I probably lasted through at least half of both tunes. The first song was Sade's "No Ordinary Love," followed by Madonna's "Justify My Love."

The one fear I had been carrying around with me since the failed attempt at her house was put to rest, and I knew we wouldn't have that problem again. Mission accomplished.

In the morning hours, between Lovemaking and the little bit of sleep we managed, Selena and I talked *a lot*. It started off with us reminiscing about how the weekend had come together, how she had devised the plan, how I had executed it, and how we had stolen the weekend.

"Hey, you know who Colbie Caillat is, right?" Selena asked out of nowhere.

"Colbie-... no. Why *should* I?"

"*Seriously? You* don't? Mister I-know-everything-worth-knowing? *You* don't know who Colbie Caillat is! And you're *not* playing?" she asked, totally shocked.

"Mister I-know-everything-worth-knowing?!" I laughed, acting offended. "Ouch! But I guess that is fair. *And* hilarious. I do kind of act like a know-it-all sometimes. But no, I don't know who that is."

"Holy shit, I actually get to teach *you* something!" she

laughed, genuinely excited. Then she stopped, became very serious, and in an authoritative voice that sounded like a college professor delivering a lecture, she said, "Colbie Caillat is a singer. If you don't know who she is, you *should*. Your homework is to listen to some of her music. You have to know that song 'Realize,'" and she sang some of the lyrics.

"Wow, Babe. You have a sweet little voice."

"*Oh, shut up!* I do not! Do you know the song, or n-..."

"*Yes*, I know that song. Is *that* Colbie whatever-her-name-is?"

"Colbie Caillat, yes. That's her. So then, do you know her song 'Fallin' For You'? It's a song kind of about us."

"Nope," I answered.

"Well, I'm not singing it for you, so-... I'm glad you don't know it, anyway. So Babe... can I ask you another question?"

"Seriously, girl? *Yeah*, of course, you can ask me a question," I laughed.

"So," she began, and I could hear the undertones of something serious on her mind. "We don't have to talk about this. Just stop me if this isn't cool to talk about... "

"Go ahead," I encouraged her. In that place, at that moment, together with her, naked and tangled under a sheet, I felt like talking about whatever *she* wanted to talk about.

"It's about you and Lily," she warned.

"Okay. Shoot," I said reluctantly.

"That night we met at Crusoe's – the Sunday night after my birthday party, when you met me to explain why you fucked up my party so bad [she laughed] – you told me about how the day and night of my birthday party went between you two. I know you didn't tell me the worst details... I could tell you were leaving things out... and I respect that you didn't tell me all that stuff... and I don't *need* to know all that stuff, unless you want to tell me sometime. And that did sound like things were absolutely crazy before you got to the party... but-..."

She paused. I looked her in the eyes to let her see into me, and I nudged her nose with mine for her to continue.

"I know now that you were already planning to divorce her before that. *But why? Something else* must have pushed you over the edge, like beyond the point of no return. What *did* it? What *was* it?"

"I just told you all about the Florida Fiasco on the way up here," I reminded her. I had given her the Cliff's Notes version, but I thought she knew enough for it to make sense.

"Yeah... *that* is some crazy shit. But you forgave her for all that, which is even crazier! I still can't believe you didn't divorce her right *then*.... and I know she had a ton of shit fucking with her, and she was depressed and all, but *still*... I can't believe you ever trusted her again, took another chance on her after that. I mean, I'm glad you *didn't* leave her then... I would never have known you. But between Miami Beach and my birthday, something *else* big had to have happened. Or maybe just *a lot* of little stuff. But *something* had to have happened that changed you... *something*."

"So you're asking what pushed me past trying to make it work. You're asking what made me decide for certain I'd be divorcing her someday," I clarified, getting to the point. I saw where this was going, and I knew there was a considerable story to share with her.

"Yes," she answered, eyes locked on mine. She was nervous. "Is that an okay question to ask?"

"It's a fair question," I said, trying to put her at ease. "There's no reason you can't ask about it or about anything. I'll tell you. I've never told anyone who didn't already know about Miami Beach, and I've never told anyone who wasn't directly involved with what I call the Drunken Barn Dance. Sometimes I call it Logan-Gate... same thing. It's kind of a long story, and you seem kind of tired. But if you're up for it...?"

"Holy shit, I *knew* it. *Was his name Logan?*"

"Slow down, Vasquez," I laughed, and she backhanded me. "So you're up for it? The whole story?" I asked, just playing.

"*Fuck yeah... spill it!*" she insisted excitedly, snuggling herself into me, throwing a leg over me, and settling in for the story in a position that was comfortable but also where she could look into my eyes. And so I told her the story of the Drunken Barn Dance, one of my top five *least* favorite stories from my life.

# Chapter Fourteen:
# The Drunken Barn Dance, Revisited

One Saturday night in the fall of 2008, when I was bartending and my wife was waiting tables at The Hunter's Den, there was a wedding after-party for a waitress coworker of ours. As always, I was working past the 2 am bar time to do dishes, conduct general cleanup/prep for the next day, and lock-up. I also had to open the club at 11 am the next morning, Sunday. So I declined the invitation to go to the wedding after-party bonfire at a nearby farmhouse, as it would probably be over by the time I locked-up the dinner club.

My wife was supposed to be headed to her parents' house to pick-up the boys after work, then head home. She didn't. She decided to go to the after-party, and though she passed it by me, and my spider-senses warned that something didn't feel right, I didn't really have any objections to her going. My only request was that she'd only have one drink and she'd clear it with her parents that it was okay if she showed up a little later than usual to get the kids. Remember, wait staff was typically done working and eating by around ten o'clock, and bar time was 2 am, so I was typically locking up for the night at around 2:30 or 3 am.

On my short drive home after work, I called my wife. She was still at the party, and she was clearly *very* drunk. I told her I'd see her at home, that I was going to get the boys, and that she should be home when I got there. She wasn't. I called her two more times from home over the next hour, and she just yelled at me for checking up on her, showing clear signs of becoming increasingly drunk. The second of those two calls, I couldn't even understand most of what she was yelling.

Then, she stopped picking up my calls. I called and woke-up my father-in-law to let him know I was dropping my boys off and going to find his drunk daughter at the farmhouse bonfire party (what I now refer to as the Drunken Barn Dance) before she tried to drive herself home in that dangerously inebriated condition.

I went looking for her. Didn't pass her on the only road to or from the party. Didn't see her vehicle in the farmyard, but there were many, many vehicles spread around the dark, rural property. The abandoned bonfire was still burning low. I stalked through the bonfire area, finding no one and no sign of her. With rising fury, I busted into and stalked through the dark farmhouse, tripping over drunk party-goers passed out all around each room, on the furniture, and on the floors. I rudely woke quite a lot of people out of drunken slumbers, and I heard someone in the dark mumble that she had left and driven Logan home.

"I *knew* it!" Selena jumped in, and I nodded.

I saw on her face that she was just then realizing how very difficult this story was for me to tell, so she apologized and snuggled back against me. She told me I didn't *have* to continue with the story if it was too hard, but I smiled a fake smile and just continued on.

Logan was a 19-year-old cook at The Hunter's Den and had

told all of us *at the club* that he was definitely not going to that party. I heard him say more than once that he didn't have money to buy beer, so if he couldn't drink, why go?

So, I drove home and found my wife's vehicle in the garage when I pulled in, but it took me a bit to find her in the house. She was on a couch in our sunroom, in pitch darkness, in a sort of slouched/reclined/sitting position. Half in/out of wakefulness. Dazed and almost incoherent. Crazy intoxicated. I questioned her, only to be met with drunken accusations contemptuously spat at me. After some additional prompting, she got up and pinball-bumpered off the walls on the way into our bedroom.

I called my father-in-law to let him know what had occurred and that I was coming to get the boys, but he insisted on bringing the boys to me. After the boys were tucked in, with my wife passed out in our bed, I walked my father-in-law out to the front door, and he straight up said what was on his mind.

"This means divorce, doesn't it?" But there was no question in his voice.

*"What?"* I asked.

"After this... there's no fixing it. It's divorce, right?" But again, he wasn't really asking.

"Oh, no," I disagreed with sarcasm but certainty, clearly angry with his daughter. "I'm not divorcing her." He just looked at me, unbelieving.

"How? How can you move on *now*, after *this*, and what happened *before*?"

"Simple. Fool me once, shame on her. Fool me twice? Or three times? Well, now I've got boys. That's how." He looked at me skeptically, but we said our goodbyes, and he left.

Before long, the sky began to lighten. I never slept. Never went into our bedroom where she had passed out. I just sat in the sunroom, head in my hands, and cried. And bled. This night revived and amplified everything Miami Beach had done to me, tore back open that wound. I had forgiven her for that, but for *this*, I didn't think I ever could. My father-in-law had been correct... I couldn't get past this. This was definitely the end of us. Eventually.

The wound from six years earlier was critical again – not like scratching off a scab, but rather like tearing open a scar – and as I sat in that dark sunroom, I felt like just letting it bleed out. All of that old feeling like a piece-of-shit, like I wasn't good enough, like a pussy, like a fucking *cuck*... it all erupted in me, but this time with the added insult of being a dumb ass who had forgiven her the first time... really the first *two* times.

It wasn't that I was upset at how things were... I had the two best things that had ever happened to me sleeping in the next room, under my roof. It was just my inability to affect or avoid her train wreck tendencies. To this day, she has no idea the damage she did to me that night. Maybe U2 still hasn't broken up to this day, but there was really no more hope for carrying each other to be done between us. I had carried us as far as I could, but she sabotaged us, and I knew I was too hurt to carry us much further.

It was Sunday morning, and as always, it was my morning to open the supper club at 11 am. There were always two workers on Sunday mornings, me and a cook. I almost never had a difficult time running food and drinks for the whole place during the early Sunday shift, and I knew who my cook was going to be on this particular Sunday morning. It was Derek, fellow cook and best friend of the 19-year-old Logan, the young man who I had been told was driven home by my wasted wife not so many hours earlier that very morning.

Derek and Logan were both 19-years-old, big, strong young men, old high school buddies, lifting partners, partiers, big drinkers, both using steroids and occasionally other recreational drugs. I would never fault either of them for *any* of that because they were good guys. I liked Logan a lot, in fact. And Derek and I had a very strong friendship, loved working together, talking together, and we respected each other very much. I still chat with him on occasion, to this day, though it's on social media.

I arrived at work earlier than usual that Sunday, eager and aggressive. I was more than a bit of a wild animal that morning, and I was ready to corner Derek. I had absolutely no beef with him, and whatever had or had not happened the night before between my wife and Logan, I couldn't expect Derek to tell me and rat on his best friend. Best friends have each other's backs, through good and bad, much like how I couldn't expect Lily's sister Beth to tell me about my wife in Miami Beach. Or now, like how I knew Pip and Cass wouldn't tell anyone anything about Selena for my sake. It was the same principle: you don't rat on best friends or family. But I fully planned to do whatever I had to do, to press Derek as hard as necessary, so he would call Logan and convince him to show up at the club immediately.

Honorably, Derek tried to speak for his buddy Logan, but I was having none of that. Someone was going to pay if I didn't get answers very soon, and if Logan wasn't coming, Derek was the only one there... and, of course, he *did* know what I needed to know. Derek's girlfriend was the sister of the bride; he had been working the night before, and he had surely talked to Logan that Sunday morning. He knew anything that happened. I would get answers, no matter the collateral damage. Friend or not, when faced with a pissed-off Marine, most people just want the sights set on anything *but* them if they're smart. I just hoped Derek would make the smart choice and get Logan to the Hunter's Den right away.

# Chapter Fifteen:
# Intel Collection

While I was in the kitchen having that discussion with Derek, I heard the front door slam shut. It was barely 11 o'clock, opening time, and out of habit, I had unlocked the front door right when I arrived at work. I quickly recognized the slow, metered shuffling sounds of one of my Sunday regulars. I knew who it was, just wasn't expecting anyone until right before or just after the opening kick-offs for the noon NFL games.

Then again, I should have expected *this* particular customer... Mr. Mirai was often early for Green Bay Packer games, and though I hadn't known they were playing at noon, I knew now. I'd known him for over a year at that point, ever since I started tending bar at The Hunter's Den.

"You remember Mr. Mirai, of course," I reminded Selena.

"Yeah, of course... *Sonar*... you knew him back *then*?"

"Well, like I said, at this point, I'd known him for probably somewhere over a year. But yeah, he was at The Hunter's Den that morning. You kind of have to understand how he used to fit into the mix at the bar, though. At least a little. I'll tell you whatever else you want to know about him later."

She'd met Mirai more than once by this time, but I explained some more about him, anyway. As I'm sure you recall, Reader, Mr. Mirai was a very small, extremely old, abundantly kind, sometimes funny, considerably mysterious, very likable, totally blind Japanese-American WWII Veteran. There were no people of Japanese or other Asian heritage living in the multi-county area surrounding the Den, so far as anyone seemed to know – none but Mr. Mirai.

By this time, I probably knew more about him than anyone in the area, maybe in the world, other than his driver, Walter. His arrival at the Den that morning ended up proving very important for my story, but I had to get back to Derek, Logan, and the capital 'T' Truth about what happened at the Drunken Barn Dance the night before.

Derek called Logan, tried to persuade him to get to the Hunter's Den, then told Logan exactly what I'd *told* him to say... that if Logan wasn't coming, I'd be on my way up his one-lane dirt road to Lake Whitetail in seconds. Logan was a bright kid, and he came. He was a tall, athletic, muscular young man. But when he walked in the back door by the kitchen, probably trying to meet Derek before meeting me, his eyes were round, and his face was pure white under his long, yellow-blonde locks. I was waiting in the kitchen with Derek, and I knew I was the most dangerous thing he'd seen in a long time, maybe ever. Derek took his leave, I cornered Logan in the second dining room, and he told me what he had surely practiced saying.

I heard Logan's story, which incriminated my wife's intentions with him. He said that when they pulled-up in his parents' driveway, she gave him suggestive eyes, asking, "What do you want to do now?" He claimed he hadn't allowed anything to happen between them, though. He said she was wasted, and he was pretty drunk, but he would never do that to me. He said he knew I'd kill him, and besides, he said he respected me too much. I asked where he got the money to buy beer, as he had told all of us he was broke. He said he didn't get the money... Lily had bought beer for him, a 12-pack.

Trying not to look surprised at this news, I threatened that if he'd left anything out, he'd better tell me now because I wasn't done yet, and I *was* going to find out *everything*. He swore that was it. I shook Logan's hand, thanked him for his honesty... and then I let him go about his Sunday. So next, I called Derek's mom, Tina, who was a waitress at the club and had been working at the restaurant the night before. She had also been at the Drunken Barn Dance.

From Tina, I found out that my wife had snuck her own money into my register *right behind my back* to pay for that 12-pack of beer for under-age Logan... beer that she snuck out of my bar coolers, also behind my back. She told me that Lily had been flirting with Logan all night behind my back during the prior night's shift but that *that* was not *un*common at all. It happened all the time. She sounded surprised that any of this was even news to me.

She told me that the night before, in the kitchen, my wife had literally *talked Logan into* going to the bonfire in front of everyone but me – said she'd get him beer, said she'd drive him to the party and home. Tina said everyone had been whispering about Lily's intentions as they watched her talk Logan into going with her. She'd seen Logan get out of Lily's vehicle at the bonfire, and though she didn't actually *see* Logan get into Lily's vehicle at the end of the night, everyone knew that had been the plan.

I asked if there was anything else I should know, and she said to call and ask anyone else working the previous night, but that was just about everything. She expressed strongly that she didn't want to be any part of it all and didn't want her name mentioned at all, of course. I told her not to worry about it and that I was grateful for her openness and help. She just sounded glad to be getting off the phone.

I didn't need to call anyone else for info. By then, I knew at least as much as anyone else could tell me, plus what Logan had said. I would ask individuals whenever I saw them, face to face. But I did have one more call to make.

# Chapter Sixteen:
# Logan-Gate

I called Lily's cell phone. Like a total smartass, I rubbed everything in her face that I had learned in no more than an hour. I was furious at the pure disrespect of it. I'm the guy that busted her cheating six years earlier, from 1,400 miles away, and she thought I was so stupid I wouldn't piece this one together right behind my fucking back, in the same building, in front of all our co-workers?! Mo-ther *fucker*, I was hot, but I was running the supper club, so I had gone into the empty dining room by myself to talk to Lily in the dark, looking out the front window, and I was pissed off but keeping my volume down.

She yelled and screamed at me, denying every last detail. I knew that this was exactly the reaction I would have received six years earlier if I hadn't tricked her into admitting everything herself. Now, I had heard it from first-hand accounts, from an eyewitness to all of it, and from the very guy involved. Tina's story had pretty much mirrored Logan's, and neither of them had any reason to make any of it up. Tina liked Lily quite a lot, in fact. She told me later she'd heard the danger in my voice, though, so she wasn't going to lie to me about it when Lily hadn't even tried to conceal any of it.

And how about that? How stupid could my wife have been to think no one would tell me? And to think that *I* wouldn't figure it out *after* the Florida Fiasco? This was the best she could do? Just call everyone a fucking liar about all of it? And how did she think this was going to make *her* look in their eyes? It was all just so stupid and sloppy. I had always respected my wife's intellect, but sometimes she just went off the rails like this and did stupid shit.

I got off the phone, went back to the bar, and hung out with my few customers. Now, at least I knew the capital 'T' Truth. I would eventually be able to get past this and move on in Peace. Just as I would never tell my little boys about the Florida Fling, I would never tell them about this. And when the boys would eventually grow up, they'd move out, and so would I. For good. My father-in-law had been correct... this *did* mean divorce. Just not yet. I was content with that, ready to just get back to bartending as best as I could, considering the circumstances.

Until... Lily jumped in her vehicle and sped the ten miles from our house to the supper club, showing up at the restaurant while I had those few customers sitting at the bar. She came in the front door and stood between it and the bar, shifting her weight forward and back like she would do on the very rare occasions when she was intoxicated and agitated, a look in her eyes that said she was ready to start some shit. She began making a loud scene, accusing everybody and their mom of lying about her, all those *fucking liars*.

She denied buying the beer, denied the flirting, and denied convincing Logan to go to the bonfire with her. She even tried to argue that she hadn't driven Logan home. I pointed out that if she had gone straight home from the bonfire, I would have passed her on the road on my way there, but I hadn't, so she had to have gone somewhere else.

She acted like I hadn't even said it, repeatedly insisting that everyone I had talked to about it was a *fucking liar*. But she didn't know I had *only* spoken with Logan and Tina. Everyone else who had worked at The Hunter's Den and attended the Drunken Barn Dance the night before knew everything Tina knew, and Lily knew it, so it was like she was assuming I had spoken to everyone. I hadn't... yet.

So I pressed her further about people saying she'd driven Logan. I think she knew she couldn't deny driving Logan, as she had done when I confronted her at home. And she must have realized on her way to The Hunter's Den that morning that she couldn't lie about that much further. So, I pressed harder.

"So if you didn't drive Logan home, where did you go, Lil?" I put her on the spot. "If everyone is lying about you, answer that one question. You weren't at home. You weren't at the farmhouse. You weren't on the road between home and the farmhouse. There is no alternate route to get home from there. So where did you go, Lil?"

Although denying *any* of this was ridiculous (given how many of our co-workers witnessed all of it), denying that she'd driven Logan was just *too* absurd. She could make her stupid arguments that what everyone had seen was *mistaken* (such as putting money in my register for beer), or *misunderstood* (such as her talking Logan into going), or a matter of *subjectivity* (such as the flirting), but not Logan physically getting into and out of her vehicle. Too many people had seen the exact same thing, and there was no room for subjectivity. And, of course, she couldn't answer my one simple question: where had she gone? This was all just a smokescreen, a meltdown, unprecedented damage control rivaled only by the events following Chernobyl or Three Mile Island.

"What's *that*?" Selena interrupted.

"What? Chernobyl and Three Mile Island?" I asked. "They were horrible nuclear power plant accidents in the seventies and eighties. One was in Ukraine; one was in Pennsylvania. The Drunken Barn Dance was like the worst nuclear disaster of my life, and Lily was just trying to do damage control." Selena understood and tucked her head back into my chest.

The fact that Lily had to admit to driving Logan further infuriated her, I could see. I was almost certain that she was intoxicated when I spoke to her on the phone earlier, but now I was certain. She was considerably intoxicated, especially knowing how wasted she had been as she had just arrived home a bit before dawn. She wasn't one to start drinking again in the morning, but maybe this time she did, I don't know. Everyone at the Hunter's Den knew she was intoxicated that morning, though.

When Derek poked his head out of the kitchen, she struck out at him, surely assuming he was part of my information grapevine (though he had said *nothing* to me, and I hadn't asked). She accused Derek of flirting with her behind my back at work, and she did all of this with Mr. Mirai and now a couple of other regulars sitting at the bar, Derek standing in the door to the kitchen, me behind the bar, and herself standing between the front door and the bar. Derek was instantly furious at her allegation, and he lashed back.

Derek accused her of flirting with *him* and hitting on *him* at times ever since she'd been working there, divulging that she had even grabbed his ass behind my back one time, too. She called him *a fucking liar* and said Derek had grabbed *her* ass, but I could see right through her. After repeatedly telling her to leave the club, I had to threaten to call the police and even picked up the phone to start dialing. I hoped she would give up this foolish scene before my hand was forced. She made some threats, left, and I called my father-in-law. He informed me that, yes, they had the boys. Shortly afterward, I went for just a ten-minute drive to cool down.

"Where do you think I went, girl?" I asked Selena. She thought for a few moments.

"Probably to the scene of the crime. The farmhouse? Or up to that lake where Lily had driven that Logan guy home?"

Where do *you* suppose I went, Reader? Yep. I drove up into the hills behind The Hunter's Den, up that one-lane dirt road, to the place where anything that *could* have happened between my wife and Logan *would* have happened... a small park on Lake Whitetail, near Logan's parents' house. I slowly rolled through the small parking area, pulled-in where I imagined *I* would have chosen for secret deeds, and *there it was*. Right fucking *there*. A discarded, used condom on the ground. And maybe ten or so feet away, the wrapper. *Magnum.* That's all the evidence I have to this day.

Neither Logan nor my wife ever admitted to any physical wrongdoing. He said she said. What the fuck ever. I already knew everything I needed to know, and I never questioned Logan about it again. Why would I?

Lily never admitted to Derek's claims of flirting, hitting on him, ass-grabbing, etc., but she did eventually admit to buying Logan the 12-pack of beer (out of my register, right behind my back), talking him into going to the party, and driving him home. She acknowledged that everything she had done was stupid and wrong and kept saying it:

"I know it was stupid, Honey, but-..." She stuck to her guns about what she deemed to be the most important, or perhaps the most dangerous, parts. She insisted emphatically that nothing physical happened. It probably did happen, but maybe it didn't. I didn't care. It didn't matter much. She had gone to great lengths to put herself squarely into a cheating situation, and at the very least, Logan had been the one to hit the brakes. So who cares whether they fucked or not. I wasn't taking any action, and I wasn't going anywhere anytime soon. I had my boys to raise.

# Chapter Seventeen:
# The Secret

I looked down at Selena, and her eyes were fixed on mine. "You okay?" I asked. "I know that was a lot."

"Ho-ly shit," she simply said. After a long pause, she continued. "You have been in such a crazy fucked up marriage for so long. I seriously don't know how you've stayed with her."

"Well, I knew she would always live in the house with my boys, so-..."

"You did it for *Lee and Ronny*... ho-ly shit. That's *a lot*."

"Well, it wasn't totally unselfish... I did it for me, too. I don't even want to think about how terrible it would be, living in my own place without doing their grocery shopping, cooking, sharing meals, putting them to bed, checking on them through the night, full family breakfasts on the weekend, looking for double-yolks with every cracked egg... it would be the hardest thing I've ever done, and I've done some hard shit in my life, so that's saying a lot.

"Yeah. I can only imagine how hard it would be for you to live apart from them. You guys are so close, and, I mean... you just..."

"I know what you mean," I said, saving her from trying to articulate it.

Then she got a kind of devious look to her, saying, "Is Lily *at least* good in bed." I could tell Selena was interested, but she was also getting very tired. "You don't have to answer that... *but is she?*"

"Ummmmm... I wouldn't really know," I replied. "Since Ronny was conceived in 2005, she and I have only had sex twice, two days in a row, a couple of years ago. I mean, *sometimes* she would take care of me in other ways. Every couple of months, maybe, if the planets aligned and Punxsutawney Phil didn't see his shadow that year."

She popped up onto one elbow. "Wait! *What the fuck?!* You are *not* serious right now! Isn't Ronny *five? FIVE-years-old?*"

I just made a pathetic smile and nodded. "I don't really want to talk about all that, but yeah, it's been like six years or whatever. And it was extremely rare before that, so all that has been a major issue between us, too. My thirties have been mostly sexless... *ten years...*"

"What... the... *fuck?* No offense, Babe, but your marriage just keeps getting more and more fucked up. The more you tell me, the worse it gets.

"And for years, you've just gone about your life," she continued. "Teaching students, coaching players, singing in front of thousands, out in the community like you two are the perfect couple. I don't even know all the details, but you've been *acting* all along... for like, literally *years!*"

I was nodding, more sadly than I let show. I tried not to think about it all most of the time.

"You have this whole *world* of bullshit going on in your personal life, but you never let on to it. And you never talked to *anyone* about it?"

"Well, my siblings know about Miami Beach. So does Cass. I think I told my mom once that I'd be divorcing Lil someday. Pip, Ron, Jess, Katie, and Cass know that, too. My brother Ken doesn't know. And my father-in-law is a smart dude... he probably still believes that I'll divorce her, sooner-or-later. He won't be surprised when it comes."

"But down around here, I mean... *no one* else knows about Miami Beach?" She laid back down with a yawn. "Not even your coaches? They're your friends."

"Nope. Her parents and siblings know. She never had the guts to tell her grandparents, even though that was one of my conditions for us staying together after Miami Beach... that she tell her grandparents, so they'd know what I'd gone through and why I'd almost divorced her. I didn't want them to think I'd just suddenly decided I was through with their granddaughter, which is what they probably still think to this day. She agreed to tell them, then when I agreed to stay with her, she just changed her mind. She just decided *fuck me*, and she never told them. And I chose to allow that. It wasn't important enough to me.

"The other condition was that she had to end her friendship with her bestie, Abby. The one she went on the first Miami Beach trip with... the one who fucked that guy with a wife and kids within ten minutes of being at the hotel. I wasn't letting that one go. And she *did* end that, but she never had the guts to tell her grandparents."

"And almost nobody knows about... that Logan guy and the Barn thing?"

"Heh-heh... Logan-Gate... the Drunken Barn Dance... same thing. And nope. I never told anyone about that, not even my own family. Only her parents know... oh, and everyone who worked at The Hunter's Den. Oh, and the patrons at the bar that Sunday morning knew some kind of bullshit happened. But her siblings don't know about that one. I didn't tell anyone, and I'm certain her parents wouldn't tell that story. It'd be another embarrassing smudge on the family."

"Can I ask why you've never told anyone? Like, about any of it?" she asked cautiously. "I mean, *I* would have. I would have told *everyone*."

"Oh, it's simple, girl. I didn't want my two young boys to know those things about their mom. Little kids shouldn't know about problems like that between their parents, and they definitely don't need to hear shit like this about their Mommy. I also didn't want the community my boys were growing up in to know that their mom had done all that stuff. Little kids can be very cruel. So can adults. And you know... it's embarrassing for me, too. As a husband,

I mean. As a man."

"I keep learning new, more amazing things about you," she said, kissing my shoulder where she had left a bite mark earlier. "And she doesn't even know how lucky she is."

"Well, thanks, girl. There's a whole shitload more craziness about me to learn if you want. You'll have to stick around a while for all that, though," I said, testing the waters, joking but not joking.

"Cal, whatever this is that we're doing is already a thousand times better than I hoped. I'm not going anywhere anytime soon. You're just going to have to cope with my hotness for as long as you can take it."

She bit me on the shoulder again, softer this time, snuggled in close, her breathing slowed, and just when I'd thought she was asleep, she spoke again.

"Cal, I have another question. *Last* one, I promise," Selena said after a minute or two of quiet thought. I knew she was really asking for permission to be nosey.

# Chapter Eighteen:
# The Region Beta Paradox

"Go ahead, send it. You can ask anything, as many questions as you like."

"I just can't understand *how* you could stay in that marriage all this time... I know it's been for the boys and for yourself, but the situation is just *so* fucked, and it has been for *so* long."

"You know *why* I've done it, but you want to know how I haven't divorced her by now."

"Yes."

"Do you *really* want to know how? The answer is kind of... well, *involved*," I offered.

"What do you mean? Like, there's actually a *real* answer?" she asked, posting up on an elbow to look me in the eyes again.

"Yeah. It's more objective than being about the boys or about me. It's a more scientific way to look at it."

"*Scientific* and *marriage* don't seem to fit in the same sentence," she said. "But tell me. I gotta try to find a way to wrap my head around this whole thing. I just can't understand it."

"Eh, I just hope it doesn't confuse it all even more. Let's start with this: do you know what a paradox is?" I asked. Her face looked like she was wondering if she could stay awake for this.

"Ummm, honestly, no," Selena answered. "I think I've

understood it in the context of people talking before, but no, I'm not sure what it means right now."

"So, this isn't perfect, but think of a paradox as something that seems like a contradiction *at first*. So, a paradox appears to contradict itself... but with further thought, you find there is Truth behind it, or a lesson. Have you ever seen the movie *Fight Club*?"

"No. Sounds cool. Did it come out before or after I was born?" she asked, being a smart ass.

"I can't tell you that," I volleyed back.

"You can't tell me when the movie *Fight Club* came out? *Why not?*"

"Because the first rule of Fight Club is... you do not talk about Fight Club."

"Cal, we were already talking about *Fight Club* before you said we couldn't talk about *Fight Club*. *You're* the one who brought it up in the first place."

"Exactly. And we're still talking about it right now. But then you have to ask yourself, *Does it make any sense to have a 'club' that you can't talk about?* I mean, how would you recruit new members? So there's the contradiction. In the movie, one of the two main characters is named Tyler Durden – played by Brad Pitt – who starts the Fight Club as a way to teach men to break society's rules.

"But to spread the word about Fight Club, you'd have to talk about Fight Club, right? Yeah, so he's really teaching them that rules are meant to be broken, that those men should break them. So he starts by telling them that the First Rule of Fight Club is that you do not talk about Fight Club, knowing that they must. That's part of the paradox that actually teaches them to break the rules. Get it?" I asked.

"Mmmm, kind of. I see the contradiction. But then I see how the contradiction actually serves a purpose. It teaches a lesson."

"Good. Stick with the idea of that kind of contradiction and you'll understand *paradox*. Well, outside the movie, in real life, there's something called the Region Beta Paradox. Don't worry about remembering the name. But the Region Beta Paradox is a concept that kind of explains my marriage to Lily. Remember when you hurt your ankle in basketball?"

"*No. I forgot,*" she said sarcastically. "Of course I remember."

"When did it *start* hurting?"

"It started sometime toward the end of summer. I kind of rolled it and started having pain on the outside of my ankle."

"So you hurt your ankle before basketball season, but you still joined the team, right?" I asked.

"Right. Of course."

"Did you go to the doctor?"

"No" she said, a little defensively. "Are we gonna start talking about this agai-..."

"Just stay with me on this. So it hurt, but not bad enough to keep you out of basketball and not bad enough to get medical attention."

"Yeah, I guess."

"So, how *did* your sprained ankle finally get diagnosed?"

"During the season, it started hurting worse. I was worried about it being a problem next July when I go to the Marines, so I got it checked out."

"And what did you find out?" I asked.

"It was a mild sprain, they said."

"And what did you do about it?" I asked.

"I told my coach I was injured and sat out. The doc said I had to rest it."

"And then, eventually yoooouuuu... you did *what?*" I led her to the point.

"And then I quit basketball."

"And do you feel better about your situation now that you quit basketball?"

"Yeah. I was just in basketball because I've always been in

basketball. When I realized my ankle was really injured, though, I had to quit," she yawned.

"So if you think about it, you had hurt your ankle, and it was bad, but not terrible. I mean, it wasn't bad enough to keep you out of basketball, right? And you would have kept playing if it hadn't become worse. But when it *did* get worse – bad *enough* – *that* was what actually forced you to get it checked out. And when you got it checked out, and you found out it was sprained, *that* caused you to quit basketball. And by quitting basketball, you allowed it to heal so you could go to the Marines in July. So that means that if your ankle had *not* become worse, you still might be playing and potentially hurting your chances to be healthy for the Marines."

"Okay," she said, nodding, and she seemed to understand.

"*That's* the Region Beta Paradox in a nutshell. Things getting worse actually forced you to put yourself in a better place. So your situation getting worse is what *caused* it to get better. But if it *hadn't* gotten worse, you'd still be stuck in a pretty bad situation."

"So... I think I get it. With your marriage, it was really bad, but you're a stubborn motherfucker, and it wasn't bad enough for you to divorce her... until it *was* bad enough."

"Riiiiiiight," I smiled. That was a quick pick-up on her part. "So when I realized I couldn't act the part of the Happy Hubby anymore, and when the boys started being negatively affected by the situation, I knew I had to divorce her. But before that, things were bad, but nothing I couldn't cope with. It wasn't bad enough to force me to take action, so-..."

"So *it getting worse* was what pushed you to start looking for a divorce lawyer. *That's* what put you in a better position... a position to open up and give *us* a chance. So the marriage getting worse actually made things better because now you have me. And now you can be happy. And divorce would really be better for the boys than how things were going, too, right?"

"Yes. I realized it late last summer, the day Lee came into the kitchen and asked Lily and me to keep the yelling down. The whole charade had gone on too long, and I was faltering under the weight of always accepting blame, always keeping my head down, always being the Happy Hubby. It was a breaking point. In order to get better, it had to get worse. That's the apparent contradiction that is the paradox. But we can't depend on thinking things will automatically get better just because we took action to change them. Often, things get worse, still, before they really get better."

"I think *you're* a paradox sometimes."

"What the fuck is *that* supposed to mean?" I laughed quietly because she was starting to get really sleepy.

"You're such a good person... but you're not somebody to fuck with." She was getting quieter and slower, though. She was almost ready to fade off... "But when I look deeper, I see that you being somebody to *not* fuck with is actually part of what allows you to be a good person."

"And where did *that* come from?" I asked, half expecting her to be asleep before she could answer. What an interesting thought.

"I don't know," she whispered. "Cal, I'm tired."

"*After.*"

"After *what*?" she asked.

"The movie *Fight Club*. You asked if it came out before or after you were born. It came out six years *after* you were born. 1999."

"*Shhh*," she warned.

"What? What's wrong?"

"First rule of *Fight Club*..." She buried her face in my chest, giving me little kisses until somewhere in there, we faded off to sleep.

# Chapter Nineteen:
# Stomping Grounds

The next morning, while Selena and I were enjoying a long shower together, the alarm next to the bed sounded, playing music from some Chicagoland radio station I wasn't familiar with. After all, I had been living in central Illinois for almost six years. When the song "Steal Away" came on by Robbie Duprie, I laughed a little.

Selena asked why I laughed, so I had to explain that it was a very appropriate tune for what we were doing. It's a song about two people stealing away into the night to be together. She listened a little, but she didn't like the tune. It sounded too old, she said, looking at me sideways.

"I know what you're doing, Babe," I smiled. "I know you're really calling *me* old."

"Yeah, but I *like* you... even though you're old."

"I'll show you old!" and I dragged her playfully out of the shower and back onto the bed.

***

Later, I called Lily to tell her I had some places from my childhood that I wanted to visit while I was up north. That was a lie. I just wasn't ready to start heading back down south. I wasn't ready to admit that this little steal-away was coming to an end. Selena had taken control of the radio dial by then, and appropriately, Taylor Swift's "Today was a Fairytale" was playing on the radio when I made the call.

I had traveled back to my old stomping grounds to visit sites from my youth several times before over the years, so Lilith was used to it. I'd drive through the old neighborhood and visit my childhood home. I'd revisit Seminole Park, across the street from that childhood home, with the old glory days of those baseball diamonds, where I had been the best pitcher and batter of my league (I still have the original typewriter-typed stat sheets to prove it, lol).

I had more innings pitched and far more strikeouts than any other pitcher in the league, but you'd have to keep in mind it was only a 10- to 12-year-old league. I was in 6th grade that year. Though admittedly not a "fast" pitcher compared to many others, I could put the ball just past your chin to back you off home plate or just a hair above your sweet spot to fool you into a strikeout, anywhere I wanted, and I knew how to trick the best batters.

My batting average was a ridiculous .799 at the All-Star Break and .769 at the end of the season. For reference, a batting average of .300 is considered to be very good. So my batting average meant that if I stepped up to the plate, I was going to get on base from a hit (as opposed to getting on base from a walk or getting hit with a pitch) 76.9% of the time, not to mention hitting eight home runs in the season and more doubles, triples, and Runs Batted In (RBIs) than any other batter in the league. I was exceptional at aiming my hits, and I almost never hit singles. I had more doubles than triples and more triples than singles. So not only was I going to bat myself on base... I was going to bat myself at least to second base a majority of the time.

Over the years, Lily also knew I'd visit Maine West High School, the football fields, reminiscing on old wins and defeats, touchdowns, interceptions, memories, laughs, coaches, and teammates. I'd drive past friends' and old girlfriends' houses, revisit the sites of crazy shit that happened growing up. The Chicago MEPS station, where I'd signed and been sworn-in for the Marine Corps, across the street from my high school.

I'd drive past the businesses where we'd all spent time growing up. McDonald's on Oakton (yes, I know, *I know*), Kmart, Brandy's (used to be Yankee Doodle Dandy), Stan's Liquor Store (for soda and candy in junior high, and literally right next-door to where serial killer John Wayne Gacy took his last victim in the late '70s), Slurpees at 7-11, nachos at Rollie's, pizza at Nick's La Cantina, Barnaby's Pizza, Dairy Treat, etc. I'd visit Radishes Bar and the Beacon Tap, where we'd go in later years.

Visits like these were about as close to a time machine as I ever got. But I wasn't really planning to drive around the old stomping ground with Selena, reminiscing about glory days.

Selena and I never visited any of those places or shared any of those stories because it was really just about spending more time with her. I was definitely planning on taking our time to get home because once we got back there, "being together" would mean we had to go right back to sneaking around. Have I mentioned that I hate *sneaky*?

We talked about how Selena had managed to get out for the weekend without detection. She was in the habit of telling her mom that she was staying overnight at a friend's... sometimes she did, sometimes she didn't. She had likewise told Homeboy that she was headed up to Chicago with a girlfriend of hers to visit the friend's extended family. We got a late checkout from the hotel, and we stopped to grab some Chipotle before getting on the road back down south.

Chipotle was a newish thing, at least for me. I knew it was a Mexican-American twist, but my Mexican twists only stretched as far as between Taco Bell and BurritoVille at WIU. My wife and I had had our favorite authentic Mexican restaurants through the years, and as my first boy loved his Mexican food, we sometimes spent his birthdays at Agave's, the very same Mexican restaurant where I had met with Selena to talk to her about the Marines the previous summer. But I had never been to a Mexican-American twist like Chipotle.

We were sitting in the Chipotle parking lot, eating in my vehicle, when Selena's phone rang... it was Homeboy.

Selena muted the radio. I didn't feel good – felt bad, in fact. I wasn't the kind of guy to pursue another guy's girlfriend, but if she pursued me, I wasn't afraid to meet her halfway. In fact, that was how I first got together with my wife.

# Chapter Twenty:
# Study Buddies

In college at WIU in the mid-1990s, I didn't normally attend many general education classes. Keep in mind, this was before the internet became mainstream, so there really was no distance learning as we know it today with the internet, and physically going to classes was the only way it worked. I wasn't introduced to the internet until probably the fall of 1996, my senior year of college.

So, instead of going to classes regularly, I'd only go the first few days, paying attention to which of the prettiest girls in class were consistently in attendance, paying attention, and taking copious notes. Out of 100 or so female students in a general education lecture hall, that would leave me with three to five potential study partners. Then, I'd assume a seat next to the prettiest and/or best choice of those. After another couple days of befriending them, I'd offer them an arrangement that worked every single time.

If they were willing to attend every class, pay attention, take notes, and sign me in every day (if a class took attendance), I'd be at home aggressively reading and highlighting/annotating the textbook assignments, which were hundreds of pages. Then, we'd get together to share our efforts and study before each test. I'd assure them that if they agreed, I would walk away with an 'A,' and they could, too, if they were dedicated to it.

My girlfriend of several years (yep, Kay, my female best

friend from high school that I told you might show up in this story again) was fully informed and cool with all of it. Of course, she trusted me, as I didn't cheat with any of these study partners (thank God she almost never *saw* these girls – *whoah*), and the arrangements worked like a charm. I coasted through four years of college with an overall 3.89 GPA without attending Gen Ed classes. Well, Lily was the very first study buddy I met at WIU, for a Film History class my first semester there.

Toward the end of that first semester, Kay and I went on a double date with Lily and her longtime boyfriend (much, much later, after Lily and I got together, I started calling him *Fuckstick*). After that semester, for about the next year, I'd cross paths with Lily here and there around campus, say a quick hello, and go our separate ways. But as you know, when Kay and I ended it in October 1995, Lily knocked on my apartment door.

I later learned that Lily had found out about the breakup from a girl named Becky, who sat next to me in a non-Gen Ed class and who had a crush on me. That semester, every day I had that class, Lily would be walking into the classroom that I was exiting after class, and we'd stand outside the door and chat for a few minutes. I had absolutely no clue that Lily was interested in me.

I also didn't know that she was then talking with Becky, playfully encouraging this girl to ask me on a date. Becky never did, thank goodness, but when I didn't show up to class one day, Becky informed Lily that I had called and asked her to take good notes. I had also told Becky that Kay and I had just broken up, so she told Lily that she was excited because now she could get up the nerve to ask me out. But Becky was waiting to make her move because she felt bad, as she could hear in my voice that the breakup was terribly hard on me. Lily heard this and had plans of her own.

Although Lily had been with her boyfriend for like two years at this point, she convinced her roommate to move into my apartment building the summer after we had met... *because I lived there.*

Yep, Lily was a genuine stalker, but not like the stories you hear in the news. She wasn't being creepy – following me around, hiding behind bushes, taking photographs from across the street, prank-calling me in the middle of the night. None of that. She admitted to stalking me, but she was no psycho about it. No, Lily was the patient, fairly harmless kind of stalker.

I didn't even know she had moved into my building until she told me that morning after the breakup when she came knocking. She had just strategically positioned herself to attain something she wanted *if* and *when* the opportunity arose, and then she waited for the breakup. I was impressed by her patience and determination.

Coming right on the heels of the breakup with Kay, Lily's attention was distracting and flattering, and I wasn't opposed to a little *something-something* without commitment, something with no strings attached. I'd never played the role of the side-piece before, but so long as neither of us caught feelings, I figured she'd get what she wanted, and it could help me regain my equilibrium.

It was like mid-October, and I was getting in the habit of drinking daily from these super-sized cups that held a pint of Seagram's VO Whiskey on the rocks, probably two pints a day on weekends, drowning out my sorrows. VO was what my dad used to drink when I was a kid.

It started as "coping" relief for the breakup with Kay, as although we had both been 100 percent behind the breakup for the right reasons, it was terribly hard on both of us. I was certain that the drinking was *as* necessary as the breakup; it felt right when I did it, but it hurt immensely after-the-fact. It sucked, but it just *was*. So I'd sit in my studio apartment, sipping my whiskey, reading my textbook assignments in my recliner, and teaching myself both Japanese *Hiragana* and *Katakana* alphabets for my next semester of Japanese language class.

The day after I'd told Becky that Kay and I had broken up, there came a knock at my door, so I figured it was the wrestlers down the hall asking me to come over and hang out, which I often did. Usually, late at night, I'd go to their place, they'd all get blazed, and I'd get drunk, laughing our asses off, watching *Mystery Science Theater 3000* or *Beavis and Butt-Head*.

But it was Lily at my door that day, with no car keys or jacket, wearing sweats, a T-shirt, and just slippers. I was extremely surprised to see her. We both laughed, and I asked where her shoes were.

"I live here," she answered.

"You live *where*?" I asked, puzzled.

"*Here*," she said. "In this building, around the corner, but up on the third floor."

Her Tinker Bell pillow soon became a permanent fixture on my bed. Yeah, she closed the distance and marked her territory faster than I've ever seen.

I spent quite a bit of my time becoming fluent in reading/writing/speaking Japanese while my *sensei* was setting me up to teach English at the University of Tokyo, Japan. And, of course, I was reading and annotating hundreds of textbook pages every week. And then at night, usually when I'd caught enough of a buzz that it was hard to focus on reading, instead of going down the hall to the wrestlers' apartment, I'd float up to the third floor and hang out with Lily (and sometimes her roommate, who knew what was going on).

*Where is this hottie's boyfriend?* I asked myself, night after night. When I eventually asked her, she said she didn't see him much. They lived apart, and he went out a lot with the guys, leaving her home alone, channel-surfing on the TV.

*Fuckstick.*

Very early on, like within the first two to three days after she came knocking, I made her dinner. It was skinless chicken legs, some mashed potatoes and veggies, or something (she would tell me like a year later that she hated eating meat off the bone, but she hadn't wanted to offend me, so she had just smiled and eaten it).

Before long, I could tell she was catching feelings, which concerned me a little, but she kept Fuckstick around for a few months until *I* caught feelings. Then I got tired of playing *that* game and gave her an ultimatum. I insisted that if she was keeping Fuckstick around, she and I were not going to continue with any kind of contact. So, as I'd expected, she opted to end it with Fuckstick. He was a real piece of shit to her, anyway, which had been making it all easier on my conscience.

But Lily had done her share of deceiving Fuckstick in those few months before ending it. It was fucked up the way he'd sometimes show up at her place and find me there, sitting on the couch, giant whiskey cup in hand, wearing only jeans that were practically falling off me (I had stopped eating from the trauma of the break-up and was getting shredded) – no shoes, no socks, no shirt.

I was behaving like a savage after that breakup with Kay, and Fuckstick never said a word to me about hanging out with his girlfriend... which also eased my conscience. It took him *way* too long to become assertive and get after Lily about hanging out with me, but by then, it was too late. The guy deserved to have her snatched away, and I'd be lying if I said it didn't feel like I was the white knight in shining armor rescuing the princess from the evil clutches of her captor. It was a real ego-stroke, but I had caught feelings, all the same.

# Chapter Twenty-One:
# Same Story, Different Decade

And then, sixteen years later, in November of 2011, here I was, listening to Selena lie to *her* boyfriend while I tried my best not to feel like a dick. That was when it occurred to me for the first time how similar my wife and I began as compared to Selena and me.

In both cases, I was in a bad place emotionally. They advanced on me, they had boyfriends that they weren't planning to break up with, I was okay with being the side-piece, and then... I kind of wondered how it would turn out for Selena and me. I did not like listening to Homeboy on the other end of the phone, suspiciously asking her very pointed, probing questions. He was more than a little bit suspicious, and I didn't like how it made me feel.

Granted, I had eventually stolen Lily from Fuckstick, but I wasn't necessarily *stealing* Selena from Homeboy. She and I were technically just kind of borrowing each other despite the very real, growing connection between us. She had pursued me, and we were sharing time together. I had only the faintest designs of this relationship lasting. I mean, it couldn't, right? Twenty-two years apart in age? Her, being a former student of mine?

Though exploring a divorce, I was married with two young boys who were closer to her age than I was, as Lee was only 11 years her junior. Society would never allow this relationship, and besides,

I figured it was just a matter of time before the thrill was gone and one or both of us would grow bored or lose any genuine feelings we had for one another. But, on the other hand, that also sounds exactly like how Lily and I started out...

In the meantime, though, here was Homeboy on the phone, being suspicious, telling Selena he couldn't help feeling like she was being less than honest with him. Her defense was to become angry with him, ridicule his suspicions, and hang up on the guy. It was something my wife would have done. I said nothing. I really just wished I hadn't even heard any of it, that I had vacated the vehicle and gone for a walk. After all, by then, I knew exactly how it felt to be the dude asking those questions.

We finished up our Chipotle, and we got back on the road down south to central Illinois. I recall that when I turned the radio back on, just as I was getting on 53 South by Woodfield Mall, I didn't like the song that was playing: "I Don't Want to Know" by Mario Winans and a few bars by P. Diddy... so I flipped stations. No way was I going to sit there and listen to *that* song with Selena next to me right after talking to Homeboy.

# Chapter Twenty-Two:
# Odyssey

Reader, please keep in mind that XM radio began in 2001, and Sirius radio hit in 2002, but listeners had to pay a subscription for the services. I was on a small country town teacher's salary with a daily 15-minute commute, so I never cared to be a subscriber, especially with free FM radio still common and a CD player in my van. So, as I was flipping through radio stations, I came upon some oldies.

"Do you like oldies?" I asked Selena.

"What do you mean? Like stuff from the 80s?"

"Well, no. Not *really*," I tried not to laugh. "*Before* the 80s, before Classic Rock... I'd say oldies would be like 50s and maybe some 60s, though I'd label some 60s stuff as Classic Rock. I guess there's some overlap there. So, I guess I'm asking if you like 50s and 60s stuff? Like, around Elvis's time?"

"I doubt it. I don't really know any. Maybe, though."

It was another one of those moments that reminded me of the serious age gap between us. She was born in 1993, the same year I was medically retired from the Marine Corps and just six years before I married my wife. I was born in 1971, around the same time as her parents. *I had tattoos older than her.*

When Selena and I were together, though, we almost always

felt like we were about the same age. Looking back, when she and I would talk about it, we chalked it up to how cognitively mature she was for her age and how socially playful I was for mine. It was just a good combination that melded incredibly well, almost seamlessly and effortlessly.

"Well, I'm not a huge oldies fan, but if it's okay with you," I suggested, "I'll switch it up and try this oldies station. Cool?"

"Cool. But can we change it if I'm not into it?"

"No," I laughed. She backhanded my arm and laughed, too.

"Easy, Vasquez," I warned, and she hit me again. "Oh, good tune! It's called 'When a Man Loves a Woman.' This is like 60s R&B. It was a major hit at the time, and it's been redone a couple of times by other singers. I think Michael Bolton won a Grammy for his rendition in the early 90s."

"I was *born* in the early 90s."

"Yeah, Selena, I'm *aware*," and I gave her a *no-shit* look, smiling. "Some songs are just timeless. You might or might not like the sound, but check out these lyrics."

We quietly listened to that song, the confession, the painful timber of Percy Sledge's soul conveying just how deeply, hopelessly, and even foolishly a man can fall for a woman. I waited for Selena to ask me to change it, but she didn't.

I watched her, and she just concentrated on the lyrics and

looked out at the human geography of West Suburban Chicagoland passing by outside her passenger-side window. When it was over, she turned off the radio, but she didn't say anything or even look my way. She seemed to be thinking, but I thought maybe something in that song had touched a nerve or something.

"What'd you think?" I asked finally, almost afraid to hear what she'd say.

"Is it really like that?" she asked, still looking out at the suburbs.

"Is *what-*... I'm not sure what you mean."

"Cal..." She looked at me like I was stupid. "When a man Loves a woman? *Duh,*" she laughed. "Is it like that, like the song says?"

"Ummm... that's a really good question. I don't even know if I can answer that very well. But yeah, I mean, I'd say it's pretty accurate when a man *really* falls deep, *really* falls hard, and especially if he *really* falls fast. We can become kind of like dumb animals at times. I'd say that sometimes a man can become almost intoxicated by it, by *her*, and it can make him kind of foolish.

"It's gotta be some evolutionary mechanism or something," I continued. "Like how bucks go into rut in the fall and lose their fucking minds. You probably already know this, but that's why deer hunting season is in the fall – they're out of their minds in rut, looking to mate. Almost toxic doses of testosterone stop males from foraging, making them more active, more aggressive, and less wary of predators.

"Except in the song, it's not talking just about sex. It's talking about *love*, so add oxytocin, endorphins, serotonin, and dopamine to that elevated testosterone. I've heard of those together called the pleasure cocktail. I was high as hell off it the night you convinced me to give us a chance outside of wrestling practice. When you drove away, I walked back into the gym a little dizzy from it."

"*Really?*" she asked, smiling large. "You didn't tell me that."

"Yeah, uh, sorry... I mean-... wow, this is *weird*... I'm not trying to say I love you... it was just that hormone cocktail that got me. I was like that plus Hulk-like doses of gamma radiation for my girlfriend of over five years, Kacey. I called her Kay. I might have mentioned her before. I felt that way about her the whole time we were together and for a very long time after we broke-up. Except I loved Kay. I mean, I *loved* her like-..." I looked over, but Selena didn't stop me. She was looking right back at me, eyes wide, ears open.

"*Anyway*, I always thought I'd marry her, but maybe that whole story is better for another time. But yeah, she had been my best friend my senior year of high school – her junior year – and we got together when I came home for my ten days of leave after Boot

Camp. So I was gone in the Marines for the early part of our relationship, then had part of my skull removed in Hawaii and the whole dark aftermath of that, then through most of college. My love for Kay was deep and powerful, and it made me more foolish at times than I'd like to talk about."

"Like a dumb animal?" Selena asked, smirking.

"Uhhhhh, yeah. Probably. Yeah, sometimes I was like a dumb animal with her."

"I think that's sweet," Selena said, thinking. Then: "Okay, so I *gotta* ask. Did you ever cheat on Kay when you were away in the Marines?"

"No. Never. Never even felt a little tempted to. Other Marines fucked with me about it, but I had the sweetest angel waiting at home for me. Having sex with some Camp Pendleton base baby, or some Okinawa buy-me-drinky girl, or some Hawaiian hottie... not a chance. Even with *my* libido, I abstained without any difficulty at all. Kay was too important to me."

"What is *that*... that Oki-... Oki*nawa* girl you mentioned?"

"Oh. When young men go into the Marines and get stationed in Okinawa, Japan – and they're halfway around the world from friends, family, and everyone they've ever known – almost all get really lonely. They also have a steady paycheck for the first time with almost no bills. So they go to these little titty bars, and the dancers are called *buy-me-drinky girls* because they'll approach these young, lonely Marines – sit with them, whisper sweet things to them, maybe rub on them, so long as the guys keep buying them drinks. The drinks were tiny, like just a few ounces, and they were made up of like 7-Up or 7-Up with a splash of Coca-Cola, and they would sell for ten bucks a drink back in 1991. I know, *I know*, you were born in 1993.

"*Anyway*, at the end of the night, these girls turn in all of the straws they've collected from those drinks, and the Mama-san running the place pays them a commission for how many straws they turn in. So the more drinks they get Marines to buy them, the more commission money they make."

"*Buy-me-drinky girls* is a fuckin' hilarious name," Selena said, entertained.

"It's because they walk up and ask, 'Buy me drinky?'" I clarified. We laughed.

"Do they have sex with the guys?"

"Sometimes, but it seemed like almost never unless the guys paid for it. Then, yes. I knew a guy who regularly slept with them for money, but I don't know how routine that is in those places. I only stopped out to one once, secretly, with a sergeant in my unit so he could show me how it all worked and where my fellow Marines were going off-base and blowing all their money. None of my friends would tell me, mostly because they all did it."

"Wow. But you didn't cheat... you're not like most guys. Most guys would pay for it in a heartbeat. I thought *all* guys would."

"No, I'm not like most guys in that way. I've always known that. But I did have a close Marine buddy in Okinawa named Manny who was freshly married – Kay and I went to his wedding when Manny and I were home on leave after Nuclear-Biological-Chemical School, before he and I went to Okinawa together – and he never cheated on his wife. Good dude. But, I mean, I guess I'm not *that* different because... *here I am,* right?"

Selena clearly didn't want to talk about that, as she changed the subject.

"I want you to tell me more about Kay sometime. I think I could learn a lot about you from it. Anyway, I kind of like that song on the radio, but you're right. I mostly like the lyrics. It's kind of a window into this man who knows he's too far gone for this woman but can't help it. It's almost like he's apologizing for it, but he's not."

"Wow. Yeah. *Exactly.*" I was extremely impressed by her quick analysis. I knew then that we'd have to talk a lot more about music. And movies. And everything.

"And what about that part with the best friend?" she asked.

"What do you mean?"

"Like in the song. Did you ever have to defend Kay against any of your friends or anybody who, like, *put her down*, as the song says?"

"Uh, I don't think so, no. Even if any one of my friends *could* ever find something to *not* like about Kacey – which was just about impossible – they would never say anything to *me* about it. That would have been a problem. When you're *that* far gone for a girl – like how I was that far gone for Kay for five years – stand the fuck by, tread lightly, and do it carefully. I was a fighter in those days, and I was in *way* deep for her."

"So, don't take this the wrong way," she said, carefully, "but what about, like, your best friend Cass or your brother? They just met me. What if one of them said something about not liking me?"

"Well, I wouldn't worry about that. There's nothing to not like about you. But I could understand one or both of them saying something to me about our age difference or maybe even about you being a former student of mine. Or about bringing you to Cass's place unannounced. I'll have to talk to Cass about that and apologize. I don't know what I was thinking, not filling him in first. I can't deny that I've made some questionable decisions lately, kind of like the song is talking about."

"You mean questionable decisions about *me*?" she asked,

surprised.

"I mean, yeah. Definitely. Not anything that is your fault. I make my own decisions, period. But since last Sunday, I've been acting increasinglyyyyy... let's say, lately, I've been increasingly risky and less cautious, less thoughtful and vigilant than I usually am. Bottom line, if I really wanted to take you to Cass's because I wanted to spend more time with you, then I should have at least given them both a heads up. So, to answer your question, Pip and Cass might share some concerns about you and I and about tonight.

"But those are reasonable concerns for them to have," I continued. "I'd just talk it out with them, though. Once they understood the details of us and why it's more of a taboo or stigma than a real concern, they'd understand. We'd work it out, no problem. They'd forgive me for taking you there unannounced. They're smart, and I trust them... they'd just talk to me about it, and we'd work it out. They'd probably just call me a dumb ass, and we'd laugh it all off."

***

On a related but separate note, I found out later from Pip that Cass was pretty upset over that Saturday night. He was pissed that I was cheating on Lily. He had recently gone through a divorce from the girl he'd been with forever because she'd been cheating. He was pissed that I had let Selena have some alcohol in his house, too.

After we left Cass's place that night, he had let loose on Pip, saying how pissed he was, saying that they had a responsibility to report me to the authorities – that I am entrusted as a teacher to teach youths, and I had broken that trust. There had been follow-up calls to Pip about it, too, and they had met out for drinks, where Cass doubled down on his views.

*Who you talking to, Cass? Who you trying to turn against me, Cass? My* real *brother? Pip? My most trusted partner on the entire goddamn planet? Good luck with that one, motherfucker.*

# Chapter Twenty-Three:
# The First Casualty

They say the first casualty in war is Truth. I'd say the first casualty in betrayal is Trust.

When I learned of this bullshit with Cass from Pip, I was shocked, then furious, then *irate*. Cass never said a word *to me* about any of it. Although I was already of the mind that I had made a mistake by bringing Selena to Cass's and by potentially putting my two brothers in an uncomfortable, compromised position, and although I had already conceded to myself that I needed to apologize for being so stupid about it... I couldn't believe the level of Cass's betrayal.

He was pissed about one wine cooler Selena sipped at while eating her dinner... *big deal, Cass*. He thought perhaps he should *REPORT ME TO THE AUTHORITIES*, that I had broken the TRUST as a teacher?! *Fuck you, Cass.*

I had only broken the stupid social norms and taboos that said an 18-year-old can sign up to potentially give his/her life or life-long health for our country, but an 18-year-old can't always choose which adult they want to be with. And, as we already know, she was far removed from being a student of mine or in my school, and she wasn't a minor. I held no power over her. She chose me of her own free will with nothing to gain for it and everything to lose.

*That's fine, Cass... roll the bones and see, player.*

He never asked for an explanation. He never asked for an apology. He just went straight Judas Iscariot mode. I never even had an opportunity to apologize. And after hearing of his betrayal, I'd be damned before I'd apologize to that motherfucker.

He didn't care that she was 18, an adult. He didn't ask if this had started in any way back when she had been a student of mine or at my school six months earlier or when she was a minor. He didn't care to find out who had pursued whom. He didn't care that he *would* have been right about me breaking the trust *had she been a minor,* or *had she been a student of mine* during this senior year, or *if she was even still going to the school where I taught.*

Any one of those situations would warrant being reported. But there was not a word said to me nor a question asked of me, and yet he was instantly trying to turn my *brother* against me, to *report* me... after Pip and I had treated him like a brother for over twenty years! *Oh, fuck that.*

And the motherfucker didn't care that, during *his* divorce, I had his back and wanted to defend him with extreme prejudice. I was infuriated that his wife had betrayed him, pissed at the girl who had been my close friend as long as Cass had been, since high school, 22 years, a woman I would have fought to protect like she was my own wife. He was a great guy, a loyal soulmate to her, and that bitch fucked him over royally. I had been ready to go on the warpath for Cass, doing everything I could to talk him up, keep his outlook positive, show him support, keep myself from murdering the bitch. *That's* what a best friend does. *That's* what a brother does.

And our two stories were nothing alike. Cass *knew* how bad my marriage had been. He *knew* about my wife's transgressions over the years, in detail. He *knew* she and I had no sex life for all those years. He *knew* I planned to divorce Lily when the kids were out of the house. And that fucking turncoat was going to judge *me?! Fuck you, homie.*

I had stuck with my wife *after* forgiving her for Florida, and I treated her like a queen, with breakfast-to-order in bed on Saturdays, for a handful of years *after* she forced me to give up on her.

Those two, Pip and Cass, were my brothers. One brother accepted my mistake that night and, by telling me about the other's betrayal, supported me even though I was doing something I swore I'd never do... cheat on my wife. The other was no best friend, no brother of mine; he had no idea how to be *my* brother.

I didn't burn energy on Cass; I just ended communication with him. He had made his choice. I had been his Best Man at his wedding, but there was a reason *my* Best Man was Pip. Cass had stood up for me at my wedding with my closest lifelong friends and biological brothers. His now ex-wife had stood up as a bride's maid for Lily. Him, his ex-wife, me, and Lily had gone on whitewater rafting vacations together in the Rockies and the Smokies. He and I had done all New Year's Eves together since 1993. But I had no use for him anymore, not after this.

His bitch-ass had always been the weaker friend between the two of us, but I had been happy to always work harder to maintain the friendship. He never wrote to me in the Marines, though I found time to write letters home to my friends *from fucking Marine Corps boot camp* where I was in charge of almost a hundred recruits.

I never heard from him after having part of my skull removed, all the complications I suffered through, recovering for a year in my parents' basement... and the motherfucker lived a handful of blocks away. I didn't even get a quick visit to say hello, didn't get a goddamn phone call! It was as if he'd forgotten about the friendship as soon as I'd left for recruit training. It was *me* that called and visited *him* after I returned home, after I started healing up and getting out in public again.

Now, *this* nailed it shut. Cass became the first casualty of the age taboo between Selena and I. He would not be the last.

On a side note... against my better judgment, I agreed to meet with Cass a couple of years later. We stopped out to an Irish establishment called the Kerry Piper where I used to meet him after work many years earlier, up in southwest Chicagoland. We sat at a table in the darkened dining area, having a few Guinness, and admittedly, I had gone there with a bad taste still dank in my mouth.

There was really nothing to be done here but walk away with some closure. I didn't want to bitch at him for any of it – no sense in that – and I knew he would just stammer out some weak excuses for why he felt the way he did or said to Pip what he had said on several occasions. He'd have no valid reason for his choices, nor for why he never talked to me about his problem with me. And the meeting went as expected.

When I decided it was time for me to go, that I was indeed wasting my time, he handed me an invite to the upcoming marriage to his soon-to-be new bride. I took the invite, but I was so unimpressed by his uninspired and disingenuous discussion that night that I don't ever remember seeing that invite again after he handed it to me.

I didn't give it – or him – a second thought. I don't need a best friend or brother like that. Pip is and will always be a pillar in my life, but Cass never really was. As they say, with friends like that, who needs enemies? Cass and I do not speak to this day – not out of anger or hatred on my part... just out of practicality. And I haven't missed him a day in my life since.

# Chapter Twenty-Four:
# Week Two

Upon my return from Chicagoland that Sunday evening, I was met coldly by my wife and joyously by my boys. The three had already eaten, as I had cooked and left meals in the fridge, ready to reheat in the microwave. My wife simply said I should have been home to make dinner, and though she wasn't wrong, I recognized it as bait for a fight, but I wasn't biting. She was extremely angry with me, and I knew to just weather the storm.

We tucked the kids into bed separately that night, her first, me keeping a wide berth from the Gorgon that my wife had seemingly so quickly become. She was onto *some*thing, *some*how, and though I couldn't blame her suspicion and harsh feelings toward me, I knew that she didn't *know*-know. If she had, she wouldn't be creeping around me like Medusa stalking her prey — she'd be tearing shit up like the Kraken.

After wrapping up Ronny Taco and Lee Burrito in their blankets, hugging and kissing them at will with some tickles once they were wrapped, I went to my den, only once venturing out into the boys' room to check on them. The cold shoulder, accompanied by a couple of turn-you-to-stone glares, and Lily retreated to her lair for the night.

When the coast was clear, I checked my phone, as I had been

purposely avoiding it since I got home, keeping it on silent. There were two texts from Selena. She wanted to know if I could duck out of practice the next night and head to her place for some alone time, as her mom had taken on an extra shift that day.

I told her I couldn't do that, as I wouldn't be at practice the next night. I had been spending less time grading lately, mostly because of wrestling season and *us*, and I was beginning to fall behind. My father-in-law was taking the boys to wrestling the next evening, as I had to stay at the school so I could catch up, so we *could* see each other more. She asked if she could call me just then, and I reluctantly texted that she could not.

*Not tonight. Lily is on to something, but she doesn't know-know. She could be lurking right outside my closed den door right now, trying to decipher what's going on.*

*Okay*, she texted. *Then maybe I'll come to your school tomorrow night and bang you in the janitor's closet.*

Few ladies had ever talked dirty like that to me, like Torch and Sully from clinical school. Or Kenya, Dayna, and Trina from college during that period after Kay and before Lily and I became a committed couple. Anyway, I knew well that Selena might just be serious enough to show up at my school for a little fun, for the thrill, and that could *not* happen. She was probably just looking for a knee-jerk reaction, but on the other hand, there definitely *was* a chance she could be serious. She had that streak of daring in her that made me more than a little nervous sometimes.

And there *was* a knee-jerk reaction, as I texted *Okay, that was hot. I'll give you that. But I don't ever want you to step foot inside that school while I'm in it. I can't deal with the clashing vibes I'm getting thinking about that. I'm sorry to be a downer.*

There was a long pause before she responded.

*Don't worry, no downer. I'm just playin Babe*, she replied. *I wouldn't risk your job and I get it with the grading but we'll text and call tomorrow and I'll see you at wrestling practice on Tuesday night right?*

*You're going to wrestling practice Tuesday?* I texted back. I had just assumed that had come to an end with her quitting basketball.

*Yeah*, she replied. *I'll be there unless you don't want me there. I thought I'd come after she picks up Ronny. I can wait in my car until they leave.*

*Yeah, that'd be fantastic*, I replied. *Just call me when you see them leave just in case something goes wrong or changes before that.*

*Like what?*

*I have no idea, but she's suspicious of something, and it's got to be us. Like I said, she doesn't know-know, but she's probably onto us. Please, just call first, okay, Babe?*

*Okay I'll call first. And I'll talk to you tomorrow, anyway.*

* * *

Tuesday came, and it brought wrestling practice. By then, I had noticed that my wife seemed almost totally back to normal, paying little to no attention to me unless she had something to blame me for or fight with me about. How perfectly typical that when she was on the scent of something with Selena and I, her interest in me absolutely peaked. Not because she had feelings for me, but rather in defense of her pride, defending her claim on the property that belonged to her: *me.*

But when that threat died down, she was back to not giving a shit about me one way or the other. Not that I had any false hope that her radar for Selena had stopped blipping. I wasn't that easy to smokescreen. No, her radar was still reaching out there into the landscape, scanning the terrain for any hint of what she was still determined to uncover.

Lily came to practice, picked up Ronny, and had a few words for me about being home by 8 pm, directly after practice. I confirmed that, yes, we would be home directly. Where else would Lee and I go? Except maybe to Taco Bell to grab him a couple of tacos and his favorite cinnamon twists.

I reminded Lily and Ronny of how proud I was of Ronny's progress, as this was his first year. He was picking it all up really well. And I reminded her how proud I was of Lee for his efforts and progress, though he was still at practice, transitioning to the older group. I again mentioned that we'd probably hit Taco Bell, as usual, and she just emphasized that I should be home around eight o'clock or so. We'd be later than that, of course, but I'd learned years ago to just keep my mouth shut and take her disapproval in stride when Lee and I showed up at home around 8:15 or 8:30 or whenever. It's the whole *ask for forgiveness instead of permission* thing, you know the saying. We had finished the little bit of homework Lee had right after school, before his and Ronny's 20-minute power nap, and she knew that. But it wasn't about Lee's homework, of course. She wanted *me* at home where she could monitor me.

By about 20 minutes after Lily and Ronny headed home, I started to think maybe Selena had changed plans. By now, I was well-aware of how eager she always was for us to spend time together. I was just as eager, and it was really, really nice to know someone was thinking of me, that a female wanted so genuinely to spend time with me. I thought she'd be walking into the gym two minutes after Lily walked out, just out of being anxious to spend time.

I was impressed when she walked in after those 20 minutes. She told me she had been in the parking lot when Lily and Ronny walked out. Lily had not left straight away, though. She had sat in her car, surveilling the parking lot and the roads near the school.

My wife was definitely waiting for her to show up, Selena thought. But Lily didn't necessarily know Selena's car as Selena sat in an adjacent parking lot, parked in a group of wrestling parents' cars. She didn't know what to look for. After 15 minutes, Lily must have been satisfied that the coast was clear, and she pulled away. Selena had waited another five minutes just in case Lily doubled back on some jealous hunch.

And it wasn't like I *wouldn't* tell my wife that Selena had come by, if asked. I certainly wouldn't volunteer the information, but I also wasn't going to ask Lee to keep it quiet by any means. Why couldn't my wife know that Selena had come by to visit? She was aware that Selena had quit the basketball team, and she knew that during basketball practice Selena had visited me before. Now that Selena wasn't playing, maybe she was driving by and got bored, thought she'd stop in. There wasn't a lot for young people to do in small, rural towns like that. It wasn't a crime to cruise the town and stop in to hang out with a friend.

# Chapter Twenty-Five:
# Little Boys and Their Daddies

Sometime later, Selena asked if we could go outside. I told her that as much as I wanted to, this would not be that kind of night. Tonight, I felt a need to stay and watch Lee, to see his progression as a wrestler, and to let him *see* me there watching him. I explained to Selena that one of my core beliefs about fathers and sons is that little boys absolutely need their daddies to *see* them. I explained how I had grown up never feeling like my father *saw* me.

I was in my father's presence a lot from fourth grade on, especially on construction sites and in his work truck, but he never really *saw* me. In our household, it was almost unknown that I excelled at anything. It didn't matter how dominant I had been as a child athlete or how many other people cheered me on stage from the time I was in third grade. As far as he knew, I was simply number five of six. He was never there to see me as anything else, even once. Well, maybe he saw me *one* time.

I remember one time during a baseball game, right across the street from the house where I grew up, I was in the on-deck circle, about to bat. The only teammate of mine who had ever met my father came up to the fence from inside the dugout and asked me if that was my father walking up from the other baseball diamond, nearest to the street. I didn't even look... I said no, it wasn't him. I remember being a little pissed off that this kid had even asked me that.

But after the batter ahead of me struck out, I stepped up to home plate and happened to see my father walking up to the bleachers where my mom was sitting. I swung at the first pitch and knocked a three-run homerun ball far over the fence, hitting the retaining wall of the I-90 tollbooth above right field. I knew it was a homer as soon as I connected with it, and I looked over my shoulder to the bleachers. Though he was already walking away, my father stopped, turned, and looked out at right field where that ball hit the wall and disappeared in the long grass. I guess the cheers from the crowd and from my dugout caught his attention. Then without any reaction, he turned and continued toward home. I watched him until my coach started yelling at me to run the bases for my homer.

To this day, I have no idea if he even knew I had been the batter. I never asked my mom why he had come by, and even after he became my best friend in my adult life, I never asked him about it. Instead, I have always deliberately chosen to believe that he *saw* it, that he knew it was me, and that he was impressed. I think I was afraid to ask the Truth in case he hadn't known it was me, or perhaps worse, that he had no memory of it at all.

And I guess there was *one* other time, maybe. The only other memory I have of my father's presence at my sporting events was when I was in seventh grade football. I had been playing football since fourth grade, and though my parents had always taken me to my older siblings' games, my parents never did have an interest in me playing football. In their defense, we should keep in mind that I was about ten years younger than those siblings, so my parents had already been there, done that. They had already raised a family by the time I was in sports. I don't think they *could* have been interested in me playing football unless I had been a truly phenomenal athlete, like my bother Ken and sister Jess. And maybe not even then.

In junior high football seasons, we'd play every Saturday morning at Forest Elementary School, which had a vast field that I'd say allowed for maybe six or eight shortened-field tackle football games to run simultaneously. So there'd be a large assortment of different team jersey colors packing that field. I recall a friend of mine asking if that was my father's pickup truck driving past, and when I looked, I was surprised to see that it was. There was no mistaking the custom wooden toolboxes built up on both sides of the truck bed, with ladders stacked atop them. It was him.

I watched his truck slow down and roll past the field. He didn't stop, but I didn't expect him to, as I knew he wouldn't have known which color jersey I wore. All those jersey colors probably just confirmed for him that there was no need for him to stop. I mean, I don't even know if he was aware that I played football at *that* particular field. I remember being very aware that he probably wasn't there because I was; more likely, he was in the neighborhood on a job site. Again, though... I never asked. I just chose to believe that he had at least made an effort to come *see* me.

And so here is the kicker that is so unfair to my mom – she very rarely missed one of my baseball games from second to sixth grades, and yet it is these two memories of my father being nearby for just a few moments that are most clearly burned into my memory. The idea that he *might* have seen me or *tried* to see me have stuck with me over four decades.

Let me be clear, though – I never felt the slightest bit of anger toward my father regarding my childhood, never felt neglected, and never felt like he was inadequate in any way. Quite the opposite, in fact. I innately felt proud of my father, because he was a very masculine, hard-working man, and that resonated with me despite the absence of a relationship with him. You know, the whole "My dad can beat up your dad" kind of thing that little boys argue about. But I had a constant drive to *try* to be worthy of his attention, and I absolutely believe that *that* drive existed in me exactly *because* he was a man, *because* he was my father. All the love and attention my mom showered me with growing up could never fill the need I had for my father's recognition and approval. I needed him to *see* me.

It was the single greatest reason why I had chosen to test myself against other young men in the military, and it was absolutely the *sole* reason I chose the longest, toughest, most demanding military basic training in the world as my proving ground. And yeah, my exceptional performance in Marine Corps Boot Camp *did* finally earn my father's attention, respect, and approval. As an added bonus, the Marine Corps was *why* and *where* I learned that I was intelligent... that I always had been. Especially now that my father has passed on, I will always be grateful for my upbringing and proud that I had the balls to make that relationship happen. *I earned him.*

And I honestly wouldn't change any of that at all, despite how hard that was as a kid, because it *made* me earn his attention. But maybe I just wasn't tough enough to bear putting my boys through some kind of similar hunger for my attention throughout childhood.

I think it can be very dangerous – or at least very risky – to make young boys work for their father's attention and approval. For a boy like I had been, it *might* make him stronger, and tougher, and help him realize his potential; but for another boy, it *might* make him angry and harbor an unhealthy sense of self-worth. These are the inner-workings and the delicate balance between nature vs. nurture.

So from the time Lee was born, I was constantly telling him that I *see* him (*I see you, kid! I see you!*), and I'd look deep into his green eyes. Thinking back, I find it strange that Lily never asked me why I was saying that all the time. I don't think she and I ever talked about this part of my upbringing or my philosophy on raising boys. When I'd say it (*I see you, kid!*), Lee would focus his eyes on mine, and I have no doubt that *that* absolutely was at least part of the catalyst for our telepathy, the unique bond between us. Just as I had deliberately forged a relationship with my father, I deliberately forged a relationship with my son. If only I had been around for that first year of Ronny's life to forge a similar relationship.

That night at wrestling practice, I didn't tell Selena about everything I just shared with you, Reader. In fact, I don't believe I've ever shared that with anyone. But I did try to convey to Selena my belief in the power of a daddy *seeing* his boys, the power of those boys *seeing* their daddy *see* them.

When I looked over at the practice after explaining this to Selena... *no shit, there it was*. Just as if Lee could sense me talking about him, he was standing straight up, staring at me, his partner down on the mat, looking up at him quizzically.

"See, look at *that*," I said, kind of excited. "It's like he can sense me talking about him. No way he can hear us from here, but he just *knows*."

"*No shit!* Look at him!" she confirmed.

Upon seeing Selena and I looking at him kind of excitedly, Lee said something to the wrestlers around him and double-timed it over to me. "Do you need me, Daddy?"

"No, Lee," I said, laughing. "You're just tuned into my conversation right now. I was talking about you, and it was like you heard me."

"Oh... yeah," he replied, smiling. "I didn't hear you, but I kind of *knew*. It's our thing, isn't it?"

"Yup. Like your mom always says, we're telepathic. You're a very sensitive receiver. But no, I didn't need you for any reason. You had a great first practice. By the way, good work with that over-the-top single-leg takedown you keep doing, or whatever that is... did your coaches teach you that? I didn't see them teaching anything like that, and I've never seen it before."

"No, I just noticed with one kid I could reach his knee over his back... so I fake low, he goes low to stuff my takedown, I take his knee by reaching over his shoulder, and push into him to put him on his back. I showed my friend, Billy, but he can't do it. The older kids tried it, and they can take *us* down that way, but they can't make it work on each other."

"Wow. Cool! I saw you guys messing around with it. Sounds like you created some new takedown. I think it works because you're almost always going to be taller and longer than opponents at your weight. Let me know what Coach says about it. It looks kind of weird, but it seems to keep working."

"Yeah, it works pretty good most of the time. I better get back, though. Hi, Selena," and he gave her a quick hug while she pretended he was all sweaty and stinky. He pretended to rub it on her before he went back to work.

"You two are different," Selena said, looking into my eyes. I didn't know what that meant, but when she really looked into me like that, I knew to pay close attention... she was being serious. "I mean, like, I've never seen a kid and his dad like you two. It's probably partially that telepathic stuff or whatever, but it's something else, too. Something more than that. You two are just dialed into each other or something. It makes me happy to just see that between you two, like-... I don't know how to explain it. It's just on a different level than everybody else. It must drive your wife nuts."

"Yeah, it does. And how it makes you feel happy... I feel that way with him all the time," I said. "God or the Universe or whatever just gave it to us... that *something*. It's probably the best gift I've ever received, and I'm pretty sure I've never done anything to deserve it.

"I mean Lee *and* Ronny, *both*. But the gift I'm jabbering about, *the bond*, is only with Lee right now. Just imagine if Ronny could tune into it, too? *Imagine that.* I think about that all the time, and I'm constantly looking for signs of it from Ronny. Right now, he just stares at Lee and me... he knows something is going on that he doesn't understand. As he gets older, he might develop it though. I really hope he does. The three of us might be on the same wavelength. *That* would drive Lily crazy as hell, like when we all watch that crazy *Wipeout!* show," I said laughing.

I shared with Selena an example that proved my point about how little boys need their daddies to *see* them. Once in the summer 2010, my wife yelled through the house that the boys were calling for me out in the front yard. She said they were playing monkey-in-the-middle with a friend. I went to the door, and Lee called time-out and came running up the steps.

"Are you gonna come watch us play, Daddy?" he asked, looking up with hopeful eyes.

"Yeah, kid. Let me just grab some ice water, and I'll be right out."

"*YAY!*" he called to the other two, "*He said he's gonna come watch us!*"

Sometimes, I wonder if I *ever* forget memories about my boys. I don't think I ever do, thank God, or the Universe, or whatever.

Selena said she understood, and I got the feeling that she was hinting at her relationship with her dad, growing up. She had talked about it superficially on our drive up to Chicagoland, but to someone paying close attention to every word, to her body language, to slight changes in facial expressions, to inflections of voice and tone, it seemed that she still had more healing to do than she had been letting on. So, she said she understood why I needed to stay and watch Lee's practice. She asked if I minded her hanging out with me while I did that, and I laughed and asked her to please stay.

# Chapter Twenty-Six:
## *El Quiere Taco Bell*

When practice was over and all the wrestling mats were wiped down and rolled up against the walls of the gym, Lee ran over to us, noticeably pleased, excited even. I knew I had made a good choice to stay and watch, then. He began asking if I had seen this half-nelson on that one nine-year-old kid, did I see him bridge and flip the hips to escape bottom, did I like it when he-... And then, just like that, mid-sentence, he switched to hungry-kid mode, asking if we could stop and grab some tacos and twists at Taco Bell. I assured him that was where we were going.

Lee pumped his fist and exclaimed, "Yes! Hey Selena, are you coming with us? Daddy, we could go inside and sit down for a little while so I can see my food."

That was a surprise... the part about Selena coming, not the part about sitting down inside Taco Bell. Lee had often complained that he couldn't see his food in the pitch-black back bench of my van on that 20-minute drive home through country roads, surrounded by timber and cornfields, with no road lighting of any kind. The personal overhead lights in the very back of the van weren't the best and rarely worked at all. I'd had it checked out; it was an electrical short, and the expense of fixing it didn't make sense for the minor inconvenience. But I really was tired of finding diced tomatoes, shredded lettuce, grated cheese, and taco meat all over the back bench of the van, where Lee liked to set up shop in his car seat with his Taco Bell.

I had once asked him after we got home from practice to please try harder to *not* drop food all over the bench in my van, and he said he would try, but it was hard in the dark. I couldn't blame him for that, and jokingly thought to myself *If only I had some night vision goggles for him.* In one of those too coincidental to be coincidence moments, Lee walked out of the room, mumbling, "It would be so much easier if I could just see in the dark."

Selena looked at me expectantly, smiling, while Lee gave her a quick hug. I explained that Mommy was at home expecting us by eight, but he pulled the old, "Puh-leeeeez, Daddy? (then, pointing to the wall clock) It's already past eight! I just want to sit down and eat. It won't take long."

I caved, and I warned Lee that he'd have to explain to his mom why we were late getting home, or if she called, *he* was going to have to handle it. He had no qualms about that and snagged my cell phone out of my hand, pretending to talk to his mom: "Yeah, hi, Mommy. Yeah, I know we're late. Yeah, I know we were supposed to be home at eight. I know, Mommy, I told Daddy that, but Daddy said we have to go *inside* Taco Bell to sit down so I don't mess up his van."

He was looking at me expectantly to see my reaction, smiling so huge he could barely finish his last words, and by the time I took my first step toward him to make him pay with tickles, he was already laughing and two steps ahead of me. The boy was impressed with himself. As his mom often reminded us, "He is AAAALLLL you, Daddy."

I looked at Selena, she smiled warmly back at me, and I asked if she'd like to join us for an elegant dinner at a local, high-end, ethnic dining establishment. Lee looked at me with a ruffled brow. Selena laughed and said, "Sure. You convinced me." So we went, Selena following us in her car.

All said, Taco Bell took about a half-hour, which meant we were going to be over a half-hour late getting home. Lee sat quietly eating his two tacos on this night, along with an order of cinnamon twists that, for some reason, he liked to take his time with and savor. When he was done with the first order of twists, he asked for another order, so after a moment, I allowed it and handed him some money to go order. After that one, he was clearly taking advantage of Selena and I talking, and he asked for *another* order. Totally out of my norm, I allowed a third order. They were only little bags with a handful of twists inside, without much sugar, and made up of mostly cinnamon and air. And my boys' diets had very, very little sugar, normally.

When Lee returned with his third order of twists, I made a quick decision. I had planned to wait until Selena and I were alone again to give her the birthday gift that had finally arrived in the mail. It wasn't anything that everyone couldn't know about, or that Lee couldn't see, as it had been ordered for her birthday, long before Selena had popped the question and before either of us had feelings for the other. Lily knew about the gift, though she had seemed to forget about it, as she had never asked about it after the day I ordered it, and she hadn't been home when it had arrived in the mail. So, I decided to go ahead and let Selena have her birthday gift.

"You know, your birthday gift arrived in the mail recently," I told her. Lee looked up from his crisps and paid attention. He was sitting there pretending not to be listening, but he wasn't fooling anyone... I knew he was always cued into me. Selena sat up straight in her seat, a big smile grew, and she gave me a quick up-and-down look, as if scanning for it, but it was in my jacket pocket. "I think you're going to love it."

"Is it *here*? My birthday was *weeks* ago," and she laughed a little at her own excitement. "May I have it, please?"

"Oh, so all of a sudden you're miss prim, proper, and polite?" I laughed.

I pulled it out from my jacket pocket, and she knew it was a small jewelry box right away. I reached across the table and took her hand, placing the box in her palm. She opened it slowly, almost as if she was trying to build her own suspense. When she opened it, she put her hand over her mouth and said, "Oh my gosh, I love it... um... what *is* it? I mean, I know it's a ring-... a gold ring, but-... "And we both laughed out loud. Lee looked at the ring, then at Selena, then at me.

# Chapter Twenty-Seven:
# Claddagh

"Daddy, what's *that?*"

"That's the birthday present I ordered for Selena on the internet months ago, and it just got delivered, so I'm giving it to her now."

"Oh," he said, still looking at me. "Is it a *ring?*"

"So, to answer both of you, it's called an Irish Claddagh ring. Lee, are you Irish?"

"Yep," he nodded. "You know *that*, Daddy. You're 100 percent. I'm probably 75 percent." He was repeating what he'd heard Mommy and I say.

"Well, someday you'll probably have a Claddagh ring, too." I went on to explain both the meaning of the ring and the two ways it could be worn.

"An Irish Claddagh ring consists of two hands holding a heart that is topped with a crown," I explained. As I said this, Lee scooted closer to Selena and leaned in to see the ring more clearly. He grabbed a napkin and wiped his hands, then reached down and gently pulled Selena's hands with the little box closer for inspection.

"The hands symbolize Friendship, the heart stands for Love, and the crown represents Loyalty," I explained. "It is usually worn on the left-hand ring finger. If someone wears the ring so that they, themselves, can see the hands, heart, and crown properly, it represents that they are taken, in a relationship and unavailable, possibly married. And if they wear the ring facing outward, so others can see it properly, then it indicates to others that they are single, perhaps available."

She slipped the ring onto her left-hand ring finger, and it fit. Lee bent closer toward her, as they were both sitting opposite me at the table, and he took a good look at the ring.

"Why'd you put the ring facing *you*, Selena?" he asked.

"She's got a boyfriend, Lee, remember? He was with her at our game that time, right here in Delphia? And he was with her at the Firedance Festival, by the dunk-tank? Remember?"

Selena just kept looking into my eyes, as though trying to read whether I was really talking about Leonard or myself being her boyfriend. I didn't even know, as I didn't know what she had meant by putting the Claddagh ring on that way. Selena and I weren't a thing yet, that long ago. I figured I must be misreading the look she was giving me.

Then I went on to explain to both of them that I have two Goddaughters, one my sister Jess's daughter, and one my brother Ken's daughter, Lee's and Ronny's cousins. I explained that when they turned 16, I took them shopping for their first

Claddagh rings, as every Irish girl should have a nice Claddagh. So, likewise, as Selena's mom is 100% Irish, Selena is a 50% Irish girl, so I had chosen to get Selena something that represented our friendship (and Selena looked up from the ring), something meaningful, something she could take with her when she leaves for the Marine Corps next summer.

"Well *I'm* probably 75 percent Irish. Will you get *me* a Claddagh ring someday, Daddy?" Lee asked, and it melted my heart.

"Well, kid," I replied, looking into his deep green eyes, "You are an Irishman. Your mom is around 50 percent Irish, like Selena, so that makes you and Ronny around 75 percent Irish. But for boys, it's normally a girlfriend or wife that will get you your Claddagh."

"Oh, okay," he said, looking back at the ring, "Well, *I'm* trying to get a girlfriend." I was and wasn't surprised by this. Lee had always been tuned-in to girls.

"You're *trying* to get a girlfriend?" I asked, and Selena and I couldn't help but laugh a little. "What do you mean, you're *trying* to get a girlfriend? How does one *try* to get a girlfriend?"

"You know," he replied, looking at me like I should know this. "Like other kids *try* to throw a ball, or *try* to be funny. I'm *trying* to get a girlfriend." Then he just refocused on his cinnamon twists.

"I love it," Selena said. "It's perfect. I'm never going to take it off."

And although I knew she wouldn't wear it during the 13 weeks of Marine Boot Camp, I did not say so. I simply said, "Nice. I hoped you would like it."

I was very pleased at the reaction I received from her. When I ordered that ring for her birthday, little did I know everything that would transpire well after that. I just thought it was a cool *idea* at the time, as she could take it with her to the Marines.

After the gift reveal, there wasn't much we could really say in front of Lee. And after I attempted a couple of leading questions to Lee about practice, it was clear that he was done talking about that, as he answered with one- or two-word responses. I did get it out of him that his coaches had said they'd never seen that over-the-back single-leg takedown before, that he could land it because he was so tall for his weight. They approved of it, if the opponent gave it up. Lee was pretty much done talking shop after that, though. He was content to just sit there enjoying his twists. After the half-hour, we said our goodbyes, and Lee and I headed south out of town while Selena headed north to her home.

When Lee and I walked in the house, I could *feel* the tension in the air. My wife came out from the sunroom, where she and Ronny were no doubt watching some stupid reality show like *The Bachelor* or *Paradise Island*. We had fought about how morally wretched those kinds of shows were for the boys to watch, and she would argue that it was no big deal. Remember, by this point, I had become comfortable with defending myself or even attacking issues that I recognized, as opposed to the man who had for so long tucked tail and accepted blame for almost everything.

Before she could attack, I gave her the hand and told her to talk to Lee, that he had been the reason we were late, and that he had agreed to field any problems she had with it. When she called Lee back in from his room, where he had immediately gone to change out of his sweatsuit and wrestling singlet, he came in and started telling her it was my fault, just as he had practiced. But he was looking at me, almost laughing, and when I said, "Leeeeee," he exaggeratedly hung his shoulders and told his mom the real deal.

I didn't really know what to make of the fact that Lee did not mention that Selena had joined us. He just said we went inside Taco Bell so he could see his food, because it was always dark in the back of Daddy's van, and it's hard to eat because-... I just went in, gave Ronny a hug, told him I was proud of his efforts at practice that night, then headed into my Den until it was time to wrap the boys up in bed, Mexicano-style.

# Chapter Twenty-Eight:
# Thanksgiving

The next day, Wednesday, November 23, I don't recall much, other than that – with *all* that had already occurred by this point – it was only Day Q+10. Crazy.

Though I had spoken with Selena over the phone a good bit that day, I had also explained to her that my wife wanted me to stay home that night to spend time with the kids. And my wife was right... although I didn't have much time for the boys outside of coaching them and taking them to other sports, doing homework before wrestling practice, grocery shopping and cooking/eating dinner together, etc., I rarely took time to sit down and, for example, watch television with them. Of course, I knew that it was really just a way for my wife to keep an eye on me for another night, but she was still right about me making time to spend with the boys. It was a good idea, regardless of her motives.

I stayed home that Wednesday night. Selena protested my decision, but it was the smart thing to do, the safe thing, and the right thing, so I insisted that I couldn't leave the house. That is, until the boys and Lily were asleep, at which time I signed-off texting Selena and told her I was heading to workout. Not only was my grading slipping lately, so were my workouts. She texted back that I should text her when I get back home safe, even though she'd be fast asleep. She'd see my text first thing the next morning and know I was safe.

I left the house shortly after 10 pm, as I had been doing on-and-off for years and consistently for a few months, long before Q+0. I had faintly awoken my wife, let her know I was going to work out, locked up the house, and headed to the gym for a couple of hours. The gym was located far back off the main road about 80 yards, behind an auto garage, accessed by a thin gravel drive, opening into a gravel lot that could hold maybe 15 or so cars. Throughout the day, that lot was often full, but almost no one but me took advantage of the gym's 24-hour accessibility with a FOB to open the locked door. Late at night is still my best time to work out, to this day.

When I approached my turn-in for the gym, I could see from the road that there was a car in the lot, which was rare that late at night. I pulled off the main road, onto the long, gravel drive that led back to the gym, and as I approached the lot, I recognized the car. It was parked in the far corner of the small lot, as far as possible from the lone parking lot light post, surely an attempt to camouflage the car from the road.

I pulled up and parked next to Selena's black Nissan Altima, looking over with a goofy face. She immediately got out with blankets, and I figured out very quickly what she was doing. It was genius. I remember being glad she always thought of everything, as we couldn't leave the van running for heat if we were concerned about police patrols. I got out, and we embraced briefly but tightly, then I followed her into the back of the van.

"What do you think you're doing?" I asked her playfully.

"I'm *doing* what you pussed-out on," she replied, smirking, all proud of herself. "Making sure we get to see each other tonight." And we laughed.

It was pretty immediately apparent that the back bench/bed of my van wasn't going to work for our purposes. We had talked about using the van as a place to be together, but we had never really checked the feasibility of it. The bench/bed, when laid flat, was hard and too small. After all, it was only a minivan, nothing like the full luxury van I drove in high school. This bench/bed could work for a quickie, but we weren't there for that.

Other than that third-row bench, there were two second-row captain's chairs, and the two front seats. Selena asked if the second-row captain's chairs were removable, and I admitted I had no idea, I'd never thought about nor needed to remove them, if they did. She was pretty sure all minivan backseat captain's chairs were removable. A lot of her friends' parents had minivans, and she'd seen the chairs taken out many times.

"We'll put them in my backseat," she said, and she set herself to figuring out how to take out the chairs. It only took her a couple of minutes, and we were hefting the two chairs into the back seat of her Altima. I was amazed at how much space that allowed in the back of the van. She quickly set up our nest on the van's floor, we snuggled up, covered up, and clung to each other for heat. It wasn't as great as the hotel up in Chicagoland had been, of course, but it was pretty fucking great.

We laid there, holding each other, talking and giggling, kissing and caressing, warming each other for some time. I'm sure it was over an hour before our interactions became intimate. Looking back later, I was amazed that the two of us did not fuck wildly like two kids in the back of that van... no, we made love, which only reaffirmed my deepening feelings for her, and I'm sure, hers for me. She had brought a couple of towels, as well, and after all was calm again, we laid back and snuggled as we had been doing before.

The time allowed by the van and this gym parking lot was precious. So long as we didn't get caught by a police patrol, no one would ever guess. What else could we have done to spend this kind of time together without spending any money, without a paper trail, without anyone finding out, being alarmed, getting hurt (or just pissed, as would have been the case with my wife).

I was good on this night, disciplined, explaining to Selena that my "workout" couldn't last more than three hours. I had worked out for that long plenty of times before, but not longer. If my wife woke up and I was not home in that timeframe, she'd be right back onto us heavy, and we wouldn't be able to use this plan again. Selena understood.

As we rolled up the blankets and began to pull the chairs from her car, I mentioned that the windows on the van were all fogged up, that it could cause a patrol car to check it out... *if* a patrol car ever came by in the future. I didn't know if police cruisers ever patrolled the gym property at night. I had never seen one, but I had always been working out inside.

We weren't too worried about it. But something else was worrisome, though, as in the dark, neither of us could see how the chairs went back into the van, secured in place. Selena hadn't known what she'd done initially to free them, she just knew she'd pulled a small lever on the bottom of the chairs to release them. It took us maybe ten minutes to figure it out from the underside of a chair and the slits in the carpet on the floor of the van, laughing nervously about what would happen if we couldn't lock them in. Once we figured it out, though, we made our goodbye for the long holiday weekend, and we drove our separate ways.

***

The next day was Thanksgiving Day, Q+11, and Selena and I had already conceded that there was no way to see each other on the holiday. She wasn't exactly sure what she and her mom were doing, but she was thinking that they might have plans to head to Fort Clark to spend the holiday with a large family of friends so close to Selena's family that they were considered extended family, complete with prefixes like Aunt, Uncle, and cousin.

As usual on each of the big three holidays (Easter, Thanksgiving, and Christmas), Lily, the boys, and I would also be headed up to Fort Clark to my wife's maternal grandparents' home. All my in-laws would be meeting there, as the grandparents loved hosting the holidays. So around 10 am on Thanksgiving morning, we headed up to the grandparents', and I always enjoyed that.

The guys would sit in the living room, sprawled on couches and recliners, watching football and talking about whatever. The ladies would be out in the kitchen playing cards or board games, kept warm by their own raucous discourse and laughter, and by the bird and pig in the dual oven. The ladies were always by far the louder of the two groups, so we'd eventually turn up the TV to near-blasting, and then the women would all chime in that it was too loud.

There was no alcohol at these occasions, as my wife's parents and grandparents were Methodist, strictly alcohol-free. Before long, it would be time to eat, as this family always ate close to noon, which years ago was new to me and very cool, because that meant we would eat leftovers for dinner again before we went home. Gramma was an excellent cook. But eventually, home we went, Lily and the boys napping in a blood sugar crash by the time we were leaving Fort Clark proper.

Throughout the day, Selena and I had snuck texts back and forth. No one on her end found it strange for her to be on her phone texting on the holiday, but for me, it was extremely out of the norm and dangerous, particularly considering that my wife's radar was still scanning my every move. Keep in mind, my flip-phone had no capabilities that would attract my attention other than texts. So, I'd sneak outside to check on the boys, or I'd head upstairs to the restroom, or I'd go lay down in the spare bedroom, none of which seemed to blip on that radar. I always did those things on holidays.

The next morning was Friday, Q+12, and we engaged in our family tradition of Christmas tree hunting. My father-in-law's family was *extremely* wealthy and influential in the area, and he had an acquaintance who owned a Christmas tree farm about an hour west of town where that owner allowed us to walk out onto his property and choose our own trees to cut every year, so long as they were marked with a neon green ribbon.

My wife had always liked the evergreen trees with the soft, feathery, wispy, effeminate, long-needle branches, and when Ronny was born and grew old enough to understand, he agreed that those were the trees he wanted for Christmas. I, on the other hand, preferred the evergreen trees with the neat, firm, sharp, masculine, short needles. When Lee was old enough to understand, he agreed with his daddy that the short-needle trees were what he wanted for Christmas. In the beginning, when it was just my wife and I, we agreed to alternate every year, her choosing a long-needle tree one year, then me choosing a short-needle tree the next. As the boys came into our lives, it became teams of Mommy/Ronny and me/Lee. This year was Lee's and my turn to choose, with Mommy and Ronny as the support team.

Late in the afternoon, after a smallish Thanksgiving breakfast at my in-laws' place and tree-hunting, the fam and I headed home. We were already home when I felt my phone vibrate in my jacket pocket... I'd thought it was set on silent... but I didn't dare pick up. I couldn't risk it, so I quickly silenced the phone. There was music playing, and luckily, my wife and boys were catching a nap.

# Chapter Twenty-Nine:
## *Xenia*

I waited until we got home, settled in, and my wife and the boys were safely in the sunroom, watching television. I watched TV with the fam for quite a while, and then I retreated to my den, closed the door to "work," and called Selena. She was upset, but not at me for not picking up her call earlier. She explained that she and her mom had gotten into a serious altercation, over what I don't remember, and Selena packed a bag and had Homeboy come pick her up.

For some reason, she could not stay with Homeboy at his place. He must have still lived with his parents or something, but I'm not sure... was his dad an alcoholic or something, was that it? There must have been a legit reason, I just can't recall. Selena's mom had taken her keys, so Selena had to call Homeboy. Just then as we spoke, they were in Fort Clark, parked in a grocery store parking lot, trying to contact me to help figure out what they should do. They had gone shopping for a bit, and they were about to get something to eat.

My feelings for her were triggered. I did not like hearing her upset at all, and although I was happy that I was not the cause, the male problem-solver in me made himself known. I was also triggered by her being with Homeboy, by him coming to her rescue, but I knew that I was the man she had come to for a solution. I was racking my brain on how to solve this problem, how to ease the turbulence I could hear storming inside her. Perhaps I could pay for a hotel room for at least one night, if my wife would go for that.

"Is there ANY way I might be able to stay at your place for a day or two?" she asked.

"Oh, shit. *Seriously*?!" I remember whispering. "*Here?!* Shit, girl, I-... I don't-... I don't think that's a good move for us... "

"I *can't* go home," she insisted. "I *won't*. I'll go break into the school or something-... "

"Hold on, hold on, Vasquez... slow down," I urged. "Just... I'll give it a shot... Just give me like 20 minutes or so. I'll find a way to pass the idea by Lily. Even if she allows it, and I *highly* doubt she will, I'm not feeling great about even asking her this... but I will... *for you.*"

I'm not going to pretend I remember how this all transpired. I remember a lot, but not everything.

I know I went and found some way to approach my wife with Selena's situation. I know that the two of us put the boys to bed first, then we discussed it further. Very strangely, I don't remember my wife having much of an issue with Selena staying with us, as there was no big fuss about it, and I remember thinking that maybe she *didn't* have suspicions about Selena and I. Had it been my imagination all along that my wife was catching on? Maybe I was way off the mark. Maybe I was just that far along the tiptoe toward paranoia.

So I did end up going back into my den to call Selena and let her know that she could stay the night, or "through the weekend, if necessary" (according to my wife). Together, Lily and I had decided that through the weekend would have to be enough... that would be two nights. I was shocked at even *that*.

Selena asked me to keep all this from her mom. I told her that she was 18, an adult, and that although I would not be contacting either of her parents, as this fight was none of my business, I would also not lie to them. If they contacted me looking for her, and if they asked directly if I knew where she was, and she was still staying in my house... I would be honest with them.

I also recall feeling like a fish being lured with some spinner bait for the first time. I remember feeling like "that was too easy," like my wife was using this opportunity to attempt to catch Selena and I doing something wrong, or at least to get a better feel of the two of us together. Maybe she was testing the air to see if her radar, her suspicion of "something," was on point. At any rate, I figured, Selena and I were going to be on our 'A' game, however long she stayed.

Selena and Homeboy arrived late, and I couldn't help but wonder where they had been and what they had been doing in the meantime. I realized that I was jealous, and I was trying to come to grips with that. When they arrived, my wife came directly to my den, anticipating that I would lead the greeting, and we both met them at the door.

As Homeboy had most likely heard of my impressions of him from Selena, he had left the car running and didn't stick around. I remember he leaned in to kiss her goodnight, and she slipped the kiss, taking it on the cheek, eyes flashing at me and then away. I wondered if my wife had caught the slight and/or the glance. He looked at her kind of strangely, but with me standing there, he just uncomfortably told her to call him when she was settled in for the night, turned, and left.

Selena came in the front door from the porch slowly, cautiously. My wife greeted her with a fake-friendly voice, smiles, and a hug, but she pulled it off cleanly. I acted my normal self, though my brain was wigging out a little, realizing that my mistress was going to be staying under my wife's and my roof for a few days *and a couple of nights*. I gave her a very quick, very light hug, a bit of a slight of my own.

Part of me was a little excited, part was pretty damn concerned. The excited part came absolutely zero percent from any kind of thrill from the dicey situation; I never felt any buzz from the deception of what Selena and I had been doing. I was excited simply that I'd be around her. Surely my wife wouldn't be glued to us, and we would have time to talk, something Selena and I never seemed to get tired of. I genuinely loved that kind of quality time with her. I was concerned because I knew that I couldn't let anything physical happen in my house with my wife anywhere around, but as far as ensuring that nothing *did* happen... that might prove to be tough with Selena's care-free, risk-ready sense of carpe diem.

We set up Selena in the guest bedroom, which happened to be located on the opposite side of one of my den walls. The bed was a double, and I'd slept in it once or twice, so I knew she'd be comfortable. Then came the tour of rooms and explanation of routines, given that there was no school for any of us, as it was the weekend. I also gave her the lowdown on where everything she might need was located... glasses, plates, silverware, microwave, fridge, pantry... and encouraged her to make herself comfortable and to wake us for any reason. Then I gave her a glass of ice water, asked if there was anything she needed, ignored the look she gave me (yeah, you know the look), and wished her goodnight.

I had noticed that my wife had actively participated in very little of the tour, but she followed closely behind and seemingly assessed how I went about this task. I knew, and I sensed that Selena knew exactly what Lily was doing... she was assessing us... and both Selena and I played it cooler than cool.

When Selena was in her room for the night, my wife retired

to our bedroom, and I went to my den to try to wrap my head around the fact that us three were going to be sleeping under the same roof. I closed my den door, but as I was honestly concerned that Selena might come to my den in the night, I went to bed a short time later. I couldn't work with her on the other side of my den wall, anyway. I was going to need some sleep for the next day and the next, but I didn't sleep much that night.

***

Saturday morning, I was out of bed and in my den trying to get something productive done when I heard the boys' bathroom toilet flush... twice. The boys were awake.

Then, as usual, I faintly heard the boys goofing around in their room. Then a little louder in the living room. Then quieter again in the sunroom. And then I heard their voices back in the living room, just around the corner from the door to my den, whispering. I always knew when they were sneaking up on me, usually to ask permission for something or to make them something to eat.

I wondered if they would remember the few words my wife and I exchanged about Selena's visit the previous night, just before we put them to bed. As always, there wasn't much you could slip past those boys. And then I heard Lee whisper *yadda-yadda-yadda Selena yadda-yadda...*

"W h a t are you two *d o i n g*?" I drawled out quietly,

knowing the two were standing just outside my open door. Lee came swinging slowly around into my open doorway, hand clutched on the side of the door jamb. Ronny shimmied into view behind him. Both were smiling the cheesy smiles they used when they thought they were being sly.

"*D a d d y*," Lee said slowly, interrogatively.

"Yes, boys, Selena stayed the night here last night."

The two shot each other a quick glance, Ronny's brow furrowed with a question on his face, and Lee pulled his fist into his side, saying, "*Yes!* Told you Ronny! I *knew* it!"

I then went on to explain that it was still pretty early for people other than rascally little boys and workaholic daddies, so they could head into the sunroom to watch TV or play, so long as they kept the noise down.

"There's no school today," Lee reminded me, asking, "It's Saturday, so are you-... "

"Yes, I'm making breakfast in a while, kid," I assured him. He pulled his fist into his side again, "*Yes!*", and then he paused, looked at me, and asked "Daddy, how did you know-... "

"Because I'm Daddy, I rule... and I *always* know what you're thinking, Lee. This is nothing new to you." He nodded, knowing exactly what I meant, and went on his way.

# Chapter Thirty:
# Telepathy

You see, Lee and I really were telepathic. It wasn't like we could speak actual words and sentences to each other with our minds, like in the movies. It's kind of hard to explain, as I've never heard anyone talk about experiencing what my boy and I had, and I have never otherwise experienced it.

It was as if we felt one another's general thoughts, feelings, and perceptions. And it wasn't something that was 'on' all the time, like a constant flow of understanding each other. Our minds were not constantly streaming content back and forth. It just seemed to 'turn on' by itself sometimes, and other times it seemed we could kind of activate it. In highly emotional times it was triggered, too, I sometimes noticed. It's so hard to explain. But here's just one of a million examples.

Once, during the summer of 2011, as we were walking out of Walmart into that huge parking lot, I held out two fingers on both hands for the boys to hold onto while we headed to the van, as always. Ronny obliged, but Lee quietly protested to himself, then to me, "Why do I *have* to do this, Daddy. I'm *seven*... I can walk by myself."

*Here we go, again.*

As I had done countless times before, I explained to both

boys that I was not a gambler. I trusted myself and Mommy supremely, and I trusted them for the most part, but I did not trust anyone else around us. I would not risk my boys' lives in a parking lot that large and bustling, and so, we would not be stepping off to go to the van until Lee took my fingers. Begrudgingly, he did.

About 20 feet into the parking lot, I saw a pretty lady about my age and her cute little daughter walking toward us. The girl was probably a year or two older than Lee. I opened the two fingers in Lee's fist and said, "Lee, let go of my fingers and stay *very* close to me."

It took him a moment, but he let go, smiling, eyes in wonder, and Ronny just kept looking at me like he was expecting the same directive. I told Ronny he'd have to be quite a bit older before he could let go of my fingers in a parking lot. And though I wasn't looking directly at Lee, I kind of sensed that Lee just then saw the little girl. I felt him look at me, and then look back at the little girl, who smiled at him. Lee gave her a big smile and wave, and she reciprocated. It was cute.

When we got into the van, Lee moved up toward the front, leaning forward between the two front seats, and said, "Daddy-..."

"You know *exactly* why I told you to let go of my fingers."

"But how did *you know*?" Lee asked, looking right at the side of my face.

I gave him a sly sideways look and said, "Because I'm *Daddy*, I *always* know."

"Is it because we're telescopic?" he asked.

"No, kid," I explained, "It's because we're tele*pathic*."

"Oh, yeah, tele*PATHIC*."

# Chapter Thirty-One:
# Juice Boxes and Shoe Boxes

While I worked in my den that Saturday morning (and yes, I was actually writing some curriculum, even *with* Selena on the other side of that wall), I was remaining keenly aware of the sounds in the house, listening to detect any sound from the room on the other side of the wall to my left, the guest room. I could hear the Wii game system in the sunroom – bowling. Around ten o'clock, I decided it was time to start getting everyone ready for breakfast.

As my wife was used to sleeping in on weekends when the boys had no sports, enjoying breakfast-to-order in bed on most Saturdays – *and* as Selena was apparently just used to sleeping in – I had to wake up those two for their orders. I knew what the boys wanted... they were always happy with whatever Daddy decided they wanted to eat that day, unless they had the odd hankering for something specific.

Today both boys chose cheesy scrambled eggs, Selena and I both chose two eggs fried over-easy, and it was a ham/cheese omelet for my wife, all with sides of sausage/bacon, cheese, toast, Kerry Gold butter (the "block o' sin"), etc. On this particular morning, I even broke-out Winston's Irish bangers and rashers (sausage and bacon), which was something we did about once a month. We'd go to Winston's Irish Market up in Chicagoland once a year to stock up on the Irish breakfast supplies, and we'd pick up twelve of everything.

While I prepared breakfast, of course Lee was at my side finding things to help with. On that morning, Ronny and Selena sat at the kitchen table and watched us cook. On mornings like this, we had little things we just tended to do. Sometimes we'd turn on the radio and sing songs together, which sometimes brought Mommy out of bed to join us. Sometimes we'd put on dance music and dance around like wackos.

Sometimes, without the radio, I would start singing a song that I knew the boys knew, like Bruno Mars's "The Lazy Song." Sooner than later, the boys would start singing the song, I'd stop, and they'd keep singing. A minute or five minutes later, it didn't matter, I'd start singing a different song to myself, and the two of them would start singing *that* song. I'd switch it up again and again and get my kick out of it, and the boys never caught on to what I was doing.

On this particular morning, Lee and Ronny started singing a song that I didn't even know they knew, a song old enough that I had no idea how they *could* know it. It was "I Love Rock 'n' Roll" by Joan Jett and the Blackhearts, from when I was young.

"*... so put another dime in the juice box, baby,*" Ronny sang, and Lee and I looked at each other, strange looks on our faces. Telepathy, kind of.

"Ronny, those are NOT the words," Lee corrected. "It's '*so put another dime in the SHOE box, baby.'* NOT juice box."

Now I looked at Selena, and she and I both had wrinkled brows. No telepathy. It was an old song when she was born, but even she clearly also knew those words weren't right.

"No, Lee, stoooooop. It's *JUICE box.*"

"Ronny... *one* more time... it's *SHOE box.*"

"Lee, that doesn't even make any sense. Why would you put a dime in a *SHOE box*?"

"Ronny, why would you put a dime in a *JUICE box*? HOW would you even put a dime in a *JUICE box*?"

I ended the argument by turning on the radio, and we were all back to singing. Even Selena sang with us for some song I don't remember. The singing brought Mommy out of bed to join us.

As always, the boys were happy and sat eating their breakfast like adults, with just a little playfulness. Selena was surprised at how easy the boys were, how happy they were to just go with the flow. She told me later that it's difficult to have perfect kids in public, but it's possible... but to have perfect kids *at home*? Doesn't happen.

I explained that a lot of that came from the security of the routine I had instilled... they knew exactly what to expect and how this would go, every time. They knew the rules and consequences, and they knew I never allowed a strike two. So they followed my lead, and I almost never had to impose consequences. It was amazing, as a father.

My wife, obviously, was not in bed, but rather ate with us at the table, seemingly happy and pleasant. She kind of jokingly bragged to Selena that when the boys had no sports, Daddy made and brought her breakfast in bed, where she would watch her shows. Selena was very surprised to know that my wife routinely got breakfast in bed on Saturdays, especially with such a spread. She shot me a quick *WTF?* look that no one else saw.

"One time I remember," Lily offered, "the boys were in bed with me while Daddy cooked breakfast. I think we were watching Saturday morning cartoons, or something. Anyway, Lee asks me 'Mommy, wouldn't it be cool if we could order room service right here in bed, at home, just like at the hotels?' And I told him, 'I always order room service here in bed, at home. I just yell DAAAADDYYYYY.'"

We all laughed at her little story, but Selena looked at me a bit strangely as she laughed. The smugness of my wife's comments were not lost on her.

"Oh, Selena," Lily practically interrupted herself. "I love your Claddagh ring. Your mom is Irish?"

"Yeah, I'm not sure what the percentage is, but I'm pretty

sure she's *mostly* Irish. Her maiden name is Kelly."

"That's nice. Did she get you the Claddagh?" Lily asked.

I looked at Lily incredulously, wondering if she was just kidding or if she could be serious. Lee took note of it. Lily knew I got Selena a Claddagh for her birthday. We had talked about it at the time. She had thought it was a good idea.

"Um, well, no. My mom didn't get it for me."

"Lily," I interrupted. "You are *not* being serious right now, *are you?*" Lee looked at me. I knew he could sense my mood.

"What? About the ring? Yeah, I'm serious. Why, Honey?"

I knew she added in "Honey" because Selena was there. But I couldn't read whether she was joking. Either she was trying to be funny and was keeping a serious face remarkably well, or she was pretending not to know I'd given Selena the ring for her birthday. I wasn't quite sure which.

"Mommy is just joking, Daddy," Lee tried to explain, practically reading my mind. "She knows you got Selena that clad-... umm, clad-..."

"Cla-duh," I said.

"Yeah, *that*. Mommy knew you got that clad-... Clad-*duh* ring for Selena. She was just joking."

He was right that his mom knew I bought Selena that ring, but he was wrong about her intent. She wasn't joking; for some reason, she was *pretending*.

"Lil... I know it was a while ago, but we talked about this... that's the Claddagh that I ordered online for Selena's birthday present over a month ago. That's the Claddagh I gave her."

"*What?*" Lily said. "Oh... yeah, I guess I forgot. I didn't know it arrived. I didn't know you'd given it to her. That's a really nice Claddagh, Selena. Nice choice, Honey." I just shook my head, and Lee kind of shook his with me.

"Thank you," Selena said. "I never heard of a Claddagh ring before this. I love it."

My wife gave me a look that was... kind of a glare. I ignored it, but Lee stared at her, not seeming to understand. My view was that if she had a problem with that ring, it was her own problem. I had checked with her before I ordered it, and besides, there had been absolutely nothing romantic between Selena and I at the time.

"Everybody here is Irish," Ronny pointed out, and I had a very strong feeling that he was just diffusing the tension in the air. "Daddy, I-*rish* I could have another Irish sausage." And we all laughed as I handed him one. My boy.

"It's a *banger*, Ronny," Lee corrected his brother, almost as an afterthought.

"*Duh*. I *know* that, Lee. I said it like that so Selena would know what I meant."

Those breakfast mornings with the boys were an absolute joy for me, every time. If I ever had the chance to time travel, to go to just one place and time, a Saturday morning breakfast with the boys would be in my top three.

But, of course... there are no time machines.

# Chapter Thirty-Two:
# Little-Man Mantra

I think Selena spent some time in the guest room through that day, and I went to the gym to get in a workout (like, a *real* workout, with weights – not captain's chairs, lol). I could have invited Selena to go with me, but part of my reason for going to the gym was to burn what could otherwise have been a pretty awkward afternoon, and I didn't want to make it any more awkward.

My wife watched TV with the boys for a while, but when I got home, she unexpectedly decided to go to her folks' house for a visit.

That left me with the boys... and Selena. I decided to stay in the sunroom with the boys, so if Mommy came home and started asking questions, they knew I was never out of their sight. Selena joined us shortly, and we put on a movie: *Star Wars IV: A New Hope,* Lee's choice and his favorite flick. Selena had never seen it which absolutely blew my mind.

I thought about telling Selena that the movie came out in 1977 and was probably the first movie I saw in a theater, as I had been only Ronny's age, 5-years-old. I decided to not bring that up, though, until Selena eventually asked when the movie came out, and I told her and the boys. Ronny couldn't seem to grasp that I had ever been his age, and he asked how old Uncle Pip was back then. I explained that my little brother wasn't born or even thought of, yet.

Everything seemed to be all fine and good, until we had just about finished the movie, the Death Star had just exploded, and the electricity in the house went out. We did not have a generator.

*"That was awesome!"* Lee cried. "Did you see that, Daddy? Luke blew up the Death Star, and our lights went out! *That's crazy!"*

The house was pretty large for a ranch at just over 3,500 square feet, with vaulted ceilings, 12 feet in the living room, about sixteen feet in the sunroom, and there were a lot of very large windows throughout the house. As we liked to keep the house pretty cool year-round, the house very quickly became pretty cold. My wife would be unaware, because her parents' house was just outside of the town limits, and so they were not on the same electrical grid as us.

Selena had been giving me the eyes from time to time through the movie, and it was killing me, though I knew she was just playing with me. I did not want to end up in the dark and cold with just the boys and Selena. So I called my wife, just to let her know about the power outage, as it was already late afternoon, and it would be getting dark soon. My wife needed to be there. Evidently, she thought so, too, as she came home directly. At some point later, my wife pretty much interrogated the boys about what had gone on without her in the house. Lee mentioned it to me, days later. I wasn't concerned, as I knew there had been nothing of note for them to report.

We had a gas fireplace in the living room that had only been lit once by us when we did our final walk-through inspection on the home almost six years earlier. That Saturday afternoon with no electricity was the perfect time to break it in. As it grew dark outside, it was unseasonably cold in the low 20s, and it became straight-up freezing cold inside surprisingly quickly.

The fire was a hit with everyone, and they all went to their rooms to grab blankets and pillows while I whipped up some hot chocolate, as the stove was gas fueled. Lee helped me out, of course, pulling up a chair and using his toy flashlight to find the marshmallows and cocoa in the pantry.

Selena fit right in like one of the family, and I must admit, I felt terrible guilt once I looked at the three of them wrapped in blankets, sitting or lying in front of the fire. I noticed that Selena was very observant on this whole visit, watching everything, really seeing how the family worked. I stayed at the kitchen peninsula, overlooking the living room and fireplace, trying to rid myself of the guilt of allowing Selena, my mistress, to mingle so closely with my family.

What the fuck was happening here? How did this happen? But I knew exactly how it had happened, and to a large degree, I just wanted to get through the weekend without any problems, to put distance back between these two separate parts of my life.

Earlier that day, I had taken ribeye steaks out of the freezer to thaw for dinner, but I put them back into the fridge. It wasn't like I couldn't have made steak dinners, as the oven/stove ran on gas, but the whole dinner thing would just have been too major of an ordeal. So, the talk came to what we were going to do for dinner, and I'm almost certain it was my wife who suggested that we should go to the best steakhouse in the area.

It was our favorite, a high-end prime steakhouse that was known far and wide to be very family-friendly, as opposed to so many prime steakhouses that tended to be kind of stuffy and snobby, almost exclusively catering to adult dining. My boys were super easy to take anywhere, but they preferred the family-friendly environment of our favorite: Optimus Prime Steakhouse. It was exactly 23 country miles west of us.

I loved the idea, as did the boys because they knew this place well, and it meant that they got to help my wife and I grill their steaks of choice and to make garlic Texas toast over one of four huge, open, grated fire pits in the restaurant. I thought it was a great idea, mostly because it would burn quite a bit of the evening/night that could otherwise turn awkward.

And so, we all piled into the van, and we went.

Usually, I'd take Lee to the meat coolers to get his choice of beef, and my wife would take Ronny. Today was different, though, as Selena had never been to a steakhouse where you selected and cooked your own beef. So, my wife took the boys to the steak coolers to choose their cuts, and I took Selena over to the opposite side of the coolers, as there were many, where she could find all different cuts of beef: seasoned, marinated, steaks, kabobs with hearty cuts of vegetables... there were options.

After Selena initially protested that she wasn't really hungry due to the late, large breakfast, I got her to admit otherwise. She tried to talk about our strange situation with me quietly at the meat cooler, but I kept redirecting her to her choices of beef. She, of course, chose whatever I chose... an eight-ounce, teriyaki-marinated NY strip, as I didn't feel like messing with cutting out the fat of a ribeye that night. Of course, Lee was floating around Selena and I, saw what I chose, and so he went back to Mommy and chose the same. Ronny went with the same as Mommy, a five-ounce filet mignon.

At the end of dinner, everyone was satisfied. On the way home, Selena commented from the back of the van that she couldn't believe how well-behaved the boys were. I guess while we were grilling our steaks, the boys headed back to the table to start in on the garlic-buttered Texas toast they had made with Mommy, Selena, and me. At this place, we limited the boys to one piece of Texas toast each while the steaks grilled, and then we'd say grace together when we were all ready to eat. Lee said Grace for us: "Thank you, God, for this food and drink to nourish our bodies. Thank you for us all being healthy and safe, and for Daddy making us our secret hideaway." Selena, Lily, and I laughed, of course.

Before that, though, while Lily, Selena and I were grilling the steaks, Selena had paid attention to the boys as they sat down, tucked their napkins, and kept their Texas toast over their plates while they munched. When a waitress came by and asked the boys if they were okay, Selena said Lee had replied, "Yes, we're okay. Thank you." The waitress had commented to the boys about what polite little men they were. Lily and I exchanged glances, smiling at another one of our many small parenting victories.

I sensed Lee smiling big at Ronny, as they were always very pleased to be called good boys. It went back to the morning mantra I had begun with Lee when he first went to preschool, and even younger with Ronny as he joined in with Lee and I. Every morning, before leaving for school, I'd ask the same question: "Boys, what are you going to *do* today?"

And they would respond, in unison: "Today, I am going to be a good boy, so I can grow to be a good man, so I can become a good husband, so I can become a good daddy, so I can raise good boys... "and sometimes Lee would continue this mantra round and round the cycle, cracking himself up. Once, when I was driving him to school, he continued it despite my joking protests all the way out the door, into the van, and five blocks to school.

From time to time, I would ask them to explain the meaning

of the mantra and why we say it. It was always extremely rewarding to hear them articulate it in their own words. They understood why it was important to be a good boy, as it was the first step and the best thing they could do to make sure they could be good men who would one day raise good boys.

One might wonder how I felt about that mantra now that I had blatantly been a bad husband, was cheating on my wife, and, in fact, had my mistress with my family at dinner and as a guest in our home. I can say it bothered me quite a lot... but I tried my best to reassure myself that I had been the best husband I could be for *as long* as I could be, far beyond the scope of what the vast majority of men could be or would be willing to do in a sexless, betrayal-themed marriage.

After everything my wife had done to betray me, embarrass me, disregard me, ridicule me, abandon me, cuck me... and the years I had spent playing the part of a very good, happy husband beyond reason, and a GREAT daddy beyond measure, I had reached the end of what any man could endure. I was left with that small consolation for the discord within me regarding my recent choices... that I had performed beyond any reasonable expectations, and I was still doing the best I could with trying to balance it all.

The end goal was to raise good boys, and at least I knew we were doing an outstanding job of that.

# Chapter Thirty-Three:
## *Muy Mal*

When we arrived home, we found the electricity was restored, and we all watched some TV for a while before the boys' bedtime. When it was time, the boys changed into their pajamas, and I invited Selena to join my wife and I, tucking them in. She thought the Ronny Taco and Lee Burrito thing was adorable. And she thought the fact that I went in to just watch them sleep from time to time through the night was very sweet.

To this day, I wonder how Selena felt about "us," knowing what she then had learned about my family. I never asked. I imagine she must have been impressed by how the boys and I interacted, and she probably watched my interactions with my wife, carefully considering the ways in which I played my role without exposing my true condition. Did Selena ever wonder if there was a future for her and this man, or was she solely interested in keeping things going the way they were? Gotta say, questions like this sometimes help me learn from my reflections on those sunsets behind us.

Shortly after that, my wife decided it was time for her to go watch her shows in our bedroom before bed. It was probably around 10 o'clock, already a late night for her. She lingered only a bit, then asked what my plans were before I'd head to bed. I told her I just figured Selena and I would watch some TV, talk, then when Selena hit the rack, I'd go to my den, and then I'd hit the rack early in the morning, as usual. She asked me to wake her and let her know when I came to bed, and she took her leave.

With Lily gone to bed, I didn't ask Selena about the fight with her mom, but I had to ask, "Does your mom have any idea where you're at?"

"No way," she replied. "I'm sure she'll call my dad, or she already has, thinking I went there. He'll tell her to just call me, but she won't do that. This kind of shit happens with moms and daughters. They fight. *We* fight. It's normal. It doesn't happen much, but when it does, my mom knows that sometimes I just have to get away from it, especially now that I'm an adult. And she knows I'll be somewhere safe with someone I trust."

"She would never think you'd be here?"

"Oh, fuck no. You'd never even cross her mind, no matter how hard she tries to think about where I'm at. And we don't know anyone else in this town, so she'd never think of Kent."

That response kind of made me feel like Selena *wanted* her mom to be concerned, *wanted* her mom to be wondering where she was, who she was with. But I also knew she was right – an adult daughter under mom's roof? They're going to fight. There's nothing wrong with walking away to clear your head for a while.

"Would Homeboy-... would your boyfriend tell her anything? I mean, she's *gonna* call him, and of course, she knows that *he* knows where you are. And *he* knows *she* knows that. Let's just imagine that he does tell your mom because he doesn't want to lie to her, right? If she found out you were here, would she ever suspect anything between us? Because if she would, we might want to start thinking about how to handle that."

"Whoah, *whoah*, slow down, Sherlock Holmes. She would never think something was going on between you and me. Who would ever just guess that? It's crazy. And he would never tell her I'm here, anyway. And she would never call him about it. But if she *did*, and if he *did* tell her... I told you before, Cal, that would be THE bad. *Muy mal*. I don't even want to think about that."

So we didn't.

Selena and I sat near, but not next to, each other on one of the sunroom couches, a few feet from one another, facing the sliding glass door that led into the living room and the rest of the house. It was an excellent spot, as my wife could check up on us and see us sitting apart on the couch through the glass of the patio door, but we wouldn't be able to see her because of the reflection of the sunroom lights (unless she stepped over by the open doorway, where we could see into the main house). And she did come to check on us several times throughout the night. I could hear her creeping around out there, and once when she stepped too far over, I saw her through the open doorway.

"Lil, do you *need* something?" I called with sarcasm in my words.

"It's getting late, Honey. You should let that poor girl get some sleep. What are you guys *doing*?" She was showing little restraint.

"We *were* talking about movies and actors. But *now* Selena is testing me to see how much Spanish I know. *Why?*"

"It's just getting pretty late-..."

"Well, I kind of know a lot of Spanish, so..."

"Don't forget you are bringing Selena back to her *boyfriend* in Delphia tomorrow at noon... you'll both want to get some sleep."

"Of course, I didn't forget, Lil. We're cool," I replied. "She'll head to bed whenever she's ready, and I'll either head to my den or to bed. No worries... thanks, though." And she disappeared.

And that really was what we were doing. We were keeping track of how many Spanish words I knew. She would say a word in English or Spanish to see if I could translate it. Selena was surprised and impressed, as we had stopped counting around 200 words, and we were still going strong. I was proud to show-off my Spanish knowledge to her. But eventually, we tired of the game, and she suggested we go downstairs.

"*What?* Why would we go *downstairs*?" I asked, clearly suspicious of her motives.

"Let's play some pool, or we can play some Xbox," she said, with an attitude of "relaaaax," which was a good response. AND it would be pretty cool to play a game with her, fire up a little competition, see what she's got. I had told her what the basement was like when I'd given her the initial tour of the house. It would have to be Xbox that night, though, as the pool table was too loud, situated sort of below the boys' bedroom.

"Hey, Lil," I called quietly into our bedroom. She was wide awake. "We're gonna head downstairs, play some-... "

"*Downstairs?!*" she shot back. "To do *what?*"

"Selena challenged me to one-on-one Halo," I replied. "I'm about to teach her a lesson."

A long pause.

"Teach her a *lesson*, huh?" and that response seriously surprised me. She was not hiding her suspicions at all. "Don't wake the boys, *Honey*," and I couldn't see if she was looking at me through the darkness, but I figured she was, and I felt like the *Honey* was forced for Selena's sake, as she was standing behind me by the door to the basement. So, I closed the bedroom door, and we went downstairs.

# Chapter Thirty-Four:
# Lesson Learned

I went to what the boys called the Xbox TV, as that was all it was used for. Selena then said, "Hey, Master Chief, we're not playing Halo. Come here," and she sat down on the couch just around the corner from the view of the stairs. It was the safest strategic place for what she wanted to do.

I walked slowly over, and she was giving me those eyes. Before I sat a few feet from her, I said, "No, Babe," very quietly, and she scooted over to me and took my hand. She tried kissing me a little, but again, I stopped her and told her, "No. Not in *this* house, especially with my *wife* right upstairs. That is *not* okay." Then I motioned for her to stay quiet, listening for movement from the upstairs floor, basement door, or stairs. Nothing.

She stubbornly leaned in to me for a kiss, and I caved a bit. She stopped, motioned to the couch in front of and perpendicular to the one we were sitting on, and said, "Don't you want to just bend me over that couch and fuck me?"

I was learning that *that* kind of talk absolutely aroused my inner animal and outer hardware, and it seemed I wasn't getting used to it. I growled, low, deep, looking at the back of that couch.

"*Yes*, I *do*," I admitted, "But *no*, we can *NOT*... that is absolute and non-negotiable."

She forced a very frustrated, harsh breath for effect, and soon after, we both agreed it was time for bed. We were meeting Homeboy in Delphia at noon, and although I could go days without sleep and had done so many times, Selena clearly liked her sleep. So, we called it a night.

When I settled into bed, my wife, wide awake, said, "Who *won*?" I thought it was packaged with a sexual innuendo.

"Um... *I* did." I answered.

"*Congratulations*," she said, thick with sarcasm, and that was that for the night.

***

The next morning was unremarkable, really. The sleepyheads actually got up fairly early. We had the normal routine for breakfast, except Lee wanted three fried eggs like me. I limited him to two, though. As usual, Lee would decide which eggs were chosen for my fried eggs and which eggs were his as we cracked them and hoped for a lucky double yolk. He got a double yolk, so he laughed out loud and cheered that he was getting three eggs after all.

And the day was underway. Selena had texted her mom that she was coming home that evening. Her mom had replied that she'd be there when Selena got home. They agreed to talk about whatever it was they had fought about. Either I never asked or don't recall what that had been.

In coming to really know Selena in the almost two weeks

since Q+0, I had discerned that she kept her private life private, meaning her life with Homeboy, her life with her mom, and her life with her dad. She never ever talked about her little sister. Those were topics for which I quickly learned to accept anything she chose to share, but to ignore anything she chose not to. I didn't ask questions about those things. As open as she was about everything else, those things stood out as being left deliberately vague and off-limits.

There were some thinly veiled hostile vibes coming from my wife that morning, and so Selena and I decided to leave early to meet Homeboy in Delphia. Selena thanked my wife for helping her out so much, allowing her to stay, and we headed out. We ended up burning some time at a park in Danverston where our Saturday home football games were held. We parked far off, around the far end of the tennis courts, and we talked a little about the prior day and a half. It had been a trip.

"You wouldn't touch me at your house," she played, "so are you gonna touch me now?"

She leaned over the space between the two front captain chairs, and we made out a little. She threw her legs over, stood between the two seats, raised my armrest, reached across me to hit the lever to lay my seat back, and threw her leg over, straddling me face-to-face. There, we made out a bit more, and she began grinding on me.

"I could just fuck you right here, just like this," she said, and she was really sort of asking for permission. When I just growled a little, she said, "So let's go." I had to slow her down, cool her off some, cool *myself* off, and let her know that was not going to happen.

"No, Babe," I replied, laughing a little at her persistence. "Look, we're going to see Homeboy... I'm not really comfortable with fucking my girlfriend... *his* girlfriend... and then just watching you two drive away together. Too many things just feel wrong about that. It's shitty enough that I have to let you go with him."

"Awwww," she teased, "Are you jealous?"

"Fuck yeah, I'm jealous... okay? I am..." and she pulled away and looked me in the eyes.

"You really *care* about me that much?"

"Oh, fuck off. You *know* I care about you that much. What I'm afraid we both might be learning is *how much* I care about you."

"*Awwww,*" but this time, she seemed genuinely touched. *Didn't she?* "So, what, are you just going to let me go with him and let him have me all to himself? I mean, if *you* don't want what I've got-... "

That hurt. I mean it *really* hurt. It wasn't funny to me at all, and she knew it. She had just purposely taken an emotional stab at me, joking about what that motherfucker would do if I wouldn't. She knew me more than well enough to know by now that those words would hurt. It was the first taste of meanness from Selena I ever had.

Why would she say that to me? *How* could she say that to me? Especially after what had just been said about me *really* caring about her? I suddenly felt pretty alone again, as though I was the only one catching feelings. I remember my brain went a little foggy, I got more than a little upset, inwardly, and I told her we should get going to Delphia. She pulled away, *hmph*ed, and moved back into her chair, out of reach. It was our first spat.

I don't really remember the ten-minute drive to Delphia. We didn't talk. I was foggy, to be sure, stung by her cruel jab. Was I supposed to think it had been *funny*? Or did she *mean* to sting me? Was that her way of letting me know I was getting *too* deep, *too* serious for her intentions? Was she trying to back me off? It was a lesson I didn't plan to learn twice.

# Chapter Thirty-Five:
# Galaxy S II

When we pulled into the grocery store parking lot in Delphia, Homeboy's aged Ford pickup was already there, parked and waiting for us. He got out and opened my passenger door for Selena. She and I looked at each other, both of us seemingly surprised that this was how we were going to leave each other's company.

"Hey, Sweetie," Homeboy said.

*Sweetie?* I thought to myself. *That's lame. This motherfucker...*

"Sounds like you guys had a cool couple of days," he added. There was not even the slightest bit of suspicion in this dude's voice or demeanor. Of course, why would there be? He was just glad to see her.

"Yeah," Selena said to me. "When I woke up, I filled Leonard in on yesterday's breakfast and dinner and all," she said to me. I nodded. Then, to him, she said, "Cal is gonna come with us to Fort Clark if that's cool."

*What?! What is this?!*

"I'm gonna ride with Cal..." and she shot me soft eyes and a thin, apologetic smile.

"Wait... *what?*" he asked, standing outside her door, looking totally confused. "Selena, I thought we were-... "

"I know. I know, but this morning, I was thinking about the Marines, and I haven't had a chance to ask Cal a bunch of questions I came up with. I don't know when I'm going to see him next, so we need to talk a little shop." She leaned out and gave him a peck on the cheek, then buckled up.

"Why don't you just call h-..." Homeboy began, but she cut him off.

*"We'll follow you."*

The next thing I knew, the three of us were headed north to Fort Clark. I called my wife to let her know, and she didn't seem to care so long as Homeboy was with us. I had known that the two of them had plans to head to Fort Clark so he could finally surprise her with a birthday gift. Why the gift was so late, I had no idea. But she did not know what the gift was going to be.

"Did you think I would let you head home with us kind of pissed at each other?" she asked.

I stammered something like, "I-... I don't know."

I was still wafting away the tendrils of fog in my head. And I know how this must sound. I know most people would look at the little spat we just had and blow it off, thinking I was making more of it than it was. But the facts were the facts. She knew her words would hurt, but she chose to say them anyway. Now, she had chosen to steal a little more time with me in order to try to undo what she'd done. After so many years alone, I was just getting reacclimated to sharing feelings with a partner, and admittedly, I was a little over-sensitive.

"Look, Babe," she tried to sound soft, sweet. "You and I have nothing to stress about and nothing to do but enjoy each other."

She reached over and took my right hand from my side, lacing her fingers in mine. In theory, she was absolutely right, but I realized that I might be falling too hard for her. I might have to start distancing myself or at least safeguarding my feelings so I wouldn't end up hurt. It was an important lesson I was just being clued into. If she was more into us *fucking* than actually *caring*, maybe I'd just have to find a way to work with that.

"And don't start pulling away from me after my stupid shit at the park, either, okay? I really love how much you care about me, and I care about you like that, too, in case you can't tell. I should know by now how sensitive you can be, the badass Marine who is in touch with his *feelings*, and I love that about you. I'll try to be more careful with your feelings, okay?"

Damn, this girl's intuition was scary sometimes. She was reading me like a book, probably knowing what I was thinking almost as soon as I did. It was one of the many things I liked so much about her, but it was also a little... troubling.

*Damn,* I thought, *This girl reads me almost like how Lee and I can read each other, almost like...*

*"Okay?"* she repeated.

"Okay," I replied. But I was still thinking about how I could keep myself from getting hurt by all this.

"Good. Now let's forget that stupid shit and refocus on just being what we are. *Us.* I'm not going to hurt you, Cal."

*... almost like... telepathy.*

***

In the long and short of it, we ended up going to a small, independent tech store in Fort Clark. I dropped her in front, where Homeboy had parked, and I pulled around to park in the back. By the time I entered the store, Selena sounded excited. I followed her voice and found that he was buying her a smartphone, the first I had ever seen. They were ridiculously rudimentary as compared with anything we've got today, but at the time, for us, they were like something out of a sci-fi movie. I didn't even know what "smartphone" meant... like, *what,* did it form its own opinions? Could it make a valid argument or throw a curveball? Did *this* thing run on some kind of new Artificial Intelligence?

She was extremely excited, and he was beaming with pride.

It made me want to reach out and strangle the motherfucker, but I reeled my feelings in and reminded myself of what I had just learned not an hour before.

Oh, I had agreed to let us just be *us*, but I also knew I wasn't in this to get myself hurt. I was going to have to be more careful from now on, to protect myself... this was clearly *not* something that was built to last. It was temporary, light, fun... a fiction. Make-believe. It was everything we had agreed on at Q+1. And if I was going to play a game, I had better remember the rules.

As Homeboy was showing Selena the smartphone's features, he suddenly stopped mid-sentence. I saw him reach out and take hold of her left hand. I guess he hadn't seen it before. I decided to take my leave and head back home to my boys, and just as I was about to step up and tell the other two, my phone rang. It was Lily's phone, but I *knew* it wasn't Lily.

"Hey, kid, is everything okay?"

"Hey, Daddy," replied Lee. "Can we play some Wii when you get home?"

"Yeah, little man. I'm about to head home right now. I should be there around two o'clock. Two-thirty at the very latest. No warming up before I get there unless you play your little brother."

"*Sweeeeeeet,*" he replied, and I could hear the big smile in his voice. "Mommy got me a new Wii Sports game. Remember? You snapped the last one in half and threw it in the garbage? Remember? Now I can smoke you at home run derby again."

"Kid... if Mommy bought you Wii Sports again, I am going to be so-..."

"*See you when you get home, Daddy!*" and he hung up on me.

That kid. The Wii Sports home run derby is a story for another day, Reader. There was trouble brewing in the smartphone section, aisle two.

"So hold on," Homeboy was saying, not happy, still looking at Selena's left hand. "He got you *a gold ring* for your birthday?"

Selena and I never really had a proper goodbye that day, but that was okay. She had made it there safely, and I didn't need to see any more of this. I said goodbye to them, told Selena I'd see her around, and headed out before she could object. I don't know why, but when I got to the exit, I glanced back at them. He was still looking at the Claddagh, face red now, and she was looking longingly after me. We made eye contact, and she tilted her head and smiled just a bit as if to say, "smile." So I smiled a smile that wasn't fooling anybody, and I headed home.

As I pulled out of the parking lot, I turned on the radio to try to drown out everything on my mind. I didn't want to focus on anything, so I turned up the radio to distract myself for the forty-five-minute drive home.

A way down the road, just as I was exiting Delphia to the south, the song "Just a Dream" came on, by Nelly. I had to wonder... was that the Universe speaking to me, or was this my imagination? Whichever, I turned off the radio and drove the last 20 minutes home in silence.

Until my phone told me I had a text.

PLEASE FORGIVE ME FOR EARLIER. I'LL MAKE IT UP TO YOU.

It occurred to me that it was probably her first text from the new smartphone he gave her.

# PART II:
# MICROCOSM

*"Man is the microcosm of the macrocosm…"*

– Carl Jung, psychoanalyst and founder of Analytical Psychology

# Chapter Thirty-Six:
# Q&A

*March 15, 2012*

*Welles County Courthouse*

*Danverston, Illinois*

*Mr. Callahan, what do you think I've asked you here to talk about today?*

"Detective, you haven't asked me here to *talk* about anything. You've asked me here to answer questions."

*Fair enough. And what subject matter do you think we'll be asking questions about?*

"About my relationship with Miss Selena Osorio. You'll ask when I first met her, what her personality was like, what kind of student she was, and if she stood out to me from other students initially. You'll ask about any significant changes in our teacher-student relationship over that first school year. You'll ask me why she and her mom chose to move her out of the school district during her junior year. You'll ask-..."

Hathcock realized that I was about to summarize everything that she was, indeed, going to ask me about, so she cut me off

*Now*, I thought, *she has learned her first important lesson about me. She just learned that I am a thinker. She learned that I won't be as easy as she had anticipated. She learned that she isn't the only carnivore in the room. Silly rabbit.*

# Chapter Thirty-Seven:
# Sonar

*November/December, 2011*

*Central Illinois River Valley*

Monday and Tuesday of the following week were almost unremarkable, but then Wednesday hit. On wrestling practice nights, I would head to the gym afterward to *work out*, where Selena would be waiting for me so we could move my van's captain's chairs into her backseat. Then we'd nest up and spend a couple of hours of sex, embracing, talking, and laughing together.

She also took a little time to show me the ins and outs of her new smartphone. I thought it was pretty cool, but my shallow ass couldn't help but point out that there'd be a new version out in no time. Of course, she knew I was just jealous, but she agreed that, of course, it was just a phone.

"*And,*" she pointed out, "a phone isn't a promise."

"A promise?" I asked, surprised. "The Claddagh is a promise?"

"Not a *promise*, I guess. That's not what I meant. It's something *real*, though. Something *between* us. It *symbolizes* us. Friendship, Love, and Loyalty. We've got the Friendship. We've got something *more* than just Friendship, now. We'll have to wait and see about the rest. But this phone is just a phone. And like you said, there'll be a new version out in no time."

***

On both non-wrestling weekday afternoons, Wednesday and Friday, we met at McD's to work on *homework,* to share time, and to share what we now called *Iced Caramel Mocha Frappe Macchiato Choco Latta Thingies.* Similarly, sex had come to be known as "coffee," as Selena had shown up Tuesday night at the gym extremely tired, but after sex, she had remarked that "That shit will wake your ass up better than a pot of coffee."

This was the way in which we were creating our double-meaning inside jokes. *Going to work out* meant nesting up in the van, *homework* meant getting an Iced Caramel Mocha Frappe Macchiato Choco Latta Thingy, and *coffee* meant sex.

"You going to *work out* tonight?"

"Can you help me with my *homework?*"

"You just need some *coffee.*"

We were really beginning to gather a collection of things that were distinctively *ours.*

Throughout that week, I was careful to keep my feelings in check... or, I convinced myself I was doing so, anyway. I wasn't trying to forget about the lesson at the park: this wasn't real. It was all make-believe, and I was not in it to get myself hurt.

Wednesday, when we went to McD's for what Selena also

sometimes shortened to our *drinky-drink-thingy*, we had a strange visit. As usual, she had one of her schoolbooks out on the table in front of us as we sat in our nook along the side of the place, toward the restrooms. She was in the middle of saying something when she stopped mid-sentence, her eyes looking suddenly up and past me.

"*Sonar!*" she called.

I looked to my right and could barely believe my eyes. Standing there was the small frame of an old man with a bald head, a McD's takeout bag in one hand, an Irish blackthorn cane in the other hand, and large, black shades covering his eyes... or rather, *eye*. He had snuck up on me somehow, and that's not usually an easy task.

"It's good to see you, Cal san," he said more cheerfully than I had ever heard him. It was a little odd because he couldn't *see* me. And I hadn't said anything to him, so how did he know I was there?

"How did you-..."

"I heard your voice a moment ago, when I was ordering," he said. "I'd know your voice anywhere. And I heard *you*, Selena san. Good to see you, again."

"Heeeey, good to see you, too, Mr. Mirai," Selena said, and I realized that she knew quite a bit more about him than the last time they met.

"What are you doing *here*?" I asked, perplexed.

"Ummm..." with sarcasm, "You, know... I *live* here in Delphia? You knew that." He was right. I'd known the answer to my own question as soon as I'd asked it.

"So is your driver around here, somewhere... Walter?"

"Yes," he confirmed. "Walter is still driving my old ass around." I looked at Selena and made a face that said *Sorry!* But now she was looking at me, then outside, then at me, then outside. Her eyes were concerned.

# Chapter Thirty-Eight:
# Walter

I looked out through the wall of windows to see... well, nothing, really. The parking lot. I gave Selena a question mark face, shoulders raised, like *wtf?* She nodded toward the window again, with a deliberate, direct glare. There was an older model, dark blue car parked along the curb, right outside our window, as though it was waiting for someone. I hadn't even noticed it the first time, but I hadn't been looking specifically *for* it, either.

The windows were tinted dark, really dark, like *black.* I knew the car was running, because then I realized that we had been hearing its faulty muffler for a while, and now I could see the exhaust billowing out behind it, kind of dark, and I thought, *Damn, that thing needs to be emissions tested.*

I glanced back at Mr. Mirai and was surprised to see his head turned sharply to his right, as though he had seen us looking back and forth at that car. As though he was looking *directly at* that car. But he couldn't be...

"Speaking of Walter, he's probably wondering where I'm at right about now," he continued. It occurred to me then that *that* was *his* car. He must have been running low on money, then, or something, because Mr. Mirai always used to get around in a gray 2006 Cadillac CTS. This car outside was a pretty drastic downgrade.

"Gotta go. *Ja mata*, Cal san. *Sayonara* for now, Selena san,"

Mr. Mirai said, turning, then shuffling toward the side doors to our right. He looked a little less confident in walking than when I used to see him, but of course he was aging.

"That guy was *staring* at me," she said, concerned.

"*What?*" I asked, knowing Mr. Mirai was definitely not staring at her.

"That *guy*," she repeated, "in that *car*... he was *staring* at me." I looked outside, again.

"Selena, you can't even see inside those windows. There's nobody-..."

"There's a *guy* in there... white dude, real old, bald, with sunglasses on, and he put his window down for like a minute. He was just *staring* at me."

That description was definitely *not* Walter. Mr. Mirai's driver was a 30-something-year-old, sharp-looking African-American gentleman. She had to have been mistaken, somehow.

As I looked back out at the dark blue car that I could just then recognize as an older model Caprice Classic, that driver's side window was still shut. Just then, Mr. Mirai shuffled up to the driver's door, his back turned to us. He tapped on the driver's window with his blackthorn. The driver's window lowered about eight inches, a cloud of smoke began wafting out from inside almost as dense as the exhaust cloud coming out of the muffler, and though I couldn't really see inside very well, I could see that Selena was right.

The dude driving the car was white. I could barely see his bald head and the top of his sunglasses, but the wrinkles and sunspots meant he must be really old, and I thought either he was very short or he sat seriously low in his driver's seat. The top of his sunglass frames looked like a neon blue Oakley set, and the lenses reflected the same neon blue. And had I just seen a hearing aid in that left ear, just for a moment, with a curly, thin little skin-colored wire coming from it? Or had that been an air bud? At any rate, it looked like Mr. Mirai had a new driver... but... *also* named Walter? And around the same age as Mirai? I was surprised this guy was even still driving, at his age.

The engine revved a little, and Mr. Mirai raised the hand holding the McD's bag with authority, rigidly pointing to the road. The engine revved again, and it occurred to me that we might be witnessing Mr. Mirai having an argument with his new driver. I heard Mirai's voice raise, which I'd never heard like that before, though barely audible and not discernable from where we were sitting. I heard the driver's voice raise and clash with Mirai's. Selena and I shot a glance at each other, then back to the two men.

The driver's window started to go up, and with impossibly

fast reflexes, Mr. Mirai shot his Irish Blackthorn into the opening and lowered the McD's bag. It looked like the rubber bumper on the end of the cane might have popped the driver in the forehead, but I couldn't be sure. The window stopped when it hit solid wood, then lowered again, the man's voice rising and Mr. Mirai again pointing with his McDonald's bag toward the street, insistently. Mirai took a small but decisive shuffle step toward the car and started another when the car suddenly roared and pulled quickly away, billowing a trail of exhaust behind it. So that clearly wasn't Mirai's driver. *That dude and his car* both *need to be emissions tested*, I thought.

The three of us watched the car gain speed until it got to the road, slammed on the brakes, then accelerated out into the late Wednesday afternoon main street with a trail of exhaust behind it. Unreal. Mirai had sent that dude packing.

"Sonar just made that guy in the car leave," Selena said.

"Yeah he did," I agreed. "Did Mirai hit him with the cane, I couldn't see. And I don't know how-...?"

Mirai turned back toward us, appearing to stare in at us. He smiled and waved, and I knew that he couldn't see us but that he knew we were watching. Then he turned away, stepped down off the curb, and started shuffling toward what I just then saw for the first time was a gray Cadillac CTS parked further away in the lot. He went to the black-tinted driver's-side window, and when it lowered,

I saw a 30-something-year-old, sharp-looking African-American man at the wheel. Mirai handed Walter the McD's bag and eased himself into the back of the Cadillac.

"That's Walter," I said. "He drives Mirai around. That other guy-..."

"I'm glad Mr. Mirai told that creepy dude to fuck off. How did he-..."

"Yeah, that guy in the loud car," I said. "You said he was looking at *you*?"

"No, *staring* at me," she corrected.

"Babe," I said, warmly, trying to avoid conflict, "maybe he was staring at *Mirai*. Doesn't that make more sense? I mean, he was wearing sunglasses, and those two ended up getting into it."

"*Noooo*," she was certain. "He was either staring at you or me, or *us*, but he wasn't staring at Mirai. I could tell."

"Okay, well, he's gone," I offered.

"Your phone just vibrated." I hadn't noticed. I picked it up, and sure enough, there was a missed text message.

# Chapter Thirty-Nine:
## ROBIN I

THIS IS MIRAI, the text message read.

I wondered why it was in all caps. Then I thought, *Of course it's in all caps. The One Puka-Puka lives in all caps. He goes for broke. But how did he get my number?*

Then the next message popped up.

JUST FYI, it read, and a photo of the dark blue Caprice with its license plate appeared. It was a vanity plate: ROBIN 1.

I wondered what that meant. Something about it was familiar, but I couldn't place it. Was it from *Batman* comic books? Or the movies? Maybe it was just the guy's name, or *somebody's* name. I didn't know what to make of it.

CALL ME ON SATURDAY, was the last message. I showed the messages to Selena.

"I've never seen a real Hawaii license plate before, have you?" she asked. I hadn't even noticed, but she was right. It was right there: HAWAII on top, ALOHA STATE on bottom, with a rainbow across it.

"Wow. Yeah, I have," I answered. "Lots of them. But never outside of Hawaii." Selena shrugged.

"Hmmm. Well, I *told* you that creep was staring at us. Why else would Mr. Mirai have chased him away and sent you that pic?" she surmised. "But wait-... I mean... how did Mr. Mirai *know* that, though? Like, he couldn't have *seen* the guy looking at us. And how could he snap a pic of the license plate? Can he kind of *see*?" she asked, trying to make sense of what she'd just witnessed.

"Well," I said, thoughtfully, "*Kind of,* yeah. Somehow he can kind of see... or *something*. I don't really even know. Weird stuff like this happens with him all the time, and the only explanation always seems to be that he can see. But then I realize that it's impossible.

"Maybe Walter took the pic," I suggested, looking for a more reasonable explanation. "And maybe Mirai kicked that guy out of here when he left and heard how loud that muffler was, I don't know..."

In my mind, I flashed back to the image of Mirai's single, closed Polyphemus eye in my face as those iron-grip hands pulled me close and he told me my fate. He told me not to be too hard on myself when I cheated on my wife, because she was a bitch, or something like that. Those weren't his exact words, but it was what he'd meant. And his stupid fucking prophecy: "Your soulmate will soon find you, and you will find yourself in ruin."

*Don't start*, I thought. *That shit isn't real. That's some stupid bullshit. It was just Mirai's bullshit* saki *talk.*

But just the same, something in me started to think about Mirai's words again. Could there be something to what he'd said that night? I *had* cheated on my wife, just as he'd predicted. And I *wasn't* very hard on myself for it, probably at least partly because my wife was a cheat and had defaulted on our contract several times, starting long ago.

And if I was honest with myself, this was much more than just a fling with Selena. I had some real *feelings* for her. I knew that sounded crazy, but looking back on the short time we had been together, somehow the feelings I had realized on Q+0 were growing. Yes, the time had been short, but the time we had been spending together was concentrated tenfold. Perhaps my soulmate *had* found me. Still, all of this had to be a coincidence with Mirai's creepy words from years earlier. It *had* to be.

But – *my mind continued thinking on it* – if I was to put *any* stock in Mirai's words, Selena and I were going to be found out and scandalized. *That* would be the next step. Even if Mirai's words were only coincidentally related to my life, maybe seeing him and thinking about it again was a wake-up call that I should really take a time-out, reassess what I was doing, reconsider what I was risking with Selena. This secret we shared was about the only thing that could cause me to find myself in ruin. There was nothing else in my life that could hurt me. I had never done any kind of drug... not even weed. I didn't even drink, anymore. The worst drugs I was on were the Xanax I had recently stopped carrying and the caffeine in the iced tea I sipped throughout the day.

*But if this got found out...*

Just on the whim of public opinion alone, I could be unjustly accused of anything. I could be forced to stand trial even, and regardless of all evidence in my favor, I *could* be found guilty of whatever they wanted. And if my wife's family got on board, with my father-in-law's influence... forget about it. Done deal. His connections ran deep... police at all levels, high-power attorneys, judges, Congress people...

But even if all of this *did* end up happening, and the authorities *did* try to pin something on me, Lily's family wouldn't try to help them put me away, would they? I was the father of their grandchildren. My father-in-law was my good friend. My mother-in-law didn't exactly *love* me anymore – hadn't in years – but we'd still protect each other against all danger for the boys' sakes, *right?*

This wasn't something I had just started thinking about; I thought about the risk of it all the time. My supreme self-confidence allowed me to remain unaffected by any fear of it, but just then, considering Mirai's words brought it home in a strangely real way.

Don't forget, in many ways small town America has an easier time than urban America insisting on the down-low that the end justifies the means. And although they couldn't *lawfully* find me guilty of any of their archaic *moral violations*, even attaining a guilty verdict by working around the law could allow them to sleep easy at night.

Where would I be then? At any time, I could turn around to find that we had been discovered...

... that the local communities were up in arms about it...

... that my school was going to fire me over it...

... that the state's attorney was recognizing that a sexual predator conviction – real or *fabricated* – was good for business...

... that the police were tracking my every move...

... that the judicial system had me marked as public enemy number one...

... that it didn't matter whether or not I was guilty of anything illegal...

... that I was a convicted felon, as grooming is a federal offense in the United States.

I knew how real the risks were. Sometimes it's not just about the Law in small towns... sometimes, the law can be more subjective. And if Selena and I were discovered, that subjectivity could turn my situation into a witch hunt. Everyone sleeps easy so long as their fears of a witch in their midst are drowned out, suffocated, burned, black-listed. Fired. *Ruined*. Sometimes, people are comfortable looking the other way when the law is bent or broken *by* the system so long as *ding-dong! the witch is dead.*

It could easily escalate into a witch trial, much like a literary text I would teach during second semester in my senior college credit class – *The Crucible*, by Arthur Miller. Miller wrote the play in the midst of the paranoid *Red Scare* of the 1940s-1950s United States. The Red Scare was a modern-day witch hunt, coinciding with the beginning of the Cold War, and spear-headed by Senator Joseph McCarthy of Wisconsin. But the Red Scare wasn't a hunt for witches; it was a hunt for Communists. So Miller wrote the play about the Salem Witch Trials as an allegory for hysteria of the Red Scare.

In Miller's day, influential people were being accused of concealing Communist sympathies, being publicly interrogated in front of Congress, being blacklisted as Communists, and – in some cases – being jailed for pleading their Constitutional 5th Amendment. In effect, these individuals were *ruined*. In 1947, a group of popular film producers, directors, and screenwriters (known as *the Hollywood 10*) refused to answer questions from the House Un-American Activities Committee (HUAC, and no, I'm *not* making this up) about their alleged involvement with the Communist Party, citing the First Amendment as guaranteeing political freedom and, therefore, privacy. They were sentenced to imprisonment for one year and blacklisted in Hollywood.

Other notables who were subpoenaed, assisted, or spoke out against HUAC activities included celebrities Lena Horne, Charlie

Chaplin, (future POTUS) Ronald Reagan, Walt Disney, Lauren Bacall, Humphry Bogart, Leonard Bernstein, Burl Ives, Orson Welles, and Gene Kelly. In effect, those aiding the HUAC were exonerated while the accused were being *ruined*. But, like the Salem Witch Trials of Miller's symbolic play, there was often fluffy, ridiculous evidence at best, and much of it was based on word-of-mouth rumors, interpersonal conflicts, or foundationless accusations.

By the time it was over in the 1960s, hundreds of celebrity careers had been destroyed in search of witches...er, rather, *Communists*. This is known as McCarthyism, and the Red Scare is today synonymous with "The political practice of publicizing accusations of disloyalty or subversion with insufficient regard to evidence" (The American Heritage Dictionary).

I could see a similar series of events potentially being the case with me, if the community caught wind of Selena and I. They could label me one or all of those nasty 'p' words: pervert, predator, pedophile, perp. They could even call me a groomer. And they could find that aaaaall the evidence proved them wrong, but rumors and their hurt sensibilities could be all they needed to pin it on me.

A *groomer*. How fucking disgusting. If anybody, and I do mean *anybody*, ever called me a groomer to my face, I very likely would have broken his jaw before he finished the word. Fucking *groomer*. The word made me sick. A *groomer* is basically someone in a position of authority who attempts to gradually condition a minor in order to entrap them into a sexual relationship. As you know, Reader, what happened with Selena and I began *after* she was a legal adult. And *she had pursued me* long after I had any authority over her in teacher/student roles. She had nothing to gain and quite a lot to lose by pursuing me. And *she* had initiated sex, as an adult. She had recently joked at the hotel on my birthday that if there had been any grooming going on, it was by her.

"So, okay," Selena said, trying to make sense of what had just happened at McDonald's, "Mr. Mirai can kind of see. I bet he saw that creep staring at us and said something to him about it. They argued, and Mr. Mirai kicked the guy out," she said, certain of herself. I didn't argue. She had never seen his face under those big, black glasses, so I knew I had to just let it go for now. I would eventually talk to Mirai about it, sometime.

We spent the rest of our visit offering each other sips of our drinky-drink-thingy and talking about Mirai. She asked how well I knew Mirai. I told her that I knew quite a lot about Mirai, probably more than anyone but his driver, Walter. And I told her that Mirai knew a shit-ton about me and reminded her that he had been there that day of the Drunken Barn Dance. So he knew some of what my situation was like at home.

But I didn't tell her about what Mirai had said to me that night, about what I *now* call the taboo prophecy (sound familiar, LOL). Selena would love the part about not beating myself up for cheating, and the soulmate part, but the whole being "ruined" part would probably upset her. So it was better to leave that part out. If I told her about the taboo prophecy, chances were that it would keep ricocheting around in her head like it had been doing in mine. I had supreme confidence to keep me warm at night, but she didn't. The worry might really take hold, and I didn't want that.

She knew what we were really risking, and specifically, what *I* was risking to be with her. I knew that she had a fear of being the reason I would end up getting fired, or worse, jailed unjustly. We had talked a little about it a few times. I told her that if the world found out about us, and if they judged me to be immoral, or if they fired me, or if they jailed me... *she* would not be the cause of it. The world's ignorance and prejudice would be.

# Chapter Forty:
# Operation 40 Candles

Friday night was an important night at the gym. Selena and I nested up, and she wished me an early happy birthday, placing my cold hands under her t-shirt to warm them, where I found her trim waist was tied with a bow. She somehow knew that the following day, Saturday, December 3, 2011 (Day Q+20) was my 40th birthday. I hadn't mentioned it. Girls just *know* shit like that.

She had enjoyed calling me "old man" here and there, from time-to-time. She pointed out that night that my birthday would make us twenty-*two* years apart in age. It was funny to hear her joke about it, as I really did not feel any older. In fact, I felt younger than I had felt since my twenties before I was married. Sure, part of it was Selena, and part of it was my recently rising testosterone levels, but there was also something in me that had been dragged down by my marriage, that made me feel older than I really was and more unhappy than I should have been. It was like a part of me had been unjustly imprisoned, and I was still getting used to my newly regained freedom.

"So, what are you doing for your birthday?" she asked, all smiley.

"*You,*" I answered. "*Right now.*" But she told me I could open that gift soon enough. She had some things she wanted to discuss first.

*Ruh-roh, Raggy.*

"So, you going out tomorrow night? Hitting the strip clubs with the boys?" she playfully asked. I reminded her that we had talked about strip clubs before in one of our many talks, and she knew I didn't care for them. They've just never been my thing.

"So, are you doing the rounds at all the bars in town, getting hammered?" she asked. But she knew I had only drunk once in the last few months, and that was after my massive failure at her birthday party.

"No," I said, smiling and squeezing her a little. "No, I probably won't do anything. Lily will probably have a cake and candles, and cards, more for the boys' sakes than mine, but that's fine. I am all good with that."

"Cal, all jokes aside, I have to tell you something," she said, serious now.

"What? *What is it?*"

"Lily is throwing you a surprise birthday party tomorrow."

"What? No, she isn't... why would she-...?"

"*She is,*" she insisted. "She called me on Tuesday and asked me to pass it on to my mom, asked me not to tell you, and asked if I would take you to a movie to get you out of the house for a few hours on Saturday while guests arrive, food is delivered, and so they can decorate. I told her I would call you tonight to set it up, so you didn't have time to dwell on it and get suspicious."

I had been clueless. Lily had contacted *Selena*? Lily asked *Selena* to take me to a movie? That just seemed so... just so NOT my wife.

And here's one for you, Reader... it has never even occurred to me until right now, this instant, as I'm writing this, that I *should* have been wondering how Lily had even acquired Selena's cell number. Had she gone into my phone? She and I never looked through each other's phones, so far as I ever knew. She didn't have Selena's mom's phone number. Not that it matters now, but I wonder... Dani is gonna love that one.

"Your brother, Ron, is coming down from Chicago," she said, and that made me very happy. It would be his second visit down to Kent, and I was glad she would get to meet him. I knew that she had told me about Ron first because – of my five siblings – he would be the most surprising visitor. A road trip down to hang-out for my birthday did not sound like something Ron would find appealing. I was surprised that he would come down. He had been a divorcee for several years then, and this just wasn't his style.

"Ron and Jess are coming down together, she's driving. But Kate is upset that she can't make it. Lily called her *Kitty*, but I didn't know who Kitty was, so she had to explain. Do *you* call your sister that? Never mind, anyway, it's her health, you know what I mean.

Lily is going to make sure you *Skype* with Kate when they sing happy birthday, and you blow out candles. Pip and Ken can't make it, but Lily didn't say why."

*Skype*? I had never really even seen *Skype*. It was something kind of newish, and though I knew what it was, it had never occurred to me to use it with my siblings. I had always just wished my parents in Ireland would get a computer so we could *Skype*. I had taken the whole fam to Ireland over Christmas the previous year, but I wished I could *Skype* between them and my boys. Pretty cool idea by Lily to *Skype* Kate from this party I was learning about. I didn't think Lily had ever used Skype, either, which was even more remarkable.

Kate was the firstborn and an absolute inspiration to all of us, the toughest person I've ever met to this day. Of the six of us siblings, Kate was the one with decades of serious medical issues, ever since she had been diagnosed with diabetes at eight-years-old. She had endured and beaten so much for so long that I had started calling her a "tenacious bitch." She loved that, and when she was in a particularly tough spot, medically, she'd ask me what that name was that I always called her. I'd call her a tenacious bitch, and she'd laugh and laugh. I knew how much it must upset her to know she couldn't come down south to be with the rest of us for my birthday.

"Your assistant coaches are all coming. I wrote down and

memorized all their names: Leo Derby, Jake and Bella Busch, Mark and Ria Dunn, and Buck Lewis. I think some or all of them are bringing their sons. My mom isn't sure if she can make it yet, 'cuz she works part-time nights... *you know*. Sometimes, she takes on an extra shift for a night, too. And Lily's whole side will be there early afternoon, but they don't plan to stay much past the cake, because *your* people will probably be drinking. And she asked that no one brings gifts... she said you wouldn't want anyone getting you anything, you never do."

It all sounded very cool, and it made me happy. But it made me feel a little bit bad, too. It made me feel just a little bad to think that the wife I generally regarded as my Hell on Earth was planning this great party for me, and I was finding out about it from my girlfriend. But, then again, I knew that this was little more than Lily's way of looking like the good wife in front of everyone else. The nice things she occasionally did for me were rarely because she gave a rip about me, and they weren't even out of gratitude for everything she'd put me through and that I'd supposedly forgiven her for. Her day-to-day treatment of me was enough for me to know that. I didn't need to dwell on it long to realize that, of course, she didn't really give two shits about my birthday. This was about appearances.

"You have to promise to act surprised, though," Selena insisted.

I promised, and anyone who knew me knew I could put on an act like a motherfucker. If I wanted you to believe something, almost no matter how ridiculous, I could make you believe it. In high school, I had been that rare jock/theater guy. I was a four-year Men's Club Letterman and a Thespian. I won the annual acting award my senior year. I would be *very* surprised the next day, indeed.

Going to a movie together could prove interesting if we happened to see anyone we knew, and I use the word *interesting* loosely. If someone we knew *did* see us, we'd have to do damage control and make sure to contact them after the party to ensure they knew that my wife had asked Selena to take me out and distract me. If anyone from my school or her school saw us out together, just us, the rumors would potentially be rough, risqué, and ruinous. And they would spread as far, deep, and wide as the Illinois River Valley.

If we were spotted out together, I bet I'd even be called into a meeting with my administrators – Rick Lincoln and Brant Beckett – to answer for the kinds of rumors that could circulate. Rumors have that way of starting out relatively harmless or only mildly harmful, but then snowballing into big, scandalous stories. And they traveled faster and farther than the wind. We had to be extremely careful with this.

"So... you wanna go to a movie with me tomorrow?" she asked, and we laughed. "I'm asking you out on our first date, so, say *yes*."

"Depends. What movie are we going to see?" I asked, glad that we'd be able to do something new like that in public together, despite the risks. "And you're paying, *right?*"

"*That's* the surprise," she said. "I'm not telling you what movie until we get there. And yes, *jerk*, I'm buying."

## Chapter Forty-One:
## The Pledge

We softly caressed each other's bodies and shared soft kisses after the lovemaking (as our gym visits were mixed with some lovemaking and some fucking), and I had to call attention to the potential consequences of going to the movies together. Though I knew she was just as aware as I was, I had to point out the potential pitfalls to ensure we were on the same page.

We were taking a serious risk. I hoped she understood that – I wasn't saying that I didn't want to go out in public with her – I just meant that when we ventured out into public, we had to cover our asses and have a strong, rational explanation for what we were doing out alone together.

We shouldn't *have* to explain it, but we *would* have to. It was just part of the taboo that was *us*. *We* were the taboo.

As far as rumors about us making out, or fucking, or Selena being pregnant, or *whatever* they might say – and don't think those examples are too ridiculous – we could handle any and all of it if we could explain the *why* of our being there together. We'd be okay if we always had a *why* that was stronger than their suspicions. So we'd have to be unwavering and clear that we were just friends. Now that it seemed like we had *that* out of the way, we spent our time as usual, talking of events in the news, or music, or movies, or people we both knew, or the Marine Corps, or the meaning of Life.

But soon, Selena became suddenly quiet. Of course, I noticed right away, and I asked her if everything was alright. Was she cold? Was she thirsty? Should I get her some water? She assured me that she was fine, just thinking.

"Are you sure you don't want some water? *Selena... I, too, know what it's like to be thirsty.*"

It was a line from the basketball movie *White Men Can't Jump*, with Wesley Snipes, Woody Harrelson, and Rosie Perez. As Selena was a basketball player, it was one of the only movies I was sure she had seen from my generation. That line of dialogue was from a scene with Harrelson's and Perez's characters in bed, and she was thirsty. Selena and I joked about that line sometimes, but she wasn't having it that night. She repeated that she was just thinking.

"About what?" I asked.

"Just kind of everything," she answered, not really answering at all. Then after some thought, "We've been together now for almost three weeks."

"I know," I agreed. "It's hard to believe. It's blown by, but it also seems like it's been so much longer. We know each other on such a deep, *different* level now. I don't know if either of us thought things would work out like this on that night you first propositioned me."

I realized that maybe I was talking too much. I have always been aware that sometimes I do that. Maybe I should shut up, settle in, and see where she might want to take this. Not that there had to be somewhere she wanted to take the discussion, but if she did, I didn't want to talk her away from it. Softly, directly: "Whatchya thinkin', Baby?"

"Sometimes I just wonder what we *are*," she said.

I had no idea what that question meant, but in a way, I knew *exactly* what it meant. I'd seen Joe Rogan's standup comedy special from like 2006 where he talks about girls who *tell* you they don't want to get serious or start being smothered by a relationship, but *secretly*, they're plotting how they're going to hit you with something like the line Selena had just hit me with. But Selena took it a step further.

"Ya know, like, sometime down the road, isn't this all just going to be some stories we'll never tell anyone about?" She thought a bit more, face tucked into my chest. "I mean, aren't we going to have to drift apart at some point, like, before long? Or break this off and try to go back to being just friends? I mean, people could never accept *us*, together... like at your work. I grew up with all those people, their families... they could never understand *us*. I have plenty of enemies there now, too, since the fight with Letty. They'd fire you because of the taboo of *us*, but the people who don't like me would fire you out of spite."

She was thinking out loud, and I didn't know how much of this she had thought about before or if this was streaming live, coming to her in real-time.

"I mean, *what?*" she continued. "Like I'm going to leave for the Marines and eventually marry *Leonard*? Move away? Maybe have kids? But the whole time you and I will be having visits together, my visits with Cal? And maybe my boys will be yours, and Leonard will never know that. I mean, that could be how this plays out, if we wanted it to.

"Ya know? Like, I know you're eventually planning to divorce your wife, you always were, I know that, now. But what if you never do it until the boys grow up and move out? You have the boys at home for like the next 13 or so years, and I'll be at least 31 by then. And I won't ever try to compete with them. Like when I watched you wrap them up in bed into-..." she paused.

"Into Ronny Taco and Lee Burrito?" I offered. She laughed.

"Yes. And how you love to stop into their room at night and just watch them sleep... I could see how happy that made you. And then I saw you with the boys at breakfast, with Lee helping you cook, looking for double yolks, helping you serve us, the music, the singing, the dispute about lyrics, what was it? Juice boxes and..."

"Shoes boxes." We both laughed.

"*Right*. And when the electricity went out, you being Daddy with the hot cocoa and Lee helping to find the marshmallows with his little orange flashlight. And the way they took your hands in the parking lot of the restaurant to walk in safely. And the way Lee came over to see what steak you were ordering so he could have whatever you were having. And how they followed your lead at the restaurant... perfect gentlemen... your boys are just... *special*. Like, *priceless*. You and the boys are just-... that bond is-... just something you never see, *ever*." She floated back into thought.

"Fingers," I said.

"What? Did you just say *fingers*?"

"Yeah, *fingers*," I said again. "In parking lots, the boys don't take my hands. I say *Fingers*, and they hold my two fingers, one boy on each side." That got her laughing again.

"Yeah, *Fingers*, whatever, they hold on to *you!* And for their whole lives, they'll hold onto *you*. And you'll hold on to *them*. And maybe we could have boys like that. Could you imagine what our boys would look like? Fucking *studs*. I mean, Lee is already waaay on his way to being an all-around stud, and Ronny is going to be a lady-killer, too, but if *we* had boys..." She paused again to think.

"Yeah? Well, I do know how to build good boys who will become good men," I replied after a bit.

She had been kind of rambling, but I loved that last part. She was spot on about my boys. They were exactly how I had taught them to be, and they absolutely *were* special. *We* were special. And no matter what, we *would* always hold onto each other. The divorce was imminent, but the boys and I would always be bound together, and

Lee and I would always be telepathic. Maybe Ronny, too, someday. And I don't mean to say all that to say that they wouldn't always be just as close to Lily their whole lives. Of course, they would.

But this talk about Selena marrying Homeboy and having *my* boys? I mean, I would have to understand her moving on with Homeboy or somebody eventually, since I'd probably be married until the boys were grown, but secretly having my boys? Now *that* was some free spirit thinking. Was she seriously talking about long-term cheating on Homeboy? I didn't know what to make of all that talk... shit, that was *a lot*. I *really* didn't know what to make of that. I mean, even if something crazy like that were to somehow happen, people would know because I'd have to tell my boys. I could never father a child with someone, ever, and not tell my boys that they had a brother... and it *would* be a brother. That's all I make, LOL.

But she was kind of right... you never knew. We could define whatever we were or weren't going to become, so I figured she must just be thinking out loud. My head started getting clouded with everything that could be, all the directions we could take. At the heart of her rambling, though, was her first question: what *were* we?

*What the actual FUCK?!* I thought, then. *It's only been three, fucking, weeks!*

"I don't know, I just-..." she continued. "I want you to know something. I want you to know that I will never ask you to leave your boys for me. I don't want you to worry that I might fall so deep or get so attached that I might make you choose between them and me. If there ever comes a time when that has to be a choice, I will let you go."

Her thoughts struck me deep. I was very touched that she had thought so selflessly about our dicey... *what? Arrangement? Relationship?* Whatever... our *situation*. Before what she just said, I did not know for certain if she had been falling into us the way I had been, but *then* I knew. I was pretty damn sure before, despite us getting pissy at the park that prior Sunday, but now I was sure.

Without her describing it, I could hear how much of a sacrifice it would be for her to give us up for the relationship between my boys and me. I recognized that she must have at some point wanted to ask me to push the divorce forward and move out of the house, otherwise why would she feel the need to assure me that she'd never ask for it? It would never have crossed her mind to say so, otherwise.

"Thank you, Baby," I said.

And it made me happy. Not just because she was recognizing the immensely powerful love between my boys and me. Not just because she had made a pledge to me. It was simply, and selfishly, because I then knew that she was falling just as hard as I was. We really were together in this, wherever it might go. We were forging *our* bond.

# Chapter Forty-Two:
# Spoiler Alert

I slept great that night, and for the first time in a long time, I woke up actually *knowing* that it was my birthday. My *40th* birthday. I mean, it was the day I'd get to spend with Selena for my birthday. The day my wife was throwing me a surprise party. Four decades on planet Earth. Shit, I felt like I was turning 28, the age I had turned before I got married.

Had I not known this was that day, I would have known as soon as I looked at my phone. There was a text message there from Selena wishing me a happy birthday, as if we hadn't been together the night before and I hadn't eagerly untied that bow around my gift. And there was something else. She sent another selfie, lifting up her shirt to expose her bra with charcoal gray sweats pulled down to mid-thigh, exposing hot pink and black leopard print string panties, and a purple ribbon tied around her waist.

*Holy shit*, I thought. I had the other pic she'd sent much like this one, but just the idea that she took this pic for *me*... it was a great gift to wake up to, and you could say it got the blood going.

I thought about asking her if she wanted to find someplace secluded to park instead of seeing a movie, but I knew the risks were far too great in the daytime, even with the van. I got dressed, and just as I put my phone in my pocket, it vibrated. I checked it, but there was no Caller ID name, and I didn't recognize the number.

HAPPY BELATED BIRTHDAY, CAL SAN. CALL ME TOMORROW, IF YOU CAN. MIRAI.

Oh, that was cool of him. Sometimes I just didn't bother wondering how Mirai knew things, because he must have a great memory and he knew a lot of people who filled him in on whatever he wanted to know. So I didn't even really know or care how he knew to wish me a happy birthday. His last text had asked me to call him Saturday, this day, but now he was asking me to call the next day. Good thing, too, because I would have forgotten. I made a mental note to call him Sunday. Maybe he wanted to talk about that creepy dude in the Navy blue car. What else could he want to talk to me about?

I played that morning off cool as ice, waiting for my wife to wake-up to her alarm an hour later, to wish me happy birthday, and then to fill her in on Selena's phone call. You know, the phone call I received while I was *working out* at the gym the previous night. The one where Selena asked me to go with her to see a movie for my birthday. Wink, wink. Nudge, nudge.

My wife did a good job playing it off as though it was news to her. She thought that was nice of Selena, and my God, had Selena not told me of the surprise, I never would have guessed. Lil told me that she didn't want me cooking breakfast for the fam that morning, as it was my birthday, and she called the boys in. They both had a card for me. She had apologized that she couldn't do much, as we were kind of strapped on cash with Christmas coming, and all. She had a card for me, and she promised some kind of cake by the time

I got home from the movie with Selena. Again, she noted how she thought it was so sweet that Selena was taking me to a movie for my 40th. Je-sus, she could be a good actor when she wanted to be.

I wondered aloud what movie Selena was taking me to, as I didn't even know what movies were out at the time – I hadn't been reading my *Entertainment* magazine, lately. I told Lily there was no need for cake when I got home, but she insisted. I tried not to break character. In this manner, Lily and I lied our tails off to each other to make my surprise party work out.

An hour later, around 11 am, Selena pulled up into the drive. I told her she should park on the street so our vehicles weren't blocked, but she insisted that she was driving, as it was my birthday and all. I said goodbye to the fam, and away Selena and I went to go see... whatever movie we were going to see. Selena was all excited because she could play her song playlists off the new smartphone Homeboy had gifted her. It really was kind of cool, too, because we could listen to her specific song choices on *Pandora* instead of whatever radio stations would fade in and out of reception on the drive north.

Twenty minutes later, as we were on our way north on Route 22 to Fort Clark and about to cruise out of the northern edge of her town, Delphia, she pulled into a parking lot and put the car in park out by the road. N2Deep's song "Back to the Hotel" was playing.

"Everything okay?" I asked.

"It's called *Tower Heist*," she disclosed.

"Wha-... *Oh*, that's the movie we're seeing? Cool. Isn't that the comeback movie for Eddie Murphy that everyone is talking about? I read that he's great in it."

I knew from reading *Entertainment* magazine quite a while back that Eddie Murphy had a new movie coming out, but I never paid attention to when movies were actually showing in theaters unless I could take the boys.

"He *is* great in it, but the movie isn't as good as he is," she offered. "It's alright."

"Then why are we going to see it? And-... *wait*... where'd you hear it wasn't very good?"

"It's an alright movie," she repeated, then began explaining. "There were a lot of funny parts. It's about a group of people in a condo building who are going to steal-... I think it's *billions*... from another resident who originally stole the money. It's an all-star cast, or whatever... all big names, like five of them or something. Ben Stiller and some other people you'd know. But Eddie Murphy is great as this crook that they kind of hire to help them pull off the heist. The heist goes bust, but-... "

"Wait, *what?*" I exclaimed. "How do you know all that? Why did you just *tell* me the ending?" I wasn't upset or anything, it just seemed really weird for her to tell me the whole plot through to the end. "Babe... what's up?"

# Chapter Forty-Three:
# Heist

"What's up is that I've seen *Tower Heist*, so we're not going to see it," she said. "We're not going to see a movie, Babe. I still have that cash from my birthday gifts, and we're getting a fucking room. I've got a surprise party of my own for you. *Surprise!*"

She pulled up her shirt, where that purple bow was again tied around her waist. "We're gonna fuck in a bed for a change, and this is about to be the best birthday of your life!" And she was dead serious, smiling a devious, aggressive little smile.

She pressed play on her phone, and on came Rihanna's brand-new, internet-leaked, 78 second, original version of the *very* sexual "Birthday Cake."

I looked up and realized that we were in the parking lot of the Motel 6. Selena put it back in drive, pulled around back where no one could see her car from the street, and then she had me sit in the car while she went to check us in. I was rock hard from the moment she said "... getting a fucking room."

*Now that's a damn birthday surprise*, I thought. *Sorry, not-sorry, Eddie.*

As Selena was about to close the car door, she stopped, looked in at me very serious-like, inflated her chest like a balloon, and in her best Arnold Schwarzenegger voice, said, "I'll be back."

The first time Selena had introduced me to our drinky-drink thingy at McD's, talk of *The Terminator* came up somehow, and she didn't know much about it, so I explained some things about the plot, characters, actors, and famous lines. I had told her about that line in the movie and why it's Arnold's most famous catch phrase. She knew the line, and her Arnold impression was pretty damn good (better than mine), and it was even better because I didn't know if she'd ever heard him actually say it.

"May the Force be with you," I called after her, as she went inside to pay for the room and get the key. We had watched *Star Wars: A New Hope* together with the boys on Thanksgiving weekend, as well, remember? So I knew she'd know that line.

While Selena went in to get the room, I made that call to Mirai. It was quiet, as she had taken her phone in with her.

He answered with *"Happy birthday, Cal san!"*

He then asked why I wasn't with Miss Selena, as that was why he asked me to call Sunday instead. I told him I *was* with Selena, but she was not in the car with me, she went inside to get something. He was glad, and I was confused as fuck.

"How did you know Selena is with me right now?" I asked. He ignored it.

"Do you remember what I said to you that Sunday night at The Hunter's Den? After bar time? In the entryway between the doors?" Mirai asked.

*Awe, fuck. Here we go,* I thought. I never-ever wanted to discuss that night with him. But I confirmed that, yes, I remembered.

"*Shourai.* And so you see what has come to pass?" he asked.

*What the fuck?! There is no way he knows about Selena. No fucking way.*

He couldn't have actually *seen* Selena and I sneaking around together, and there's no way he guessed it just from the few times we'd all happened to be in the same places, so if someone told him about us, that meant someone else knew. *What the actual fuck?!*

"So you *know* what you must do," he continued. "You *know* you must prepare."

"Prepare for *what?* Are you talking about that *finding myself in ruin* bullshit? Yeah, I've thought about it. Let's not go there, Mr. Mirai. With all due respect, sir, that shit has been stuck in my head ever since that night you said it. I'm ready for whatever comes, but what makes you think-..."

"*Oh,*" Mirai replied, solemnly. "Oh, but you are *not* ready, Cal san. You. Are *not*. Prepared. As long as you choose to stay so close to Selena san, you will both be in danger. You know they will never accept you two together."

"Who the fuck said we're together?! And *who* would never accept us?" I asked, becoming angrier and angrier the more he spoke. He ignored those questions, too.

"In Truth, the taboo of you and Selena does not exist on any moral spectrum; it exists on a spectrum of perspective, a spectrum that you have the ability to affect."

"Look, Mirai," I interrupted him. I didn't think I'd ever just called him Mirai directly to him before. "I'm not interested in changing anyone's moral spectrum, or perspective, or anything. I'm not-..."

"It doesn't matter what you *want*, Cal san. So long as you *want* to be close to Selena, it is the position you are in. The perspectives and opinions of society are social constructs, to be sure, and they are more closely related to stereotypes than to any degree of absolute.

"*But*... this taboo can attract the ire of those who can *never* understand, those who don't *want* to understand, those who worry more about others than themselves. You have enemies you cannot see, Cal san, and this includes those in *authority*, those in *power*... those who have the *intent* and the *means* to hurt you, to *ruin* you.

"So you see... you must prepare for the most dangerous possible adversaries. Like you did when your Grandad died the day the Gulf War began, you must focus, you must prepare your mind for the war that is coming, and you must help prepare Selena."

Just then, as if she had heard Mirai mention her name, Selena came skipping out from the motel check-in desk, smiling wide and holding up a motel key. She chose room #222. I let Mirai know I had to go, she was coming.

He said, "Take this time together. Enjoy your birthday surprises, Cal san. But then, I cannot stress it enough... you *must* prepare, as your enemies are already preparing. Before long, they will make their move. It might not be tomorrow or next week, but *they are coming for you.* Prepare." And then that motherfucker hung up on me! I really liked Mirai, but sometimes it was very hard to.

This was all some crazy shit with Mirai, but I didn't have time to dwell on it. The girl opened my car door, put out her hand, and again doing Schwarzenegger, said, "Come with me if you want to live."

# Chapter Forty-Four:
# Birthday Cake

That sent me laughing out loud, forgetting almost all about Mirai's warning, absolutely cracking up! I had told her that movie line at McDonald's when I summarized *The Terminator* a week earlier, and now she used it on me. Except it wasn't Schwarzenegger's character who spoke that line, it was the character Kyle Reese played by Michael Biehn! Arnold's cyborg character spoke that exact same line in *Terminator* 2, but we hadn't talked about that movie yet.

I already knew I was deep for that girl, but I fell a little deeper every day. And it was still such a wonder to me that not long ago, I didn't see her in a romantic or sexual light. But I knew what was awaiting us in that motel room, and I sure saw her in those ways these days.

It was two-and-a-half hours of fun. Best birthday of my life? You bet your sweet ass. We even crushed a position we hadn't tried before. It got a little wilder than ever, and a little harder, and a little louder. From that day on, we would joke about it as our Tower Heist.

"You feeling naughty?" she might ask. *Why? What are you thinking?* I might inquire. "I'm thinking maybe you wanna help me pull off a Tower Heist," she might propose. More secret code to add to our list.

Although she had other songs queued up to play while we

spent time in the room, like "Birthday Sex" by Jeremih and "In Da Club" by 50 Cent, "Birthday Cake" also became a new secret term we would not soon forget. I can still see her making direct eye contact, giving me that look, and then bouncing her head and shoulders, saying, "Cake, cake, cake, cake, cake..."

On the way back to my house, we were both glowing, holding hands, and talking about what we had just done, considering that she was about to meet two of my siblings and my friends. We knew that we were all glowing after that time together, and we'd have to shake that shit off before we saw anyone.

But when we got there, saw all the cars, and prepared for the *surprise!* things took a turn... a mind-baffling turn. An infuriating turn. There was another surprise besides the party waiting inside.

Selena said I should go in first and she'd be right behind me. We heard the *Surprise!* and caught the blur of a decent sized crowd of people inside. Balloons and other decorations were hung all around, and there was my wife smiling and beaming as though the love of her life had just entered the house... it was Oscar-worthy. She came up and gave me a monster hug, squeezed me a little too long, and I felt the repulsion in me wanting to push her away. This was all about appearances for her. I even wondered if this loving wife charade was difficult for her to enact, because I hadn't seen it in such a long time.

I saw Lily's fam there in the living room, first. Both of Lily's sisters and their husbands, then her brother and his wife, her parents, her uncles and aunts, then her grandparents (I think on both sides, maternal and paternal). I was glad that I did not see her twin brother, Asher, though I wasn't surprised. We'll talk about him later in the story.

My siblings were further back in the living room, and opposite them, I saw my assistant coaches, Leo and his son, Jake and Bella Busch and their son and daughter, Mark and his wife Ria (who, like Selena, was a rare Mexicana in a white corn town), Buck and his son... and then I saw *her*.

Sitting at the far side of the large living room on a couch were four former students who had been my seniors the prior school year. Dante was there, a young man who was the closest thing to a former student/friend I've ever had. His brother, Tim, sat there with him, another great young man.

And next to Tim was sitting Letty, yes *that* Letty, with a smug "fuck you" smile on her face, her eyes focused solely on Selena. Selena's former best friend for life who, the previous year, had beaten her up at a party over a drunken misunderstanding. The one who had caused Selena's mom to decide to move out of town.

It still surprised me. If that fight had never taken place, Selena would've still been a senior at *my* school, and we would only know each other strictly in the capacity of teacher/student. If Selena had never moved, I would never have met with her over that summer to discuss the Marines, we would never have gotten to know each other as friends, I would never have been at her birthday party, and we would never have developed feelings for one another. So strange to consider...

*What the fuck is Letty doing here?*

I threw my wife a look, but she pretended not to catch it.

On the other side of Letty sat her boyfriend, another great young man who had somehow been peripherally involved in the fight, but I didn't know the details. And it definitely wasn't like I had anything against Letty. She and I had always gotten along great for the two years I had her in class, and whatever had happened between her and Selena was between them, not us. But just the fact that my wife knew about Letty and Selena, knowing Selena would be there, then allowing Letty to attend. It was my wife I was pissed at.

I quickly came to realize that my wife must have found a way to contact one of them, who then contacted the others. My guess was that my wife had found Dante on *Facebook*, and she had encouraged him to recruit other former students who I had been close to. If that was the case, I wasn't upset with Lily, so I chose to believe that *that* was how it had happened. And Lily would never have even considered inviting any of my current students, of course.

Still, I was infuriated by the fact that she knew all about the Letty/Selena fight, and she allowed Letty to sit in my living room as Selena walked in. It was the ultimate proof that this was all smoke and mirrors on my wife's part. However, Letty had been invited, Lily knew her presence would fuck up my party, or cause an uncomfortable atmosphere, at least. She didn't care. This party was for her. But I had to stay cool, like ice, and I did.

Selena had stopped in the entryway and looked directly to me when she saw Letty. I had looked at her almost as quickly, and while I was processing all of this in my mind, outwardly greeting the guests, I put my hand on Selena's shoulder in a protective manner that I could not resist, and I directed her past the crowd and into the sunroom with me. There, already sitting in the recliner, was my brother Ron. My sister Jess sat next to him on one couch. I didn't know why, but Pip and Ken weren't there... Selena had told me the night before that they wouldn't be. I suspected that maybe Pip hadn't come because he'd met Selena, and it might be too awkward. Of course, Kate was at home, ill, as was so often the case. My coaches came filing into the sunroom behind us, as well.

# Chapter Forty-Five:
# Mrs. Osorio

Ron took one look at Selena, then looked at me with speculation on display in his eyes for all to see. Ron never pulled any punches, and I'm not sure if I've mentioned that he was maybe the most perceptive person I've ever met, and he sometimes seemed to have a very sensitive sixth sense. He called Life as he saw it, with no beating around the bush. You never wanted to lie to Ron, even if it was to protect him from something, because he sniffed out a lie or a scheme from miles away.

I remember once, right when I'd started working for Ron, when he had gone on his annual Christmas vacation with the fam down to Sanibel Island, Florida. He had called me at the office to check in. I had only been working there for like seven months at the time, and I told him everything was great, running smoothly, no issues, that he shouldn't waste his vacation time calling the office to check in or thinking about how we were doing. That was part of what he paid me for.

I remember after I said that, there was a long pause from Ron.

"Liam," he said, "You're one of the most honest people I've ever known, but you will lie like a dog when you have to."

I pretended like I didn't know what he meant, and don't forget, I can act like a motherfucker. I can fool almost anyone about almost anything, no matter how ridiculous. But not Ron, and he was right.

What I was hiding was $30K that had gone missing from our business account with payday quickly approaching, and I was working closely and desperately with our accountant to try to figure out where it went. I would end up figuring that out, myself, which was a stupid double withdrawal our bank had made for the same $30K check, once on December 31 and then again on January 2, so it showed up in two different monthly statements in two different years. Somehow the New Year had prevented anyone from catching the double charge. The money had really been there all along, but the balance wasn't reflecting it. In an electronic age, it had to be accounted for before it could be added back to the balance. But I fixed it.

When Ron got back in town, he called me and simply asked if I'd fixed whatever the problem was. I could not believe his supreme intuition told him there was a major problem. So I told him the whole story. He said he had kind of known it was something big, but he trusted me to fix it. That was the first time he told me that solving problems was maybe what I was best at, as even the company's bankers and the two generations of our accounting firm had missed the error.

So yeah, Ron looked at Selena and I with a critical eye, and my spider-senses were screaming. I knew that Ron's intuition trumped my spider-senses. Whereas my spider-senses often let me know to pay attention because *something* important was going on, and my intuition was pretty damn on-point, Ron's intuition almost always told him exactly *what* was going on. And I knew by the look in his eyes that his intuition was whispering in his ear.

"So, uh," and Ron backhand-tapped Jess on the wrist, "What movie'd you two go see?" He was just short of having accusation in his voice.

"*Tower Heist*," I answered. "Everyone, this is a former student and current friend of mine, Selena. Apparently, Lily asked Selena to take me to a movie to get me out of the way for this surprise." They all greeted Selena, and I could sense some inner speculation in them, as well.

"*Tower Heist*," Ron repeated. "I just saw that movie. What'd you think of it?" and I sensed Ron's question as a trap meant to trip me up. He didn't think we went to a movie at all... I was pretty sure he knew exactly what was going on.

"Eddie was great as the crook they recruited for the heist. I really think he's back, maybe better than ever. Did you like the movie?" I asked.

"Yeah, yeah I did. Good flick. You're right, Eddie was great," and although Ron didn't push his investigation any further, I could tell he was still sizing up Selena and me. I doubted that he had even seen that movie. To this day, I still never have.

***

Although I didn't drink on my birthday, a lot of the party is a blur, but I know it lasted until early morning. After the casual, catered, family-style meal, we did the whole cake thing, and it was very special to have my sister Kate on *Skype* for it. We used my sister Jess's laptop, as she had brought it with her for easy connection.

I remember I stopped out into the living room by myself to say hello to the four former students who I had ignored upon my entrance. It occurred to me that Lily might even have contacted Letty first, and Letty brought the three guys. I said hello and thanked them for coming while they ate their cake (*cake, cake, cake, cake, cake, cake*) and looked at each other awkwardly. I was sure my wife had told them that Selena would be with me when I arrived. They left the party shortly afterward.

I remember my wife's family leaving just after the catered meal, just as Selena had said they would. The party eventually moved downstairs to the pool table and bar. At the bar, most of the guests drank and laughed, and laughed and drank. Some played pool, and the kids were playing Xbox. Eventually, it was time for some to leave.

Jess and Ron headed out first, as they had at least a three-hour drive home. When I hugged Ron goodbye and thanked him for coming, he whispered in my ear, "Watch your ass, little brother," and I felt obligated to act like I didn't know what he meant. He wasn't buying it and just gave me that sly smile known by anyone who knew him. That smile said, "I'm riiiight."

After they left, Selena's mom showed up. It was a nice surprise, and though no one had seemed to see Selena grab my ass several times throughout the night, we tightened that shit up real quick when her mom arrived. Mrs. Osorio had had a rough shift at work, and she was happy to accept a large glass of red wine and share some laughs regarding her tough day. I'd always thought she had a great laugh, but I hadn't known that she was as funny as she was. She was well received by the group, and I was glad she had come. And then the night was over. Selena and her mom were the last to leave, and I walked them outside through the garage.

"Thanks for the movie, girl. *Tower Heist* was really good. Nice job pulling off the surprise. I guess I'll just see ya when I see ya," I said to Selena in parting, though we knew damn well we would be back in the nest in no time. Selena just gave me a look that told me I had just said something wrong.

"*Tower Heist?*" Mrs. Osorio asked, surprised, standing in the open driver's door of her new small, yellow hatchback. Selena's face turned to a glare, as her mom was about twenty feet from where we were standing in the driveway, and she couldn't really see our faces in the dark. I didn't dare reply to Mrs. Osorio.

"With Eddie Murphy?" she continued. "Selena, isn't that the

movie you just saw last weekend with Leonard?"

"Uh, yeah, Mom."

I could see by Selena's face and body language that she was nervous, and there was a quality to her voice that told me she was kind of defensive, prepared to talk her way out of whatever this was. I remember thinking that if *I* recognized that quality to Selena's voice, her mom surely didn't miss it.

"I know Leonard really liked the movie, but didn't you say you wish you'd gone to see a different movie?" Mrs. Osorio inquired. "Did you take Cal to see *that* movie?"

Then I saw the problem. *Oh, shit.*

"Yeah, Mom. Um... I didn't think it was *bad*, though... but... I mean, this was *Cal's* birthday, so... when *he* said he wanted to see it, I figured, well, if a guy like Leonard liked it, maybe Cal would, too. I didn't tell Cal I already saw it, though... you just did. Thanks a lot, Mom."

Selena had started out rough, but as she thought her way out of the jam, she gained confidence. Again, I figured that if I had noticed *that*, her mom had noticed it, too.

"Oh, *shit*," Mrs. Osorio said, suddenly. "I must have left my scarf inside. Be a good daughter, and go get it for me, Selena."

"I don't think you were wearing a scarf when you came in,

Mom. Was she, Cal?"

"Selena, it's not getting any warmer standing out here," Mrs. Osorio said in a firmer tone. Selena flashed me frustrated eyes, then turned and headed back inside. I wondered if she knew what her mom was doing. "Selena, if you don't find it downstairs, check upstairs. And check the kitchen. And the bathrooms."

# Chapter Forty-Six:
# Doublespeak

I wasn't buying it. I was certain that Mrs. Osorio hadn't been wearing a scarf when she came in. This was simply a way for her to get rid of Selena so she could talk to me, one-on-one. This could be nothing, or it could be a problem. I started walking out to the street so she wouldn't have to come to me, and when the front door closed behind Selena, Mrs. Osorio pulled a scarf out from inside her car and put it on.

"That should give us some time to talk while she's looking for this scarf," Mrs. Osorio said, almost without emotion. "Cal, I'm going to be straight with you, and I'd appreciate it if you're straight with me."

*Oh boy*, I thought, *here it comes. This is it.*

I felt that calm wash over me as it does every time I'm confronted by potential conflict. It was supreme confidence setting in, and it had always allowed me to relax, slow myself down, clear my head, and think on my feet.

"What's on your mind, Mrs. Osorio?" I asked, avoiding her request for honesty. I would be as honest as possible. When this whole thing started with Selena, I decided I never wanted to lie to Selena's parents about anything. But if the circumstance dictated that I had to protect Selena and I, well...

"Please, Cal, I don't call you Mr. C anymore, so just call me

Demi. Cal, does Selena seem okay to you?"

"I don't know what you're asking. What do you mean, *does Selena seem okay?*"

"I mean, do you sense anything troubling about her? Like, do you know if she's drinking or into any kind of drugs, or anything?"

"Wow. Um, *no and no.* Of course, if she was, I probably wouldn't know before you would, but I'd say she's not. I'd be very surprised if she was drinking or using *any* kind of drugs. Not even weed... her eyes are never bloodshot or red when I see her. And as far as alcohol, I mean, I noticed at her birthday party that she had a Dixie cup of wine with her mango, but I just figured you knew about that."

She waved that away and shook her head.

"No, not that. I *did* know about that. That's not what I mean."

"So if it's not drugs or alcohol, do you think she's having some kind of personal problem? Like at school or something?" I offered.

"I don't know, exactly," she said. "I can't put my finger on it, but yes, I have received two calls from her school lately about her skipping classes. That's no big deal, though. Everyone cuts class sometimes. I work in your district office, so you know that I know how common cutting class is. It's just something new for Selena, and I hope it's not an indication that something's wrong. I feel like she's keeping something from me.

"For instance – I hope you can clear *this* up for me," she continued. "Selena says that she often stopped in to see *you* after basketball practices, before she quit. And since she quit, she says she's still been stopping in to see you because you and your boys – they're absolutely adorable, by the way – you and your boys have wrestling practice at her school? Is that accurate?"

"Well, yeah. It's all accurate. We do have wrestling at Delphia High School – it's the closest youth wrestling program to Kent, and it's our second year wrestling there. And yes, when she was playing basketball, she'd stop in to chat after practice, and she still does sometimes now that she's not playing anymore. I figure she's a young adult with nothing else to do on a weeknight in a small town. She just seems bored with this town and the formality of finishing high school before leaving all this for the Marines."

I was trying to think ahead of her, trying to be ready for whatever the next questions were going to be. She would probably ask about McDonald's. Maybe about Thanksgiving weekend. Maybe about the Claddagh ring. It didn't seem like she was coming up with this stuff off the cuff. This could prove dangerous, and I had to be on top of my game. I was happy I wasn't drinking.

*They are already preparing*, Mirai's voice whispered over my shoulder.

"I see," she said. "So she also tells me that sometimes she asks you for help with her homework, and the two of you meet up at McDonald's in Delphia so you can help her. Is *that* accurate?"

"Yes, that's accurate, too," I confirmed.

It was possible that Mrs. Osorio, or a friend of hers, or *whoever,* could have seen us together at McDonald's. I didn't really see a downside to being honest about that, but I wasn't about to elaborate on it. Somebody had seen Selena and me together, I reasoned, because someone also had to have told Mirai about us.

"Well, you had her in class as a student for most of two years," she said. "I know she missed a lot of school in the spring semester last year, but did you ever have to help her with homework back then? Like, *outside* of class, I mean?"

"No, not once," I said matter-of-factly. She waited for me to elaborate, but that wasn't happening.

"Don't you find that a little strange?" she asked. "I mean, she's always been an 'A' student, and she's never struggled at anything academically. But all of a sudden, now she needs your help? I mean, is her coursework *that* challenging?"

It felt like she *was* trying to corner me, but then she *wasn't*. Then it seemed like she *was,* but then she *wasn't*. I mean, when she asked about whether or not Selena had come in to see me outside of class when she was my student, she might have been seeing if we were hanging out when Selena was a minor... *OR...* she might have already known that Selena never stopped in for help outside of class before, and she was just making a point about her suddenly needing help with her schoolwork, as though there might be a problem.

And when she asked if Selena's coursework was *really* so difficult that she needed my help, she might have been insinuating that Selena and I weren't really meeting at McDonald's to do homework... *OR*... maybe she was just genuinely asking whether the coursework was that difficult or if Selena wasn't applying herself. I could see both possible intents, but I wasn't making any assumptions, wasn't taking any chances, and I didn't let my guard down. I just played it straight, as if there were no ulterior motives.

"Yeah, there's some challenging stuff in senior English. It's nothing she can't handle, and I don't really think she *needs* my help. I think she really wants to keep her grades up senior year like she always has, so she's just taking advantage of having an English teacher as a friend who can help her with writing arguments and how to use the elements of persuasion. It's the same stuff I taught her, but different teachers teach the same things in different ways, and senior year just elevates the challenges and expectations, you know?"

"So that's true, too," she said, almost to herself.

I started to realize that I might be overthinking Mrs. Osorio's intentions in talking to me. Maybe this wasn't at all meant to question my relationship with her daughter; maybe this was really just concern for the changes she was seeing in Selena.

## Chapter Forty-Seven:
## You Two

"Well, you've been to our place," she continued. "You know how small that space is. I have never eavesdropped on my daughters, *ever*, but in those tight quarters, I can't help but overhear Selena downstairs or on the phone sometimes.

"For the past couple of weeks, I've been hearing Selena on the phone to Leonard, and I can tell that he's upset with her about almost never seeing each other. They've been together quite a while – what, like eight or nine months? – and this is something new. And now that I know she's not spending much time with *him*, I want to know *what* my daughter is up to and *with whom*. Thoughts?"

*Okay. Okay. I'm down for all this. Maybe she* is *being tricky. Maybe she is just confirming that Selena and I have been spending quite a lot of time together lately. But, on the other hand, maybe she has heard Selena and I on the phone, too. Curiouser and curiouser.*

If it was specific answers she wanted, she was going to have to ask some very, very specific questions. I really liked and respected this woman, so I didn't want to lie to her. But I wasn't above lying if I had to. I already knew that if Selena and I got any closer, I was going to start hinting to Selena about letting her mom know about us. But for now, my past history in sales taught me that when I find myself in a tight spot, I answer a question with a question.

"So what's *your* gut feeling?" I asked.

"Well, that's just it. My gut feeling makes me want to find out why she's almost never home... I mean, seriously, almost *never*... and not spending time with Leonard. Now I know that she really does spend a good deal of time with you at wrestling or McDonald's. Thank you for confirming that. But I pay for the fuel in her car, and she's been going through more fuel than usual since around her birthday.

"I'm not keeping tabs on her, but I'm on a tight budget, and I notice these things. It wasn't like that back in the old house or even at the beginning of this school year. Something big has changed. She wasn't out all the time and asking for gas money so often. And she's not burning fuel going to wrestling practice at her school and to McDonald's. I thought maybe she *wasn't* spending the money on fuel at all. I thought maybe she was spending it on alcohol or drugs. But I would never stoop to checking the mileage on her car – that's just now how she and I operate. So I don't see other signs of drugs or alcohol, and *you* haven't seen signs of it.

"My initial gut feeling was that she was never at home because she was with Leonard. But when I started hearing him complain to her that he almost never sees her anymore, I had to wonder where she's going that burns that fuel. Is anyone going with her, or who is she going to see? I don't want to believe she might be seeing another guy behind Leonard's back, but what else could this be? It *feels* like it's that.

"When I ask her where she's always gone to, she reminds me that she's been stopping in the evenings to visit you at wrestling practice and at McDonald's. So I thought I'd check with you and see if that's accurate, and you've confirmed that it is, so it's not that. I'm glad at least that much is true. I'm sorry, I'm rambling, talking in circles."

*Whoah, what is she doing?* I wondered. *Is she trying to corner me or not?*

"Yeah, I see her pretty often at wrestling," I confirmed. Just then, the front door of my house flew open.

"*Mom,*" Selena yelled out to the street, then lowered her volume, probably because of the late hour. "It's not here. Are you sure you had it with you tonight?"

"Yes, I'm sure," Mrs. Osorio called back. "Did you check upstairs *and* downstairs? The kitchen and the bathrooms?"

"No," Selena admitted. Silence. Then Selena closed the door again to go look some more.

"So far, I don't see a lot to be alarmed about," I offered. "She's in a new school, making new friends... I assume there's more?" I asked.

"Yes. I've always allowed my daughters a great deal of freedom. Their father and I decided when Selena was born that we would trust our kids until they gave us reason not to, and we would encourage open communication and honesty without judgment. Of course, there've been some hiccups in Selena's case, but never anything overly serious. Well, serious, yes. But not monumental.

"I'm just hoping this is all nothing," she continued. "She's just been out really late most nights, and I want to continue to trust her... she's an adult now. She's grown. She's all signed up for the Marines, and she leaves on July 8, next summer... she told you that, right?"

"Yes, she told me."

"So I don't want to give her a curfew now, when I never did *before* she was an adult. But then she went up to Chicago with a friend's family for the weekend a couple of weeks ago, and I just felt like she was lying to me about that. And then we got into a heated argument last week, and she disappeared for a few days after Thanksgiving. It all just seems suspect. Do *you* think there's another guy she's seeing besides Leonard?"

Just then, her cell phone rang, and she laughed that it was Selena.

"That's okay, Lena-Lou, I found it. It was in my car." She closed the flip phone. "She's coming back out. I'm sorry for all the questions. I hope it's just me, but would you mind kind of staying vigilant with her? Like, if you see anything out of the ordinary, can you pass it my way?"

Selena came busting out the front door before I had to commit to that, though.

"Are you serious, Mom? Cal's wife and I were looking all over for that thing, and it was in *your car*?" Then, realizing I was in the street with her mom, Selena cautiously approached and asked, "So what have you two been talking about?"

It occurred to me that Selena had just that moment figured out her mom's ruse.

"I was just asking Cal how you were doing with your English homework. By the way, Cal, thank you for meeting with Selena at McDonalds to do the homework. She's really lucky to have you to help her, and it's very kind of you to do so."

I sensed Selena looking at me in surprise, but I didn't risk making eye contact with her. Her mom could see our faces now.

"Oh, you're both very welcome," I replied. "Selena will be shocked when she gets my bill in the mail, though."

Mrs. Osorio and I laughed. Selena did not. She was still just looking at me.

"I hope this isn't strange to ask, but..." Mrs. Osorio began, "When you two are together in public – at wrestling practice or at McDonald's – do you ever draw attention? Like, do people stare?"

I was done answering questions for the night, so I looked at Selena to answer her mom.

"What do you mean, *draw attention?* You mean, like, do people think-..."

"Yes, that's exactly what I mean, Lena-Lou. Do people think you're a couple? Do people *stare* at you two? I mean, watching you two interact from my perspective isn't all that weird, because I know you're good friends and all. But to others who *don't* know you... I... I wouldn't be surprised if other people thought you two might be a couple, the way you two interact and all."

"*Mom! Stop saying 'you two'!*" Selena exclaimed, and I couldn't tell if her outrage was real or fake. "Okay, *Cal*, say goodnight to my mom, then head inside to bed. You've got a wrestling meet to get up for in a few hours."

"Okay, *Lena-Lou,*" I said sarcastically.

"*Oh my God! If you start calling me-...*"

"*See?*" Mrs. Osorio laughed. "You two *seem* like a couple."

"And you, *Mom*, follow me home. You've obviously had too much wine."

We all said goodnight, and I watched them pull away and turn the corner two doors down. The last surprise of my birthday was that Mrs. Osorio hadn't even mentioned the Claddagh ring.

# Chapter Forty-Eight:
# Challenges

The night of my party, I probably put the boys to bed a little too late, as we all had our first wrestling tournament of the season early the next morning and all day. Very early Sunday morning, we would be heading up to Fort Clark's Riverview High School to the annual Riverview Eagles Challenge, for weigh-ins.

I was not a wrestler in high school, but since 1994, I had been an avid student of MMA and its many distinct disciplines of boxing, Muay Thai kickboxing, World kickboxing, American wrestling, Japanese Judo, Russian Sambo, Brazilian Jujitsu, etc., and so my knowledge of striking, grappling, and submission fundamentals is impressive right down to the nuances of most movements, submissions, fundamentals, and skills. I've never been a practitioner, though, as my neck/skull surgery from the Marines tended to make me think twice every time I thought about training, so wrestling was a sport very different from those I had participated in and coached at all levels over the years.

I always got geared up before baseball or football games as a player or coach, but Lee starting to wrestle the previous season was a different animal entirely. Realistically, I was watching my boy in the first fights of his life. And this year, Ronny was wrestling, too. This was no team sport, not really. They struggled alone, man-to-man, and they learned the greatest lessons that sports can teach: how to win or how to lose with honor, how to work through intense suffering, how to persevere over the struggle, how to push beyond odds and overcome, and perhaps even how to execute a comeback.

My personal investment in my boys' wrestling was extremely energy-consuming, as my nerves started to hum louder and louder as the Saturday before each tournament progressed. If I slept at all that Saturday night beforehand, I'd wake-up early Sunday morning more geared up than I had ever been for my own contests in my youth. By the end of a Sunday tourney, I'd be exhausted to the point of needing a couple days to really recover. Short of Marine Corps Boot Camp, nothing in my life had ever taken more out of me in a single day.

On the Sunday of a tournament, the day began about 5 am and ended late in the afternoon. Wrestlers would first weigh-in at about 6 am, then wait about an hour-and-a-half for the tournament to begin. Each weight class was broken into groups of four. Inside a group, each wrestler would compete in three matches, one against each of the others in the group. First place went undefeated, second place lost only to first place, and so on. This tournament process took up most of the day in a hot, stuffy high school gym with six matches being conducted at the same time on different mats, all day long.

After the weigh-ins, we would typically go out with other wrestling families to the hosting town's local breakfast spot, and I was always on point for what the boys put in their bodies. When we had left the house, they were given a protein shake that I had concocted for the ride, providing some potassium, magnesium, and other electrolytes, protein, and some carbs, but balanced just right, without caffeine or refined sugar.

At the restaurant, I would order them just a couple pancakes, very little syrup, a couple of pieces of bacon (to help keep them thirsty and hydrating) and water. Later through the day, as I watched other wrestling parents jacking-up their kids with Mountain Dew and Red Bull – basically caffeine and sugar –believing it gave their child an edge, I'd be offering my boys fresh fruit, water, and parts of their Daddy-sammies (sandwiches that I made).

By noon, I'd be pointing out those other kids, who would typically be passed out asleep on the bleachers from the inevitable sugar/caffeine crash. Witnessing the other kids in a crash helped my boys literally *see* the importance of good nutrition. Then my boys would go back to playing with their Nintendo Game Boy personal game systems to await their next matches.

And my coach/dad due diligence didn't end there. Lee had started wrestling when he was six, and even at that early age, I would video tape his opponents as they wrestled other competitors. Then in between matches, I would take Lee somewhere outside the gym in the high school, sit down in a quiet corner, and analyze tape with him. I would let Lee see what his upcoming opponent's tendencies were, and every time, I would point out one offensive technique to which the opponent was susceptible and one defensive technique that could stop the opponent's primary offensive move of choice. Then we'd watch Lee's previous match so he could see the difference between what he *thought* he did and what he *really* did. The idea was always to keep doing what you're doing well, keep the pressure applied to your opponent, and focus on the one offensive and one defensive technique that we just examined on tape. If he stayed thinking and relentless, the rest would take care of itself.

Sometimes a parent on our team would ask what I was doing by filming other team's wrestlers, and when I explained it all, you could see in their eyes that they couldn't identify with it. I wasn't overly concerned with whether Lee won or lost. Rather, I was building him into a thinker, an intelligent problem-solver, a little man with a dynamic brain. It wasn't just about sports; it was about Life. It was brainwork. Brain Before Body. Mind Before Movement. And now Ronny was wrestling, too, so I was burning twice the energy. All of this was a long, exhausting day, every time.

On this particular day, I felt my wife's cold chill toward me as soon as we got out of bed to begin the marathon day after my surprise party the night before. I had no idea what was coming, though. As we sat in the bleachers, somewhere toward the middle of the tournament, my wife's emotions blew. She told the boys to stay put and play their games, that Mommy and Daddy would be right back. Then she asked another parent to keep an eye on the boys, turned to me, told me to follow her, and stepped carefully down the bleachers toward the exit. I followed, thinking that this couldn't be what I thought it was, right?

"*It has already begun*," Mirai's voice whispered over my shoulder. I literally turned, startled, but of course there was no one there. It was just Lily and me.

*Shut up, old man.*

She led me into an empty hallway, and she let me have it.

"Are you gonna *TELL* me about Selena?! Or am I going to have to hammer you with it?!" She barked at me, anger seething from her, tendrils of outrage wafting around her.

I knew what was happening. It had really come to this, and I shouldn't have been so surprised and underprepared. Selena and I had been stupid, blinded by whatever it was, and we were about to be put in check for our carelessness. I said nothing, just looked at Lily interrogatively, puzzled. Acting.

"Okay. *Fine*, Liam. I know that you and Selena have something going on. I *KNOW* it. And you are going to end it right *NOW*!"

Her voice quickly escalated into a yell. A children's sporting event at a high school venue was absolutely the wrong place to start making a scene, but I couldn't blame her for not being able to wait until later. I didn't have any real play to make, so I had to just act it out.

I went with the old, "*What?!* Lil, what are you *talking* about?! Selena and me, you mean like something going on... like, *between us?*"

"You know *exactly* what the *fuck* I'm talking about. Don't give me that stupid bullshit. I want it to end, today, *right now.*"

So I tried to de-escalate it...

"Lil, please, try to settle down. Why are you saying this? Look, think about it... Selena is like 20 years younger than me... Why would she want to be with someone *my* age? Someone almost her mom's age? Take a look at me, Lil! Would *you* have wanted *this* me when you were her age? Seriously. Shit, Lil, she's just a friend. I think I get it... I've spent a good deal of time with-... "

*"A GOOD DEAL OF TIME?!"*

"Lil, *please*, seriously, you have to calm down. Just yesterday you entrusted Selena to take me to a movie so you could get the party together. Now you think we're... *whatever*? Seriously, Lil, slow this down, think-... "

*"Are you SERIOUSLY going to CHALLENGE me on this?!*

YOU think I didn't see you two walk in all glowy and guilty-looking at the party? YOU think I didn't see you two making eyes at each other, right in front of the guests! Shit, Liam, your family probably saw what's going on, and I'm sure your friends did!"

"No, Lil... Just no. They didn't. *You* did. I guess it might look strange from your perspective, but Selena and I are just friends. You're stressed, right? You're tired? That master's degree is taking a lot out of you, I see it. Why don't you take the van and head home and-..."

And something in my words, or my voice, or my body language, or my eyes clearly started to soften her, make her question herself. As my older brother Ron had once told me, I was about the most honest person he'd ever known, but when I *had* to, I could lie like a motherfucker. Well, he *actually* said I could lie like a dog when I had to, but-...

"Lil, there's nothing going on beyond that. If you're looking for that, you might be seeing it, but you're seeing something that isn't there. You know, 'a hammer only sees a nail' and all? Do you have one piece of real, hard proof of this crazy relationship you've dreamed up? Don't answer... because no, you don't. There is nothing going on."

I really did hate lying to her like this, about this. But I had to. I couldn't just give up and admit it.

This went back and forth for about 20 minutes. As it

progressed, I was able to slowly calm her down more and more, a little at a time, until eventually she was questioning what she had thought she knew. She started to complain that it just seemed like something had to be going on. I could see some guys catching a buzz by getting away with this kind of thing, but *I hated it*. I was being sneaky, and have I mentioned that *I hate sneaky?* I just knew there was nothing else to be done.

In the end, I gave her a kiss on the cheek and a hug, a squeeze, and we walked back into the tournament in a better place than when we had walked in that morning. I never wanted Selena's and my decisions to hurt anybody, *certainly* not my wife. None of this was payback for what she'd done to me. I now knew that Selena and I had to cool some things off in the short term, and we had to be a lot smarter about our choices if this thing was going to continue.

And I *wanted* it to continue. I *needed* it to continue.

# Chapter Forty-Nine:
# Invitation Only

### *Facebook* Post: December 4, 2011

GREAT wrestling tourney today at the Eagles Challenge in Fort Clark. Lee took 1st place, pinning 2 opponents in the first period and defeating another 12-0 (almost pinning him twice, but running out of time). It wasn't his most technically precise performance, but his athleticism and pressure were relentless. I'm super impressed with this kid!!! Ronny did great in his first wrestling meet ever, coming in third place. Impressive!!! Great day of wrestling!

Of course, I was extremely proud of Lee and Ronny at the Eagles Challenge. Lee had placed first against older, more experienced wrestlers. Ronny had placed third in his first wrestling match ever, meaning that he had won one of his matches. That was all I ever wanted for the boys, just to win at least one and to never give up. And although I certainly hoped for first place – which Lee threatened to do every time he competed against wrestlers of any age and Ronny would eventually do once he gained experience – I just didn't want them to go 0-3 on any Sunday... not for me, but *for them*. Just to avoid the feeling of having all three of your opponents best you in one-on-one combat in one day. I can imagine that would have to be terribly hard to handle.

***

The next day was a good one. Selena and I texted early in the day, and we talked on my lunch break. I told her what her mom and I had talked about after my party, including the part about how she can hear Selena on the phone in that house. Selena didn't think her mom was on to us, at all.

Then, I told her all about the accusations from my wife. She wasn't surprised by it, but she also wasn't happy with my proposition that we start to cool off our soirees until things settled down. It wasn't like I was trying to bring things to a sudden halt or anything; I just felt that we needed to make an effort to allow the attention and heat from my wife to die down. Selena disagreed pretty vehemently at first, but eventually, calmer, more sensible heads prevailed, and she reluctantly agreed.

As Sunday's meet had been the first of the season, the coaches had canceled practice for Monday night to give the wrestlers and parents a night off to recover. So Selena and I agreed that we would not meet at the gym that night, and she would not meet me at or after practice on Tuesday. Once we could see how things seemed on Tuesday, we could start to talk about what made the most sense for the rest of the week. Selena protested that this would be the longest we'd gone without time together since she'd first popped the question, but she did not pursue the point.

Selena was understandably upset with me, or at least very irritated, and I tried to take it in stride. It really was hard to decide not to see each other, and I know that if I said *fuck it, let's meet...* she'd be down with that in a heartbeat. So, I was the one who had to toe the line on this one, and I was fine with accepting Selena's displeasure despite my best efforts to keep her always happy. Then, exactly five minutes after the bell ended my last class of the day, my phone vibrated. Yep, Selena.

She led in straight away with an invitation to join her and her mom in attending a high school girls' basketball game that night. She said her mom had thought I might want to join them. The game was between the team Selena had most recently played on, from Delphia, and a co-op team consisting of my school and Burroughs-Raleigh, a nearby school.

In these small rural towns, such as Bigtimber and Firedance, two towns would cooperate (or co-op) in order to have enough students to make a district. Likewise, in this case, two co-op schools would get together to have enough players to field a co-op athletic team. Co-op teams like these were often necessary with tiny schools with populations so small that they could not field a team independently.

My school had enough interested boys to field a full

basketball team every year, but the football and girls' basketball teams were co-ops with other schools. So my school (already a two town, single school co-op district) was combined with Burroughs-Raleigh (another two town, single school co-op district) in order to create a co-op girls' basketball program. Selena had played on this particular co-op team when she had been a student at my school, and the game was being held at Burroughs-Raleigh, only about 20 minutes north of Bigtimber-Firedance.

I knew that we had agreed not to see each other, and I recognized that Selena was using her mom as a front for us to do just that. But I liked her way of thinking. Her mom's invitation was about the only front we could possibly have had in order to see each other. I felt it was something with which I could go to my wife, mention the invite from Mrs. Osorio, and use *that* as my rationale to go. It was really an evidence-free, unimpeachable means to an end. I told her yes, I would be there, and (sarcastically) to thank her *mom* for the invite.

I was well-aware that Selena's mom, Demi, had almost certainly not arranged this outing. This was most likely Selena's work, as she had surely asked her mom to go to the game, and then she asked me. Sure, she had probably used her power of suggestion to bring me into discussion with her mom, guiding her mom toward asking if I might join them. Selena was certainly a clever one. I was a little touched by her efforts to spend time together, no matter the situation. That young lady was always thinking, and when she wanted something...

# Chapter Fifty:
# Games

After dinner, at about 6 pm or so, I dismissed the boys from the table to head into the sunroom, and I told my wife I was going to the game with Selena and her mom, as Demi had invited me to join them.

"Her *mom* asked her to invite you?" she asked, incredulously. "Why didn't her *mom* just call you herself? *She's* got your number. *She's* called you before."

I felt a little of that fire inside me that had been lit the day I started standing up for myself to my wife. The day we argued in the kitchen toward the end of the previous summer. The day Lee had come in and asked us to please stop arguing so loudly because he and Ronny couldn't hear the TV in the sunroom. The day I realized I could no longer maintain the facade of the Happy Hubby that I had projected for years. The day I knew I had to begin looking for a divorce attorney, *for real*, as I could no longer put my tail between my legs and accept complete blame for almost every dispute, no longer accept her tyrannical direction and correction at every turn... and doing so all in the name of keeping up appearances and the Peace.

"Look. Here are the facts," I replied, remaining calm and conversational. "Her mom knows she and I are good friends. She knows Selena and I talk quite a bit. Fact is, she simply suggested that Selena ask me if I'd like to join them at tonight's game. Selena did, and I said yes. As you know, I support my student's sports competitions whenever I can, and the Burroughs-Raleigh team roster includes many of my students. Now this delusion of yours about Selena and I having some sort of relationship or whatever, beyond being friends is going too far. Check it. I'm going to this game, and there is nothing wrong with that. I'm *going*... point-blank-period."

Before my wife could retort, I calmly strode away, went and grabbed my jacket from my den, said goodbye to the boys, told them I'd come in and give them kisses in their sleep when I got home, and gave them hugs and kisses goodnight. My wife met me at the door.

"Liam, *don't* go to that game tonight," she said urgently, almost pleading, and there was something foreboding in her demeanor and tone. Not aggressive or threatening, no... this was more like a warning.

"Go, if you must," I heard Mirai's voice over my shoulder. "But be vigilant. They are watching."

"Lil," I began, in an exaggeratedly tired voice, sagging my shoulders for effect, "I'm *going*."

"*Don't* go." A final, watery-eyed plea.

Boy, she could turn it on when she wanted to. Quite the actress, herself, sometimes. I shook my head at her, shut the door behind me, and headed four towns north to the Burroughs game. I wasn't biting with my wife's fake-ass show of give-a-shit. On the drive north, it occurred to me that lately I hadn't been looking for a divorce attorney as aggressively as I should have been. I'd have to remedy that.

Lily's pleas to me in the doorway kept playing in my head, over and over. She could always turn on the waterworks when she wanted, but I didn't think I'd ever seen her like-... well, like *that* before. Could that have been real? Why would she be so concerned? Why tear-up? The quality of her voice had been almost tragic, as though she knew something terrible was about to happen, if I attended this game with Selena and her mom. It didn't even feel like it was about Selena and me, either.

But by the time I was walking into the game, my wife's worried image and foreboding words had faded away completely. I started thinking about how me sitting with Selena and Demi was going to look, as roughly half the Burroughs team was made-up of my students.

*But be vigilant. They are watching.*

Across from the team benches, the lone set of bleachers were fairly empty, of course. Selena and her mom were only about twenty feet from me, part-way up the bleachers. Selena was looking at her phone when my phone vibrated. I picked up, as she hadn't seen me yet. I explained that I was so sorry, but I couldn't make it to the game... my wife said no. She began to protest when her mom spotted me, backhanded her playfully on the shoulder, pointed to me, and I saw her lips say, "He's right there."

Selena saw me, lit up, and lowered her phone. She gave me that fake angry face that couples sometimes make at one another, and I looked around self-consciously assessing the gym. There were a few players on both teams looking our way, which was too many, but I couldn't be certain that they were looking specifically at *us*.

I stepped up the bleachers and, for the sake of anyone watching, I reached out to Selena for a fist-bump. She thwarted my efforts by making a *fuck you* face and giving me a hug that felt a little too cozy. I sat down closer to Demi than to her. Selena crept closer and kept the conversation between us, though I kept trying to at least seem like I was including and interacting with her mom. I was putting on the act for the sake of my current students on the home team. I figured there'd be rumors flying that I was dating Selena's mom, but I didn't care about that... better than the alternative.

During halftime, when the players returned to the gym, Selena told us she'd be right back. She floated down the bleachers with athletic grace, crossed the court, and visited with the girls from the school she was currently attending, Delphia, laughing and joking for a few minutes. I hardly noticed that the sound system was playing a recent Adele song called "Rumor Has It," but I noticed.

Then Selena switched sides and visited with the girls on the team she had once played for, the team that included current students of mine. Again, a few minutes of joking and laughing, and then she came bounding back up to us.

She was in an exceptionally playful mood when she returned. She said something goofy and jokingly punched me in the shoulder. I immediately shot her a warning glance. She shot me that face of hers that said *relax*. I didn't relax.

She told me what she had been joking about with both teams. With the Delphia team, they had joked about the student team manager, an awkward, gay male student who I sensed was often the focus of their jokes. She said it wasn't about him being gay, it was his demeanor, always acting as though he was in charge of the players and better than everyone else. Before she left them, they asked who I was. She told them I was her former English teacher from her old school.

With the co-op team that included some of my students, they had joked about the trash refereeing of the first half, and sure enough, my students asked if I was there with her mom. Of course, my students all knew Demi. Selena had laughed that, no, her family and I were just close, which some of my students already knew. Still, they had teased that her mom and I looked pretty cosey up there in the stands. Selena whispered to me that she had *better not* find out that her mom and me... and I had to laugh.

After the game, Selena said her goodbyes to her former

teammates from my school, and the three of us walked out together. As she and her mom got in her mom's little yellow hatchback and I got to my van, Selena warned me not to get lost in the dark on my way home, being a city kid and all. I called out to her that I could find my way home, alright, but I wondered could she find a way to be less of a pain in the ass?

Her mom laughed out loud, saying, "*See?* That's what I was talking about. Remember? Outside his house after his birthday party? You two *sound* like a couple!"

I returned home. My wife seemed relieved. *How did it go? Any problems? Was Selena's mom there?*

I felt a little, *what?* Almost *sad* for her? But why? Why was she so concerned? What was she afraid of? It didn't seem like it was about Selena and me, and it was so out of character, so what was it? I had to chalk it up to stress... she was under quite a lot of stress with working full time as a nurse, working on her masters' degree while being married to a coach with two active little men competing for her attention.

"Was Selena's *mom* there?" I repeated, a little offended. "Of course, her *mom* was there. I *told* you, Lil... Demi invited me!"

I put my jacket in my den, went in to check on the boys and give them the kisses in their sleep that I had promised, re-tucked them in their sleep, and retired to my den. Apparently, the reason for my wife's teary-eyed concern was to be lost to history. I told myself it probably wasn't worth digging to find out what it was all about, and I tried to forget about it. And I did forget about it.

Until the next day.

# Chapter Fifty-One:
# Rumors

I arrived at school, climbed to my third-floor classroom, and left the lights off, as was my custom. There was enough light coming in through the wall of 13 huge windows in a row behind my desk, and I usually left the lights off during classes, as well. I was not a fan of those yellowish, humming, artificial, overhead bulbs. My students preferred natural light, as well.

I noticed right away that the access door between my classroom and the classroom next door to mine was open. That door joined my class with my colleague Esther McQueen' science class, the only other classroom on the third floor. Her daughter Annalise and son Peter were students in my senior Mass Media class, the same age as (and once good friends with) Selena. Esther liked Selena quite a lot, a sentiment which was not necessarily shared among the whole faculty since the fight with Letty. It was odd for that door to be open, and the lights were on inside Mrs. McQueen' room, meaning she was most likely already there.

Before I could get to my desk, just a dozen feet inside the door, Mrs. McQueen came rushing into my classroom. She whispered urgently for me to close my classroom door behind me so no one could hear us, and to hurry. So I did, bewildered for that moment, then realizing what this was about.

"Did you go to the basketball game with Selena and her mom

last night?" she forced out in an out of breath whisper, and the look in her eyes was... *panic*, maybe? She had taken my right hand in both of hers, and I felt her hands trembling.

"Yeah, I did," I whispered back, smiling. She was taking this very seriously.

"Annalise got a text after the game from her friend, a girl on the Delphia team-... "

"Lemme guess, lemme guess," I interrupted, "I'm dating Selena's mom, right?" She crazy-laughed nervously.

"Oh, no, *way worse*," she urged. "Annalise's friend told her that YOU and Selena are messing around... that YOU ate Selena out."

The words were like explosions, leaving me a bit shell-shocked. Hearing that term come from wholesome Esther seemed so wrong. I remember feeling my own hands start to shake a little. But I'd been through seriously dangerous situations before, and I was well-tempered to slow my breathing, to relax, to calm my nerves, to *think*, and to handle whatever it was that was in my way. I willed myself to slow down and to not get excited with a deep inhale, full exhale.

*I got this.*

"*What?*" I said incredulously, but quietly. "You gotta be *kidding*. That's *crazy*. Selena's *mom* invited me to that game."

"Well, that's not the story going around. I told Annalise to tell no one, to keep quiet about it," she said.

But I knew Annalise had not kept quiet about it. How could she have? She wouldn't mean any harm by it, but like everyone else around there, she was raised on gossip, so of course she had told people. I mean, I didn't know that to be a fact, but I *knew* it, and I sure couldn't blame Annalise.

As I assessed Esther, I realized that she was not trying to accuse me, and she was not excited by the small-town drama of it... rather, she was trying to help me, to *warn* me. She was concerned. Though her kids had grown-up in town, she wasn't originally from the area, wasn't raised on rumors. Of course, she didn't believe something like that... it was utterly ridiculous.

"These goddamn corn towns," I cursed, exaggeratedly rolling my eyes and looking up to Heaven, shaking my head. I was playing to Esther's city upbringing, as she had moved to the area from Los Angeles. "Nothing better to do but be in other people's business, to churn bullshit and fertilize every field, as far as they can spread it."

What choice did I have but to lie my ass off? It was similar to my situation with Lilith. I was all-in with Selena, and the only way to protect myself and Selena from personal damage was to be the most staunchly convincing motherfucker possible, to be undeniable. I knew I had done nothing unlawful or immoral, other than cheat on a wife who had been a habitual cheater from the time we started dating. But I had no other choice than to deny any and all accusations, at home and now here at school.

"Willow Braverman also knows. Annalise didn't tell her... Willow was included in the text," she whispered frantically, like a final warning shot, dropping my hand and waving her own hands in near despair.

Willow was another student in Annalise's class. I knew that this was particularly upsetting to Esther because her sons, daughters, and Willow had grown up with Selena from birth.

I remember feeling my protective supreme confidence flushing through my blood like a drug. I had stopped carrying my Xanax with me shortly after Q+0, as having the new bond with Selena seemed to gift me with the superpower of controlling my anxiety and panic response. So I began to activate it.

# Chapter Fifty-Two:
# A Blessing and A Curse

When my supreme confidence really hits, it starts feeling like general warmth at my core, around my heart and gut, and then it spreads outward through my system like a touch of general anesthesia. On the outside, it feels the way Robert Downey, Jr. looks in the Marvel Cinematic Universe's *Avengers* movies, as his nano-technology Mark L Iron Man armored suit spreads over his body.

You know, Reader, the armored suit with the artificial intelligence co-pilot he calls J.A.R.V.I.S.? I felt like this rumor situation was going to be big. Like, the MCU *Avengers* Battle of New York big. No matter how well I could handle the enemy, there was going to be lots of collateral damage to account for. The time had come to suit-up, and I knew it would be quite some time before I could take that suit off again.

I have always struggled with the difficulties that come with being both blessed and cursed with hubris, or unflinching supreme confidence. It allows most things that seem impossible to be not only possible, but *probable*, elevating me to my highest potential. I had done the impossible for the first time in Marine Corps Boot Camp, and it was like a filter was lifted from my eyes and I could see that nothing in the world was impossible. Maybe I'll tell that story someday. And now – since 2012 – I have done the impossible several more times. Maybe I'll write about those episodes someday, too. Achieving the impossible serves to accomplish almost any mission I set myself to, and to embolden me and bolster my supreme confidence's supply of potential energy.

*But*... on the odd occasion when my supreme confidence fails... the fall of failure or defeat is ten times farther than it would otherwise be without my own certainty of victory. There have only been a few, but I remember every one of those falls in my life, and the damage they did to my supreme confidence, which hits very hard and hurts quite a lot. But, then I regroup, heal that super power, and put it back in the nuclear fallout bunker for the next time I need it. Overall, I find supreme confidence to be the closest thing to a superpower that reality allows. And with this news from Esther McQueen, I was going to need every drop of it.

*Here we go*, I thought. *This is where it happens.* And then I resolved myself to a saying I had learned to believe in the Marine Corps.

*Though I walk through the Valley of the Shadow of Death, I shall fear no evil... because I'm the biggest, baddest, meanest, motherfucker in the Valley. (And, most importantly, I always added... smartest)*

It didn't matter if those things weren't True. Supreme confidence and conviction *makes* them True. So in order to calm myself so I could think most effectively, I *willed* my hands to stop shaking. I *willed* my breathing to slow. I opened up the muscles in my palms, chest, neck, shoulders, and back, allowing excess energy to evaporate from me. I *willed* my blinking to slow, my heart rate to slow. Calm. Steady. Supreme confidence. Bullet-fucking-proof.

"Relax, Esther. I've got this. Nobody is going to believe crap like this, dished out by some girl who doesn't even know me. I'll handle all of this, but-... "

"The Delphia player said Selena told her," she kind of fired at me like a kill shot. It stung, but my Iron Man defense was having none of it. My supreme confidence chewed up her words and spit... *Wait... uh, oh, J.A.R.V.I.S... what's happening to me? Talk to me, buddy.*

## Chapter Fifty-Three:
## Damage Control

Okay, that one really hurt. It just took a moment to sink in.

*Selena just talked to that team of girls last night,* I thought to myself. *This basketball player specifically said that I ate out Selena. And she said Selena told her that. How could she be lying? There was no way this girl could have dreamed this up by chance, not that specifically, and the only ones who knew about this were Selena and me. Selena* had *to have told her.*

I couldn't believe it. She had betrayed my trust and put my career in jeopardy, put *everything* in jeopardy, let alone the risk of legal accusations. I know I keep stressing this, but I had done nothing unlawful. However, in these rural areas where everybody knows everybody and justice is sometimes at least as much about popular public opinion as about Law, I knew public opinion would not be on my side.

If the law in that area wanted me guilty of something due to some social taboo, they could easily make that happen. Falsify evidence. Fabricate evidence. *Plant* evidence. Stack a jury. Apply pressure to a judge. *Pay off* a judge. Make a subjective rather than an objective, lawful judgment. And worse. Especially if my wife's extremely socially, economically, and politically influential family got involved, and they *could* get involved once word got out and the machine started running. I had always felt expendable to that family.

Why would they fight to keep me around when the law comes asking questions? It could very easily come to that.

There was no way anyone at my school was going to see Selena and I as anything but wrong, regardless of the facts that she was a legal adult, she was not a student of mine, and she was not a student at my school. My mind was rambling on about things I had already considered many times. I needed to focus. I could already see the horror in Esther's eyes. Though I saw Selena as the adult she was, they would surely see the little girl with whom their kids had grown up. Very few of them really considered their son or daughter to be an adult at eighteen, the way Demi did. They still saw their children as kids, even when signed-up for the military during ten years of two foreign wars in the sand.

"Look, Esther," I said. "There is no *way* Selena said that. Not to anyone. I don't care who says so, she has no reason to start a rumor like that, and she is *not* that stupid. This little Delphia bitch just learned my name last night during half time from Selena, then she spewed this shit within what... an hour or two? Selena knows how pissed I would be if she said some bullshit like that about me, so I know she didn't. *And why would she? Like anyone would believe that Selena would be interested in her 40-year-old former teacher?* No way.

"So, it's okay, Esther," I assured her, while my brain was preparing and planning. "I got this. Thank you for everything. For letting me know right away, for letting Annalise know to keep it quiet so it doesn't spread further, and for your concern. I'll talk to Willow briefly and gently, just to let her know not to worry about this. She must be pretty weirded out by it. It'll all blow over in no time, like so many millions of other Bigtimber-Firedance rumors."

"Will you tell Rick?" she asked, taking a step back. Did she really need to ask if I was going to spread the rumor to my principal? I was *trying* to be careful not to swear with Esther, but it's just a part of who I am.

"*No*, Esther. I have no reason to defend myself from this bullsh-... from this stuff. Besides, we all know how this goes... Rick probably already knows. This is going to get much worse before it gets better, but in the slim chance Rick doesn't know yet, I'm not going to be the one to spread it to him."

She wished me luck, and I knew she meant it. She asked me not to tell anyone that she knew about it or had warned me, and she exited the service door to her room, closing it behind her. I took a deep breath, held it, let it out very slowly. Then I texted Selena, as I didn't want her talking to me about this out loud and have someone at her school overhear.

*WTF? Mrs. McQueen just told me that Annalise got a text from a girls' basketball player at Delphia saying you and I are screwing around and that I ate you out. She told Willow Braverman, too. WTF ARE YOU DOING TALKING ABOUT THAT SHIT?*

*\Seriously? I didn't tell anyone anything!* she texted back.

Then radio silence. I could just see her starting to panic, and I got more upset.

*Bullshit!* I texted back. *She knew exactly about our foreplay. She said YOU had told her that, and we both know only YOU could tell her that. She didn't just guess that shit!*

We texted back and forth until my first class students began arriving. Then I let her cool off while I went about my day, just like any other day. I played it off cool as ice. Still, I couldn't help but wonder which students knew about the texts. I knew, though, it was out of my control. This rumor was destined to spread like wildfire, regardless of any countermeasures I might deploy. In all likelihood, they *all* knew. In extremely stressful, even dangerous times in my life, I had learned that supreme confidence could allow me to relax and even enjoy these little conflicts. It was game time, and I've always been competitive.

When Willow's English class was over, just as she walked past my desk, I quietly asked if she might hang around for just a minute. She had almost seemed like she *wanted* to stop at my desk anyway, based on her uncharacteristically slow gait from her seat toward the door, by herself. After everyone else had filed out, it was lunchtime, so I had no students coming in.

"Willow, I heard about the text," and she was looking me directly in the eye, for which I was proud of her. This must have been very awkward for her.

"Yeah," she said, nodding.

"Don't worry about it, Willow, this is all BS," and she brightened up a little. "Selena didn't say anything like that about me, I know it. This will all blow over like so many million rumors you've heard before. No worries."

"Okay, yeah," she said, and she nodded again.

"I know this is pretty weird for you, having grown up with Selena and all. But she's still the same person you knew up until last year, and she didn't do this. But thank you for not spreading it further."

She looked different just then, and I was just about certain she had already told others of the texts. Of course, I couldn't blame her. Willow headed to lunch, and I refrained from contacting Selena. Likewise, she did not contact me. Instead, I sat up straight at my desk, shoulders square, just waiting for the call to come from my principal, humming the melody to "Rumor Has It." A parent or another teacher would soon hear the rumor, if they hadn't already, and someone was sure to feel it their duty to pass it up the chain-of-command to the admin.

*Fine. Bring that shit. Biggest, baddest, meanest, smartest motherfucker in the Valley. Bulletproof. Bring that shit right here to me. I got this.*

Esther had been the flash-bang. I calmed myself and waited for the shock wave. But it did not come.

*Yet.*

# Chapter Fifty-Four:
# Impasse

I drove home after school preparing for the possibility that the "rumor" might have already gotten back to my town, because if it had, then I was certain someone would have placed a call about it to my wife. I tried not to dwell on all of the drama and strife this rumor would bring into my marriage. Wait, that wasn't True. Who was I kidding? *I had brought all of this drama and strife into my marriage. Me. I did it.* So I was solely responsible for any drama and strife that was about to afflict my marriage. It was simply the rumor that could expose it all.

There was the slimmest chance that this rumor might somehow hurt something more in Lily than simply her pride, so I didn't want that rumor to reach her before I could. And in Truth, my motivations weren't *just* about how that rumor might hurt Lily; it was also about my own need to control the narrative and deliver the news to my wife before someone else could. But I also really didn't want to let Lily get hurt by it.

I anticipated a call from her at any moment, but it never came. Selena and I had not contacted each other since our initial texts after hearing of the situation. I figured she was probably rethinking her role in how this had all come to be and how bad it could get. She was probably even trying to figure out how to tell me the capital 'T' Truth.

When I pulled into town, I went about my business as usual. I picked up the boys, took them home, fed them, worked on homework, put them down for naps, woke them, and headed to wrestling practice, where everything seemed normal. Thankfully, Selena did not visit or contact me. She was most likely feeling guilty or scared, or both, I figured. The gravity of the situation that had hit me immediately was probably just starting to really seep into Selena. She just didn't have the tools that I had to cope with it.

Curious, though, that my wife did not take Ronny home after the first practice. She seemed perfectly normal, and I was fairly certain that she hadn't heard anything about the rumor, yet. She said she preferred to stay and see how Lee was doing, which was all good. I knew that she was most likely really sticking around to see if Selena showed up. After practice, Lily and Ronny even accompanied Lee and I to Taco Bell, where I suggested that we all go inside, sit down, and do something we almost never did... have a junk food snack together. So we did.

As we walked into Taco Bell, Lee asked, "Daddy, what are *you* going to order? Have you *ever* eaten at a place like this?"

His concern cracked me up. I explained that in my youth and earlier in my adult years, I had eaten at Taco Bell and plenty of other fast-food places, countless times. But I had to admit to him that I had no idea what to order.

"Can I order for you?" he asked. I didn't trust that little prankster's sly smile for a second.

"Oh, like the time you and Mommy went to Subway and ordered me my typical foot long veggie and provolone on wheat? The time you chimed in and started asking the attendant to add everything to my sandwich that you *knew* I always leave out because of the excess sodium and fat content?!"

Lee was already cracking up before I even got that far, but I wasn't finished, yet...

"Pickles, jalapenos, banana peppers, giardiniera... *bacon!*... and coleslaw?! '*My Daddy just LOVES coleslaw on his sandwich*'," I mimicked a bratty little boy's voice. They were all cracking up by this point. "Who puts slaw on a sub? I gotta admit, though... that was the best damn sub I *ever* had!"

So I let Lee order for me. Lily did, too, as she also hadn't eaten at Taco Bell in years. Lee was considerably kind to his Mommy, asking if she liked sour cream (she did, but not too much), then ordering her two Soft Taco Supremes with easy sour cream. He wasn't so kind to his dear old Daddy.

"My Daddy would please like to order... ummmm... Mommy, does Daddy like sour cream?"

"Oh, what the hell, Lee. I'm standing *right here*," I laughed in a loud, playfully annoyed voice.

Ronny interrupted, "Lee, it's just like when Daddy makes tacos at home. He loves sour cream! *And* chicken."

"My Daddy would please like to order... three Gor-... Gor-... Gor-*dittas*... those big things, right there, please. Beef, not chicken. No sour cream, thank you," and he was so proud of himself. I had to stop the madness as soon as it had begun. Thank God they didn't have slaw.

"Please ignore my boy. We just picked him up from the pound... he's a rescue. He's still a pup, at seven-years-old, but he'll never make eight. May I please have ONE chicken Gordita, extra sour cream, thank you."

It was nice to joke with the boys and have Lil be a part of it. She hadn't been a wife for a long time and by a long shot, but she was their Mommy forever, and I'll respect that to the very end. Even if she hasn't done the same for me.

After we all arrived home, I went for a long walk around town. I needed a walk, as my new "lifestyle" had intruded greatly upon my workout schedule, both at the gym and walking the town. Of course, I called Selena and we talked about the situation. I encouraged her to just admit that she had told this girl about us.

She vehemently denied doing any such thing, or telling *anyone anything*, for that matter. She was upset with me for even half-believing that to be true... but it reminded me of sitting in my van at Chipotle up by Chicago. When Homeboy had questioned her pretty hard about not being honest with him, her tactic was to get mad at *him* for it. So now, when she got mad at *me* for believing she had said something and questioning her about it, *well...*

Taking it even a step further, Selena asked if she could play a song for me. She said she had heard it before, but she had really heard it on that Sunday morning after her birthday party, when she woke-up thinking about me. It hadn't made as much impact on her then as it had more recently, especially now.

"Selena, honestly, I love hearing you talk about how music touches you or makes you feel about us, especially when you really open up and talk about it. But I'm not really feeling like listening to anything right now, other than maybe the capital 'T' Truth from you. I can't help but believe you told that girl. How else am I supposed to make sense of this?"

But she convinced me to listen to the song. She said she wouldn't admit that she'd told that girl anything, because she hadn't. She said the song might speak to me *for* her, explaining how she was feeling about this major trust issue that the rumor had sprung up between us. So I listened. It was "Diary" by Alicia Keys. It was basically a promise song that all of my secrets are safe with her.

So we were at an impasse, and of course, I had to be the one to cave. Admittedly, the song softened me a little. If she swore she didn't tell anyone anything, then without proof, I could not rightfully continue to accuse her of it. I was just hurt that she had probably done this, hurt more that she was probably lying to me about it. And I think really, inside, I *wanted* to believe that Selena *could* be my diary, like the song said.

So, with really nothing else to be done about it, I apologized and promised her that we'd get through this. We were not backing down, but we were backing off a bit. I told her I could see her at the gym after wrestling practice on Thursday, and she was excited that I both believed in her innocence and planned to see her again.

She swore that she was going to piece up that bitch who said those things. She knew exactly who it was, and she would handle it. But I put the kibosh on that and told her to drop it. I told her not to touch that girl, to act like she knew nothing about the rumor, like she hadn't even heard about it. And if approached with it, she was to laugh it off like so much childish bullshit that is common in high school. Don't even deny... maintain an attitude of indifference and *ignore it*. Selena agreed that she would.

# Chapter Fifty-Five:
# Bend

The next day, Rick came to my classroom door during lunch and asked me to meet with him and the superintendent, Brant Beckett, in Rick's office after school.

"Of course," I offered, without showing much concern, "Is it time to debrief on my annual observations with the three of us – for my summative evaluation – already?" I asked. "It's only December."

"No, Cal," he paused and looked around, "We just need to have a discussion. We've got some questions. *On* the record."

I knew what that meant. And I was sure *he* knew that I knew. Esther had been the flash-bang. This was the shockwave. And after school, it was time for me to handle the aftermath of it all to minimize the fallout.

*Game on.*

After school, I sat in a front corner of my classroom at my computer station. It was time. I quietly played Black Sabbath's "Iron Man," gearing up for what I was about to handle. In my mind, I donned my Iron Man-style nano-suit, the *Supreme Confidence I.*

I waited in my classroom until the halls got quiet... students didn't need to know that I'd been called in by the admin. And Rick

Lincoln was solid like that; information flowed upstream to him from his daughter Amy and other students, but it did not typically flow downstream.

When the song was over for the fourth time and the halls sounded empty, I floated down the stairs from my classroom to Rick's office, stopped at the front desk to check-in with Calpurnia, the solo administrative secretary and HR department for the school since forever, and a sweet, sweet lady with a razor-sharp edge that I admired. It had taken my whole first semester to win her over with humor and kindness, and that was saying something, but she and I had enjoyed a very friendly relationship ever since. When I had finally felt like I was friendly enough with her to call her *Cal* instead of the full *Calpurnia*, we had laughed that there were *two* Cals in that little school.

I let Calpurnia know that I was there to see Brant and Rick.

"You get yourself into some kind of trouble?" she asked, without looking away from her computer screen.

"Trouble, Cal?" I played dumb. "Nah. Just some questions to hash through. You've heard the rumor. Now I've got to put it to bed, is all."

"Yeah? Well, *good*," she nodded. "I've been here long enough to see more than my share of meetings like this. The only thing I've ever seen put to bed is the teacher."

"Well, thank you, Cal. This time, it's just wind to rock the cradle, is all. But there isn't enough wind in these two towns to break the bough. Because I'm an oak, Cal. Solid."

She looked up at me over the top of her bifocals. "Well, you're certainly more confident than the others. That's good. Once that wind starts blowing around here, even the oaks give way under it."

"I bend, Cal," I smiled. "I never break. Thank you for your concern. I mean it."

"They're ready for you in there. You can go on in. Bend, Mr. Callahan. *Bend.*"

*J.A.R.V.I.S., I'm going in...*

# Chapter Fifty-Six:
# The Assumptive Close

When I walked into Rick's office, he was sitting formally behind his desk, at attention, and Mr. Beckett was semi-formally sitting in a chair he had pulled up next to Rick's desk. Both were facing me, and I pulled away the second of the two chairs set in front of Rick's desk for visitors... and set it a comfortable distance from the two men, for conversation. I wasn't making this a huddle... this was clearly two-on-one, and I wondered would one take the Good Cop role and the other take Bad Cop, or would they share roles? Didn't really matter, though.

"Okay, so what do I have to answer for? What have Amy and Jason told you two about my class?" and the two men laughed, knowing my intention was humor regarding their kids who were both students of mine. Both students were seniors, and of course, they had grown up with Selena. Mr. Beckett began the meeting.

"Cal, we are kind of in an uncomfortable position where we have to ask you some tough questions about some things that are being said around the school, the community, and nearby communities."

"No need to be uncomfortable, and no questions are tough, sir. I was expecting us to chat about this."

They both looked surprised. Rick spoke next.

"So, you know about the things going around, the things being said? About you and Selena Osorio?"

"Rick, of course I do. This is Bigtimber-Firedance. By now, everyone with a heartbeat in these two towns has heard the rumors, and probably half the ones without heartbeats, too. And of course you have to get to the bottom of it. Where would you like to begin?"

"Just so we're clear," Brant Beckett said. "You'll want to brace yourself." I motioned for him to feel free. "Well, word going around is that you and former BFHS student Selena Osorio are involved in a sexual relationship." I held a slow, steady nod, amused. "That you... *and I quote*... 'ate her out.'"

I nodded, smiling. They both remained silent, then. This meeting didn't seem to be going the way they thought it would.

"So what do you gentlemen make of that?" I asked, reversing the energy in the room. It was that tool I had learned to wield back in my junior year of high school, when I started in sales with my brother, Ron.

"Well, of course we've talked it over together... and we know how rumors get started, how they get blown up, spread around town and through the school."

"So what do you gentlemen *think?* When the two of you *first* heard of this, and when you *first* talked together about it, what was said? What do you *honestly* think about it?" I repeated.

"Well," Rick said, and the two looked at each other, then at me. "Of course, we don't *want* to believe it, but we have to be able to *account* for it. So, we had to ask you."

"I appreciate that," I replied. "I knew you two wouldn't believe it. That's why when *I* heard it, I refused to acknowledge it. I'm not going to spend my energy chasing down rumors and trying to defend myself against the accusations of some faceless kid who I don't even know and who doesn't know me. I simply won't do it."

"Yeah, well, of course we didn't believe it. So... why do you think Selena would make up something like this?" In sales, the tactic I had just employed is known as the Assumptive Close. Did you catch it?

"You think *Selena* made this up?" I acted surprised that they would think that, though I knew they would. "Guys, Selena didn't say this or make this up. I'm pretty close with her and her family, and I went to the Burroughs basketball game Monday night upon invite from her mom, Demi. Period.

"Now... Selena *did* go down to the court during halftime and talked with *both* teams, as she was on the Delphia team until she semi-recently hurt her ankle. She later told me the players had asked who I was, and she had told them. I figured the rumor would be that I was dating her mom. Some of our student players even joked to Selena that Demi and I looked pretty cozy together, up there in the bleachers. And then *this* rumor is texted later that same night by one of the Delphia players? And do you really think Selena went down at halftime and said this to the Delphia team, sitting on the bench?

"Picture it, gentlemen," I continued. "Selena goes down to the bench. The players ask who I am, and Selena says, 'Oh, that's my English teacher from my old school... by the way, he ate me out.'

"Now we have this rumor. Given *that* info, as they say, it doesn't take a brain surgeon to figure out what happened. So that's it, and I believe her. She has nothing to gain from spreading something like this, but this rumor-spreader on the Delphia basketball team evidently does. Look at what she has already accomplished. Here we are. Pardon my language, but that little bitch is already famous at my expense."

"So, *you* think Selena didn't say any of this at all? None of it?" Brant asked. They had clearly assumed Selena was the source.

"Of course, she didn't. Wow, is that really even in question? Think about it... it's not a good look for an 18-year-old to be messing around with a 40-year-old, married, former teacher of hers, with kids. Selena is practically pissed at *me*, like this is *my* fault. I advised her to ignore it."

"So, you've *spoken with* Selena about this?" They were every bit as surprised as I had planned for them to be.

"Gentlemen, come on. Of course I've spoken with Selena about it. I had to talk to her about it to see if she *had* said it. She didn't even know anything about it. It *wasn't* her. You guys hear everybody's business, so you know she has a kind of long-term boyfriend, right? She's ticked that the boyfriend is gonna be pissed off when *he* finds out. It wasn't her. Besides, what would she possibly stand to gain from making-up something like this? And then this basketball player starts texting the rumor that same night that they see me for the first time, at the game? The same night they asked who I was, and Selena told them? As though this Delphia player kept it to herself until right then? And then she just couldn't keep it in any longer, so she sent the text? *Come on.*"

The two men looked at each other, made the "I guess we're good here" face at each other with a nod. Then Brant wrapped it up.

"Well, like we said, we just had to address this with you by rule. There is obviously no evidence of any wrongdoing. Thank you for being so candid with us, and now we can officially deny any and all related rumors or inquiries about you and Selena, as they are clearly untrue."

And that was that. No real bad cop, I'd say. I walked out of Rick's office high on the fact that I hadn't seriously lied, didn't let myself get painted into that corner, just worked around the topic. And it was settled: all allegations were clearly false.

Don't get me wrong... I wasn't under the illusion that this was really over. It was just over *for now*. I assumed there would be more fallout. My game plan was simply to deny, deny, deny until the rumor would die. How could anyone dispute this with me? Prove me wrong.

And it's also important to note that those two men were far from knuckleheads. They were very intelligent, successful, intuitive, fair men, but this was just a tough situation from their perspective. I did not see them as my adversaries, and I wasn't punking them. I was actually trying to keep them out of the entire ordeal, just trying to tell them what they wanted to hear, needed to report, and be done with it.

They had to cover themselves and the school district by investigating the rumor, but everything in them was saying it was all bullshit, anyway. They'd seen more rumors, more drama, more fabricated and actual controversies than most people. And, on the flip side of that, they had also seen enough crazy shit actually go down and be confirmed to know they could not dismiss this situation without doing their due diligence.

Things work differently in small towns than where I'm from. Everyone knows everything about each other in small towns, have known each other for decades, and find themselves pumping gas with each other from time to time, or looking through the fresh cuts of beef at the local grocery store, or talking about the weather after church. Generations of the same families were born, grew-up, and passed-on in these towns. These things rarely happen in and around the big city or suburbs.

So even the most formal situations tend to lean toward semi-formal. Personal relationships tend to influence formal meetings like this one, and I had been able to use our growing relationships to my advantage. Along with the Assumptive Close, I was able to move directly from what we call the closing question to the assumption that I had already answered it, and it was settled. Case closed.

*For now.*

# Chapter Fifty-Seven:
# My Way

I called Selena directly after getting into my vehicle to head home. I acted like it was all a piece of cake, but I thought Selena might be catching onto me that our relationship had just started to wear me out a little. It really had taken great stamina to plan my defense for the admin, to wait patiently for a summons from them, to walk into the lion's den, and then to execute my plan and direct the very dangerous, potentially damaging conversation between us.

But I showed none of this. I played it off to Selena as though it was just another day in the life. She couldn't believe it had gone so well... she had been convinced that if the admin caught wind of the "rumor," that would be the end of us in a very bad way. I needed her to know that it still could be, so some things had to change.

"It's not game over," I explained. "It just means that now we have to modify the playbook. We've got to become more conservative, less risky. No more being seen together in public, less frequent and less lengthy meetups, and things like that. And when we park, we'll have to be extremely careful and vigilant about when and where."

I explained that now the local law enforcement would most likely be aware, as well. As far and fast as word could spread, it *had* and *would* continue to, and it wouldn't pass over anyone without touching them. So we were going to have to start changing up our routine. When we parked, we could choose the gym sometimes, but the Danverston gas station lots would work, The Gristmill (a bar and grill, also known as The Mill) parking lot down by the river in Kent, the Delphia Bowling Alley, *hell*, we could even drive 20 miles to the giant Walmart lot, where no one knew us or our vehicles.

We had options, but it was going to be more difficult and leave us with less time and freedom than before. And I reminded her that as far as I knew, my wife hadn't heard the rumors, so none of this was over just yet. And, of course, this little bitch basketball player might be just getting started.

"You think your wife will hear about it in Kent?" she asked, as though she hadn't really considered it.

"Ho-ly shit, *of course* she will, Selena," I assured her. "*Everyone* is going to hear about it. You know better than I do how all this works. All these little corn towns are strung together like a spider web at ten-minute intervals along country roads... texting chains and social media... word travels faster than it take to say it, these days. Shit, Lily probably already *does* know."

I paused to give her a chance to respond, but she didn't, so I continued.

"I'm going to tell her," I said. There was a longer, much denser pause.

"*What?* Babe-... What do you me-... are you talking about telling your *wife? Are you talking about YOU telling your wife?!*"

"Yeah, that's *exactly* what I'm talking about," I replied. "It's better that she hears it from me rather than someone else. Telling her myself allows me to control the way she hears it. I can control the narrative to our best advantage. If she hasn't already heard by the time I see her tonight, it'll be one of the first thing she hears from me. "

She was quiet again, seemingly thinking.

"So, what are you going to say? That there's a rumor going around through the local schools and towns that you serviced me, orally? That you *ate me out?*"

"Eh," I responded. "Not exactly. I'll sit her down without the boys, tell her that I have something to talk to her about, something unfortunate and upsetting for everyone involved... then I'll simply let her know that your old basketball teammates were asking questions and being stupid about me being at that game last night, that a girl you don't get along with got some stupid ideas, and now there are just whispers of some stupid rumors about you and me that she spread that same night.

"I'll tell her that I was called in to discuss it with Rick and Brant and that they're clear, it was exactly what they thought it was... a stupid-ass rumor."

"But you said *rumors, plural*. There's only one rumor, Babe."

"Well, maybe. For now,. But there will be more, so I'm going to try to circumvent having to do this the next time a rumor gets rolling. I'll just say rumors, plural."

"Okay?" she replied, and this time she waited for me to respond. I didn't bite. "So *then* what?"

"Then nothing. When she presses me, I will tell her that no one has really heard any details, just that there was something going on between you and me. No one believes it, I've spoken to you about it, you didn't start the rumors, and you're practically pissed at *me* about it, as if *I* started this shit. I'll let her know that all the adults in the room, yourself included, are just looking forward to letting shit pass under the bridge, so that is what she and I are going to do. I'll tell her that I will not be defending myself against this bullshit, and neither will she, and neither will you. That I am not asking, I am insisting. We are all going to play this *my* way. Got it?"

"Got it, Kowalski." It took me a second for that to register.

"Did you just call me-..."

"Yeah, *Kowalski*," she repeated. "You call me Vasquez when I get a little heated, so... *Kowalski*."

"You mean like that penguin from that one Disney movie?"

"*Madagascar*. DreamWorks, actually, but yeah. *Lieutenant Kowalski, Shock Unit!* He's in charge, he gives the orders, and everybody else follows him... just like you right now."

"Selena, *look*-..." I began.

"I'm not complaining, Babe. If *you* say that's the best way to handle this, then I'm good with that. I trust you. I'll follow you like you're Clint Eastwood in that *Gran Torino* movie."

"Are you fucking with me right now?"

"No. Well, yeah, actually. Clint Eastwood's name is Kowalski, too, in *Gran Torino*."

"You serious? I don't remember that."

"Walt Kowalski. That's a great fucking movie. We'll watch it sometime."

Selena wasn't as confident about my plan as I was, but it didn't matter to me. I wasn't in discussion mode, and I asked her to please just follow my lead with this. We would do it my way, and we would make it through the other side in the best possible condition... if we *didn't*, then we fucking *wouldn't*. Granted, Selena's and my relationship was going to take some damage, but by doing it my way, it wouldn't have to end us.

She agreed again that we would do this my way, then asked if she could see me that night. I told her we couldn't see each other, as I would have my hands full handling my wife at home, ensuring that all this didn't go sideways on us. I admitted that this was hard for me, too, but we would have to wait until Thursday night to maybe be together.

"Maybe? *Maybe* Thursday night? Are you fucking kidding me right now?"

"Easy, Vasquez," I urged, gently.

I told her about how Lily and Ronny had stuck around for practice and Taco Bell with Lee and I. I offered that Selena could call me at the second wrestling practice on Thursday night and, *if* Lily had gone home with Ronny, she could meet me at the bench outside the back doors of the gym, where we had first kissed. She was a little grumpy about it, not really liking the way I was dialing us back, surely not liking this bull-headed approach to everything that she'd never seen from me before, but she was happy we would at least *potentially* get to see each other.

And I'm almost certain that, deep down, where she wouldn't even admit it to herself, she liked how I took control of the situation and just handled it all. *My* way. She was intelligent, cunning, and ballsy, but I could tell she liked me taking control, liked that I was masculine enough to allow her to feel feminine. And we both knew she'd be there to handle shit full-tilt if I needed her.

The conversation with my wife went almost exactly to plan that night. She dug for details a little more than I would have preferred, but I stuck to my "We're not entertaining or pursuing this" guns, and I was happy with the end result. I wasn't able to tell her the details, I said, because I didn't know what they were. I would not ask, and I didn't want to know. None of it mattered... the best way to dispose of this bullshit was to ignore it, even laugh at it, but the best way to lend it weight was to show concern, ask questions about it. Lily considered this and me with skepticism, but she agreed that my approach made the most sense.

***

On Thursday, December 8, 2011, Q+25, the proof came at wrestling practice when my wife showed up, picked up Ronny, and the two went home after the first practice. No waiting around for Selena, as I had convinced her that Selena would be keeping her distance from me for quite some time so as to not fan the fires of the rumor mill.

Selena and I met at our bench outside the back doors to the gym. We talked, kissed, and laughed for over an hour. I stopped in three times to check on Lee at practice over that hour. We couldn't go to Taco Bell together, so Lee's second dinner ended up, to a large extent, littering the rear bench in my van.

# Chapter Fifty-Eight:
# Seeing Red

Spending that little bit of time with Selena was really nice, especially after how the week had started out. The logical side of me was dictating that she and I maintain the very specific, very strict rules that I had laid out for our own good, but the emotional side was yearning for her. We had kissed, and whispered, and laughed, and kissed. That was all – no excessive wandering hands or anything, just soaking each other up. Until she brought up Homeboy.

I had sensed that there was something she was trying to get up the nerve to talk to me about... it just seemed like she was looking for a way to approach some subject. And let me tell you, when you're in an "undefined" relationship with a young lady who you've just begun to realize the depths of your feelings for... *not* knowing what she is trying to get up the nerve to say is worrisome. Then she said something about being glad we were outside in the dark, so I couldn't see...

*"Can't see what?"* I asked. If she had a fucking hickey, I didn't know how I was going to respond. I was pretty sure I wasn't ready for that kind of shit.

"Well, Leonard and I kind of got into a little tiff."

*Oh, here we go with this motherfucker*, I thought.

I had really built-up quite a strong dislike for Homeboy, consisting of equal parts a straight up lack of respect for who he was and the fact that he was *my* girlfriend's boyfriend. Every time I pictured them spending time together, going out to do something together, her using the smartphone he got for her, the two of them... it reminded me of what it was like when I really started having feelings for my wife, but she was stringing along her boyfriend.

"What kind of tiff?" I asked.

"Oh, it wasn't really a big deal, but he was complaining that we don't see each other nearly as much as we used to. And we're not... you know, not like we used to be, *physically*. You know that he and I fight about this all the time now. I just didn't feel like talking about it. So we both got pissed. I told him to leave my house, I walked him to the door, and when he tried to kiss me goodnight..." She trailed off.

"*Yeah?*" I asked. As much as I already hated this story, I was dead set that I was going to get through it. *All* of it.

"I turned away from him so he couldn't kiss me. I was upset." She stopped again. I was getting frustrated with this stop-and-go approach to storytelling.

"*And...?*" I pushed.

"*And...* he grabbed me, hard, from behind and spun me back around. He squeezed my shoulder really hard, and he was mad, and it hurt."

*"WHAT THE FUCK?!"*

I hadn't seen this story going *there*, probably just blinded by ideas in my head of them having sex. "That motherfucker hurt you? I swear to God..." and I said some aggressive Marine shit, the specifics of which I do not exactly recall. I was seeing red. It was time for him to meet that other side of me. Then I realized what else she had said.

"So what is it you *don't* want me to see? *Did he leave marks on you?!*"

She nestled her forehead into my shoulder, and she nodded faintly. I just about lost my mind. I swore on what I was going to do when I saw that motherfucker next, and I... but she shook her head 'no.'

"No, Babe," she said quietly but firmly. "I'm okay, and he didn't mean to do it... he's never done it before. It's not like him. He's just mad because we aren't what we used to be, but he obviously doesn't know it's because of *you* or he would have brought it up. I know he's been a little suspicious that there might be someone else ever since Chicago, though."

"Well, maybe it's time he finds out that he's right. Maybe it's time he finds out about *me*," I spat out like a silverback beating his chest, but I regretted it as soon as it was said.

I was just acting like a little bitch at that point, upset about a relationship that I knew she was already in when we got together. I was forgetting my place in the big picture... *he* was the boyfriend; *I* was the side-piece. It wasn't my place to start having an opinion about her relationship. But *fuck!*

I asked her where her car was. She pointed. I told her we were going to the car so I could see it. We fussed about it back and forth, but in the end, we did go to the car. She popped on the overhead lights, which sputtered, and she pulled back the neck of her t-shirt to reveal her clavicle area. She explained that her overhead lights had a short or something, as they kept flickering, so she pulled out her new smartphone and turned on the flashlight, which flip-phones didn't have because they drained the battery too quickly.

Sure enough, right there, just below the clavicle bone and around her anterior deltoid, were four finger pad-sized bruises that kind of blurred together as though she had been lifted up by one shoulder. I was irate, but she calmed me down by promising me she would never let him get away with that again. Never. She'd cut me loose on him if he did.

"Then *tell* him that," I demanded. I didn't give a fuck if I was forgetting my place.

"Tell him *what?*"

"Tell him that *I* fucking *know*. Tell him that if he ever touches you in anger again, if he ever hurts you again... *I'm* gonna come take it out of his ass."

She agreed to tell me if anything like that ever happened again if I would agree to let her handle her boyfriend. It was a reasonable compromise, and so after a bit of cooling down, I agreed.

Later that night, after Lee and I got home and the boys were wrapped up south-of-the-border-style, I retired to my den while my wife went into the bedroom, as usual. I talked to Selena a little on the phone, and I sang her to sleep again. All the while, the idea that that motherfucker put angry hands on my girl had me strung. I didn't sleep much that night, and I just kept envisioning all of the potential scenarios where he and I would meet, and I would make that motherfucker pay.

***

By the next day, I was no better. I was still just as angry as when I first saw the marks on her front shoulder area. I had told Selena the night before that we would not be able to see each other that night (Friday, Q+26), as we absolutely *had* to stick to our new rendezvous playbook. So, during the day on that Friday, I learned via text that Homeboy was coming over to her mom's house that night.

*What are you guys up to?* I texted.

Stupid fucking question, and she kind of let me know it in a roundabout way. Like I didn't know what boyfriends and girlfriends did when they hadn't seen each other much lately, and they needed to make up after a fight. And I knew her mom would be working her night job. And they'd be on Selena's bed, right where I was that first night. The idea of it incited me, and burned in me all day and into late evening. Just thinking. About *them*.

It reminded me quite a lot of the way things had gone down with my wife and me. As mentioned, she had a boyfriend of a couple years for the first several months of our... *relationship*, let's say.

Just as with Selena, Lily had approached *me*, and I just started out as "the other guy." Then, I got emotionally involved. And just like those early days thinking about Lily and *her* Fuckstick... thinking about Selena and Homeboy that night... eventually, I just popped. After the night settled down as usual, boys tortilla-wrapped up in bed, wife sleeping in the bedroom, me at my laptop... I had to get out and burn some energy. I was absolutely seething inside.

So I notified my wife, locked up the house, and I took on a forced hump through town. A *hump* is a Marine term for a long, tough hike, usually at a rigorous pace and in full field/combat gear. If you went to Boot Camp at Marine Corps Recruit Depot – West, in San Diego, as I did, we had Camp Pendleton with its beaches and foothills to hump. They were the Pacific coastal foothills of the Santa Margarita Mountains, and the largest peaks held daunting names, such as Iron Mike, Recon Ridge, Old Smokey, The Microwave, Mount Motherfucker, and the Grim Reaper, among others. When Marines hump, *we fucking hump*.

Not ten minutes into the hump, my phone rang. It was Selena. She was alone, and she figured I'd be in my den, at the gym, or out walking. I told her how far I'd already gone.

"Wow," she said. "You're really covering some ground."

"Yup." My attitude was colder than the night air.

"Something got you all wound up tight to be moving like that, this time of night, in this weather?" It was about 15 degrees Fahrenheit, but I wasn't feeling the cold.

"Yeah. You could say that." I was trying to answer without making her feel like I was angry. But I *was* angry... not at her, just angry at the arrangement.

"Is it the bruises, still?" she asked.

With my wife, her boyfriend hadn't bruised her, but he had whipped a full toilet paper roll at her head once when they were arguing about me. It just about drove me wild to get my hands on him, but of course, there too, I was just the side-piece. This was like that, except Homeboy had actually hurt Selena.

There was something else on my mind, as well, and I didn't think I could keep it in much longer.

# Chapter Fifty-Nine:
# Howl at the Moon

I was just reaching a favorite spot of mine along the Kent-side bank of the Illinois River – a stony outcropping near the bridge where I often stopped along my late-night walks to watch the moon reflect on the water or to listen to the nighttime silence I had never known as a kid growing-up in the city.

Sometimes on weekend evenings, I would take the family to get ice cream and head down by the river to skip rocks, watch fish jump for bugs, watch gaggles of geese cross the road to feed on the green park grass, and/or watch the occasional barge navigating the channel or filling up the cargo hold with grain at the Kent grain elevator.

Although this night was pretty cold, November/December had generally been uncommonly warm that winter, and there was no ice on the river. I decided to stop there at my stony outcropping and watch the almost full moon shimmer on the water while Selena and I talked.

She asked if this aggressive hump and my wound-up mood was due to the bruises that Homeboy left on her shoulder, and I was weighing my options about what I should or shouldn't say. And then I suddenly *did* have something to say, goddammit.

A small voice in my head, almost totally drowned out by my

emotions, spoke up: *Are you sure about this?*

When I answered Selena's question about the bruises, my voice sounded like it dropped at least an octave, with a little growl to it. I had to be very emotionally charged for my growl to come out. It was a rarity for me, but when that growl rumbled... well, *something* was about to happen.

"No, Babe, it's not the bruises anymore. I mean, it is, but really, it's you and him. I don't *like* it. I know, *I know*... I'm not supposed to say that. I'm not supposed to say *anything*. I'm just the *side-piece*. I'm not supposed to give a shit. But I fucking *do*. I *do* give a shit, Selena."

I wasn't just acknowledging my jealousy. I was acknowledging the depth and weight of my feelings for her, acknowledging that this was more serious than I had bargained for. The plan had been to *not* make this too serious. We weren't *supposed* to define whatever it was, one way or another, because it was *supposed* to be carefree and fun. My plan had always been that we were going to be non-clingy and anti-possessive.

"*Awwwww, Babe...*" she sounded half genuine, half sarcastic, I couldn't tell which it was. "You're jealous. I *love* that. You *really* care about me."

"Yes, Babe, I *really* care about you. *Okay?* Don't act like you don't know it. I know we didn't try to make this thing serious or anything, but it *is* fucking serious. It is for *me*, and I know it is for *you*, too. I know you said you'd never ask me to leave my boys, which means not asking me to leave my wife, but I don't know if I can reciprocate anymore."

"Baby... what do you *mean*? I... I think I know, but what do you *mean*. Just *say* it."

"I don't want to share anymore. I'm *not gonna* share anymore."

*Holy shit, I said it. Holy shit.*

And then there was a very big, happy smile in her voice.

"Are you telling me you want me to break up with Leonard?"

"*Fuck* yeah, I am. Fuck that motherfucker!"

"Are you telling me that you want me all to yourself?"

"Come on, Babe, that's *exactly* what I'm saying. I'm red hot right now, and it's all me wanting you all to myself. *Fuck* Homeboy! I don't know how to define anything about this, but I know I want you to be *only* mine. I don't want to hear about Homeboy, anymore. *Fuck* that guy!"

"That is a bold statement, Babe. But guess what," she said. "I want *you* all to *my*self, too. I know I just told you last week that I'd never ask you to leave your wife and move out of the house where your boys live. But I have to break that promise. I want you to be *only* mine, Babe. I've wanted that, but I just couldn't ask you for it until you said you want me to break up with him. Because that's the only way I could really know for sure that you're committed to me.

"How do you think *I've* felt?" she asked. "When I think about you talking to her about your day, or making small talk over dinner, or telling her about how the boys did in the first practice, or making her breakfast in bed on Saturday morning? Don't you think that shit has been fucking with me? Thinking about everything she gets to have you for that I don't?

"I'm not trying to replace your boys," she assured me. "You don't have to leave them. You'll never really *leave* them. Like you've always said, you can live in town, father and coach them without living in that house with *her*."

And the anger in me, the tension, the emotions all balled up into giant knots in my gut and my head... it all dissipated like my breath on that frozen December night. I felt release, as though I had literally, physically dropped a great weight I was shouldering. I could even feel myself *breathe* more freely.

The two of us laughed, then, and we made fun of each other for being whipped. We didn't even talk about what we were both specifically going to do with this new knowledge, these new requests, or demands... as though we were content to simply get it out and to know how we both felt.

Eventually, she asked the question: "God, I wish you could come here right now. Can you get away tomorrow, like late morning through afternoon?"

"Shit, Babe... I don't know, I doubt it. I *want* to, but... there's nowhere we can safely park in any town in daylight. Ya know?"

"I want to take you somewhere," she divulged. "But it's a secret. A surprise. We probably only need a couple of hours."

And with that, I told her I would try. I could let her know in the morning if it was going to work out or not, but I'd try my best. I might be able to get a couple of hours. It was just that the next day was Saturday, December 10, and it was Lil's and my twelfth wedding anniversary. But Lily and I hadn't discussed doing anything as we had a wrestling tourney the next day. I figured I could try to get away for a couple hours to go to the gym, if I was home in time to take the fam to a nice earlyish dinner at a nice restaurant, as was our custom.

She was good with that. I told her she sounded extremely tired, and she opted to get off the phone and fall off to sleep. She told me she was happy that I had finally come clean with her about how I felt.

"*Finally?*" I asked.

"Yeah, *finally*. Don't play dumb. You know exactly what I mean. You didn't just figure this out... you just finally got up the balls to tell me," she laughed.

We got off the phone. Standing tall on that stony outcropping, I looked around at the world. I looked up to the waxing, growing moon, illuminated to 97% that night, raised my hands above my head, shook my fists at the sky in triumph, and let out a howl that surely caught the attention of the local dogs in town and coyotes in the timber up and down the far side of the river. I watched my breath dissipate like all my cares and felt something growing in me like that growing gibbous moon in the sky.

I headed home at a fast jog, what we Marines call "double-timing it," but my heart was triple-timing it.

# Chapter Sixty:
# Steal Away

The next day was a typical Saturday without sports. I made breakfast-in-bed for my wife, and the boys and I ate at the kitchen table. I let Lily believe that I had forgotten about our anniversary, as I didn't mention it when I delivered her breakfast in bed. The boys and I had our stupid moments and laughs at the breakfast table, sang our songs, made fun of each other, and filled our morning bellies.

I rarely did dishes, as Lily's and my arrangement had always been that I'd handle the grocery shopping and cooking/prepping the meals if she handled the cleaning, but that morning I did the dishes, and I thought about Selena, probably at home, thinking about me making Lily breakfast in bed.

Then I stopped in to see my wife. She was watching TV and finishing up her breakfast.

"So... Happy Anniversary, Lil... our twelfth..." I said.

"Yep. And sixteen together." She didn't even look at me, just looked back and forth between her toast, a bit of scrambled egg, a small square of bacon, and her show. She wasn't being a bitch, wasn't being rude or or even cold, not really. We had just been together for sixteen years, things had been different between us since the Drunken Barn Dance, and the routine of our lives typically made us both a little indifferent about our anniversary.

"So, what are you thinking?" I asked. "Do you want to throw something together? I know we have the tournament tomorrow, but do you want to head out tonight for a nice dinner with the boys, or something?"

"I don't know, Honey," she replied, turning up the TV.

She had always called me Honey, since back in the day when she first started working herself into my life. My memory tells me that the first time she called me Honey was back when we were early in our relationship, but after I'd met her family.

Her mom and younger sister Beth had shown up at my studio apartment unexpectedly, as Lily's roommate had told them where to find her. I think her mom knew about me by then, but we hadn't met, yet. They came knocking on the door, and Lily recognized her mom's voice and her sister's laugh. Meanwhile, she and I were trying to be quiet in the shower.

*"Honey, stop! Shhh... quiet..."* Now, I was still "Honey," though it had been many years since we were sweet on each other.

"Ya know," I continued as Lil took her last bite of breakfast. "We *are* pretty tight financially, with my birthday party, Christmas, wrestling season... we could hold off this year," I suggested.

"Okay," came her reply.

I walked up to the bedside and offered her an anniversary card. It had three of those stupid gimmicky coupons for favors I was to fulfill, and it had a treasure map to her real gift. It was a coupon for a pedicure/manicure at a new local establishment in town, and the treasure map would lead her all through the house, even downstairs and outside, before landing her in the boys' playroom, digging through their large toy bin.

I have to admit... I wasn't usually this thoughtful. I always *tried* to be romantic, and I had my moments, but at least in my mind, I often felt like I wasn't creative enough on occasions like this one. And yes, I do think I was probably creative for this anniversary exactly *because* I was trying to distract my wife from everything else going on all around me. I'm not proud of it.

"Okay. I'm good with that," I said. "So, since we're not going out to eat tonight, is there anything big going on today or tonight?" I asked. At that, she picked up the remote, muted the TV, and made eye contact for the first time.

"No. But I was going to see if you wanted to go with me to take the boys to Mom's for a few hours... "

I looked at her as though I was looking over my glasses, but I wasn't wearing any. Then I gave her the mixed nod/headshake with my palms out that asked *What the fuck?* without asking what the fuck. *Is she serious right now?*

"Are you serious right now?" I asked her.

"Yeah, I mean, if you didn't have anything going on."

I saw right through her invite. I knew she just wanted to keep an eye on me, that if I went with them, she wouldn't need me around.

She just wanted to keep my leash in hand. I'd end up hanging out with my father-in-law, the two of us commiserating over the things in our marriages that drove us nutty. He was very cool to hang with, and I really enjoyed time with him, but I had other plans that day.

"Lil, I'll pass. With the meet tomorrow, I gotta get in a good workout sometime today. Probably around noon, I'm thinking. Then tonight, since we're not spending big money on an expensive dinner for the fam, I think I'll spend a few bucks and get the UFC 141 fight card, maybe order out for dinner? It's John Jones vs. Lyoto Machida for the light heavyweight title, Little Nogueira is fighting Tito Ortiz, and Big Nog is fighting Frank Mir. Maybe I'll call your brother Paul and see if he's doing anything."

She looked a little upset, but it was in a way that she seemed to have anticipated. And what was she going to say... *no?* So I contacted Selena and told her we were a go. I'd be leaving my house around noon... but what was the plan? Like, what were we doing? Where should I meet her?

"What did you tell her?" Selena texted back.

*That I needed a couple hours or so for a hard workout, why?* I replied.

"I'll meet you at the gym. Park your van out where it can be seen from the main road, just in case she decides to drive by and see if you're there. We'll take my car. I told you... it's a surprise."

Okay, a surprise it would be, then. And a surprise it was.

# Chapter Sixty-One:
# To Boldly Go

When I pulled up at the gym, Selena was already there, waiting for me. I parked as she had directed and got into her car.

"Now you can settle in, Babe... kick back, relax, I got this," she said. I had assumed that her mom wasn't going to be home and that we were going to her house to fuck. But that evidently wasn't the plan, as she lived about ten or so minutes north of the gym. She wouldn't have told me to settle in for that short of a drive. So, I tried to stop wondering and did as I was told.

Before long, we were entering Fort Clark. I had been coming down to Fort Clark and the surrounding areas from Chicagoland for 16 years, and I had lived down there for about the last six. So I knew the city fairly well, and still, I could not for the life of me guess where Selena was taking me.

*She wouldn't have gotten us a hotel in Fort Clark, right? That'd be foolish, with the cheap Motel 6 that we used on my birthday right in Delphia.*

We had followed the Illinois River north on Rt. 22 into the city. She turned right onto Pomegranate Street, which I knew was taking us down to the city's impressive riverfront, with nice views of the river and bridges from a number of quality restaurants.

*Is she taking me out to eat? That's sweet.*

But just a block toward the river, she pulled a hard left into the parking lot of a mostly single-story, sand-colored, brick building. She parked.

"Do you know where we are?" she asked.

"Geographically, in the city, yes. But I don't know this specific place, no."

"Well then... you ready?" she asked, and I had felt her energy rising as we neared the place.

"Ready for what?" I asked. "Is it *this* place?"

The building and lot were pretty run down, and I didn't see any signage. Could she be taking me for a massage? Or might this be a tattoo parlor? It was too small to be a strip club in Fort Clark, and besides, she knew that wasn't really my scene.

"Yep, this is it," she confirmed. I had to laugh.

"So, correct me if I'm wrong, *buuuuuut* didn't you and I just recently agree that we shouldn't be seen together in public?" I smiled at her, reminding her how risky this was, but also making a point. "You know, with the basketball game aftermath and all the shit going around. And now you think we should walk Fort Clark streets together? Babe, *anyone* could see us here. Your friends, their parents, teachers... *everyone* around where we live goes to Fort Clark on the weekends."

"No one will see us," Selena assured me. "Just pretend like

we're invisible, or whatever you need to do to lighten up for just this once. *Trust me.*"

"*Warning! Warning, Will Robinson!*" I quipped, kind of flailing my arms, alternating, up and down. She just looked at me for a second, until I realized that of course she didn't catch the reference. "You know, *Lost in Space?*"

"Wasn't that a movie?" she asked.

"No. I mean, *yes*, it was... kind of. But before that, it was a TV show. The movie is newer, with Matt LeBlanc."

She just stared, with a face like she was worried about my mental health.

"Come on, Matt LeBlanc? Joey, from *Friends*? *How you doin?*"

"I've never seen *Friends*," Selena replied, matter-of-factly.

"What? *Never?* You've *never* seen *Friends*?"

"That's what I just said," she affirmed with more than a little attitude. "My mom watches it all the time, and she always tries to get me to watch it with her, but she never makes me. It just looks so *old*."

"So? *I'm* old, and you like *me*," I reminded her. "*I'm* so old, I have tattoos older than *you*, but *I* don't have to make you spend time with me."

"Ha-*HA!*" she sneered through a smile she couldn't help. "I guess I do like *some* old stuff."

"*Anyway,*" I ignored her, "The Italian guy on *Friends* is Matt LeBlanc, and he's in that *Lost in Space* flick you're thinking of. But way before that, it was a TV show, too, from way back before I was even born."

"You better explain that one to me on the way home," she said. She was always down for hearing about references to books, TV, movies, music, etc.

She got out of the car, and I followed suit, ignoring the alarms in my head warning *disaster*. She took my hand and led me out toward the street and onto the sidewalk. As we reached the corner, I finally saw the sign on the building just as I saw the obscure glass double doors.

*Lover's Playground* a small sign read on one of the doors.

*eXplore your curiosity* a large sign read on the overhead awning.

"No fucking way. *A sex shop, Babe?!*" I exclaimed.

Holding her hand firmly, I opened the door and pulled her inside. Laughing, she thought my eagerness to get inside was due to my excitement. In Truth, I just wanted to get us both off the street before someone saw us walking into or even just standing outside a fucking triple-X sex shop. And it was not that unthinkable. Students, teachers, parents, admin... they all really *did* regularly visit or travel through Fort Clark on the weekends. All it would take is one of them to ID one or both of us going into this place, maybe snap a photo... but I let her believe I was just excited.

And full disclosure, I *was* excited. Once we got in the door, I took a deep breath, and we looked at each other. I was almost instantly hard, and yes, it was in fact the idea that this little siren hottie had just surprised me by luring me into a sex shop. Selena was *full* of surprises.

Unlike the place's rough exterior, the inside was extremely clean and beautifully displayed. Bright lights, neons, striking colors, displays, even glasswork and carpentry... if you didn't look too closely, it really looked like an amazing toy store or candy shop. In fact, when you *did* look closely, you found that it really *was* a combination of an amazing toy store and candy shop.

Looking around, there were only a couple of potential customers and one attendant inside. I instantly noted that I knew no one, and no one had looked up as we entered. That was good. Behind the checkout counter, there was a smoking hot 20-something blonde in a revealing black spandex mini-dress and heels, makeup and hair done to the nines. Provocative, yet elegant. She motioned us over. Selena looked at me kind of cautiously, so I led the way.

The clerk just wanted to scan our state IDs. She explained that everyone entering at any age had to have their state ID scanned to discourage shoplifters and minors. I kept looking directly at the clerk, waiting for her to notice the age difference between Selena and I, for her to make what would become known in *my* world as "that face." But she never did. She just looked at us both, handed back our IDs, politely encouraged us to notify her if we needed her for any reason, then went back to reading her book.

I took note of the book she was reading, *Steve Jobs* by Walter Isaacson, which had just come out like a month earlier. Steve Jobs had just died about two months earlier.

*Interesting book choice*, I thought. *We're here checking out porn, and this girl could be in the industry, and she's reading a biography of Steve Jobs. Watch, she ends up changing the World someday. Respect.*

# Chapter Sixty-Two:
# A Different Kind of Ring

For the better part of an hour, Selena and I enjoyed taking our time, walking through this wonderful world of intimacy. We mostly skipped the magazines. We commented on this video cover and that, often laughing at the titles: *Forrest Hump, The Sperminator, The Domi-Matrix, Saving Ryan's Privates, Good Will Humping, Pulp Friction, Intercourse with a Vampire, Porn Star Trek (the quote on the cover read "To Boldly Blow")* ... and *Frosted in Space!*

I started laughing, but caught myself, choked it down, and looked around. One customer and the hottie behind the counter were both looking at me, then went back to their business. Selena was looking at me like a mother scolding her little kid, her face saying it all: *"Don't make me take you out to the car!"*

I quickly explained that *Frosted in Space* was a play on *Lost in Space*, the show I had just alluded to before we got out of the car. She picked up the DVD case, looked it over, then put it back, smiling.

"Now you *have* to explain this show to me on the way home."

We spent a good deal of time in the bachelor/bachelorette/gag gifts area. Likewise, we spent some time looking at and pondering the S&M/Bondage section. There were sexual edibles, games, themed lingerie, costumes, toys/vibrators... you know, the usual stuff... *so I'm told.* Which brought me to the question.

"This is some crazy fun shit, Babe," I whispered. "I never

would have guessed we were doing something like this. In my 40-year rollercoaster, jungle gym life, this is something I've never done with any partner. I mean, Lilith and I used to go to a video store in college that had one of those separate porn rooms behind a black curtain, and one time we took a quick walk through it, but we exited just as fast because we couldn't stop laughing. But never a full-blown XXX shop, pardon the pun. So, I gotta ask... like, what made you *think* of this place?" Without a beat, she answered plainly.

"We're getting a cock ring." (sustained eye contact, easily ten seconds)

(finally, nervous laughter from me)

Me: "You serious?"

Selena (hushed laughing): "Fuckin' right, I'm serious. You ever tried one? They have some with built-in mini vibrators."

Me: "And so, um... I feel compelled to ask... *how* do you know this?"

"Oh, I've never used one... never even actually *seen* one until now, but you know, girls talk. I saw some over there... I had seen them... I found them fascinating, though I hadn't picked one up or examined them *too* closely.

***

On the way home, I did my best to explain the old TV show from my childhood, *Lost in Space*. She had some questions, but by the time we got back to her mom's place, she pretty much understood the show's appeal to a young kid in the late 1970s. She asked if they had color TV shows way back then, and I said yes and no. The first season was shot in black and white for sure, but that was before my time, back in the '60s. Then maybe the second or third season it went to color.

"You are seriously a dinosaur," she said, smiling her punky smile. I didn't miss a beat.

"Yeah, well, this sexual T-Rex is on the hunt, and I'm on the trail of that tail."

At that point, we were just pulling off of Route 22, turning in toward the river on a small gravel road I had never been on before. Off to my right, almost overgrown by weeds, I saw a weathered wooden sign that said *Nysa*, and I had to ask Selena what that was.

"Oh," Selena replied, "That's just the name of this small area of homes along the water, kind of like a neighborhood name. They call this place *Nysa*."

The name rang a bell with me, but I couldn't place it.

Just minutes later, we were at her house trying out our new toy. It was alright, did everything it was supposed to do, but she preferred to lose it. I kind of liked it, but if she didn't, I didn't. So we never used it again. After that once, "cock ring" became just another inside joke in our joke bank.

As she was dropping me off at the gym to end our date, I had to let Selena know that we had to cherish the day we had just spent together. We were going to have fewer and fewer escapes together, and something like what we did that day would maybe never be possible again. As though she hadn't heard a single word I'd just said, she asked if I'd take her with me to the boys' wrestling tournament the next day.

*It's right here in Fort Clark, again, so it wouldn't be weird for me to go,* she claimed, and I kind of felt like there was a little voodoo in her words.

# Chapter Sixty-Three:
# No Easy Way Out

"Are you fucking high?" I asked. "You wanna go with me to the meet? Maybe your mom was right about you being on drugs."

She gave me the glare I was looking for, and I kissed her. She blushed and smiled.

I told her that she couldn't *possibly* go to that tournament. After everything we had dealt with in the past week, *of course* it would be weird. In fact, we couldn't see each other very often in the upcoming weeks, so we had to cherry-pick our meetings, as we really did have to sacrifice our time together for the safety of ensuring it could go on as long as we wanted it to.

If we were ever discovered, or even if there were continued rumors about us due to our own lack of discretion, it would most likely incur devastating consequences, despite the lack of doing anything illegal. I stressed, yet again, that justice was in no way promised. In those small, rural areas, public opinion often ruled the day. If they *wanted* me guilty of something illegal... you fill in the blank, blah-blah-blah. If they *wanted* to punish me for some social taboo, you fill in the blank, yadda-yadda-yadda. She understood, but she said she didn't have to like it. It wasn't fair.

And I understood that.

***

I was home by late afternoon, and I contacted my wife to tell her so. She and the boys were at her mom's. Lily informed me that her brother Paul was having the UFC 141 fight card pay-per-view at his place, and I was invited to join them. Lil was going to stay at her mom's for most of the night, so I decided to join the guys' night of fights.

About ten o'clock or so, at the fights with the guys, Selena called me. Although I knew I was being paranoid, I could not help but feel like the guys were suspicious of something when I went outside to take the call. Selena tried to get me to slip away and meet her.

I was cautious. Had Lily told her brother of her suspicions? Had he told his friends? Had someone heard about the rumor?

These were a group of guys that I had known peripherally for many years, since they were in high school, and I had bought them alcohol on more than one occasion, years earlier. I knew them each to differing degrees, but surely neither Lil nor her brother would have said anything to anyone else, right? I hoped not.

"Who was that?" one of the guys asked when I came back inside from the call. My brother-in-law walked in from the kitchen, and they were all looking at me now.

"Oh, just my little bro. Wanted to know if I was watching the fights."

"Seemed pretty important... or private," somebody added. Had he just looked around at the others before he finished his thought?

"You were out there for quite a minute," said another.

"*Every* call from my little bro is important," I replied, my tone adding that it was none of their business. "And *private*, thank you."

***

### *Facebook* Post: December 11, 2011

So proud of my two little men today! Lee defeated two opponents to take second place and Ronny! Ronny had only his second-ever tournament, and he also beat two of his opponents to take second place! Great work, boys! Daddy is super proud of you both!

The next day's tournament was a blast, as always, but relatively uneventful. My wife was pretty cold toward me since the night before, and we didn't really talk much about anything.

Part way through the tourney, I had told Lily who won the UFC fights the night before, and how. I made some guesses about what the night's wins and losses meant for each weight division, who would probably fight whom next, what the overall rankings and pound-for-pound rankings would most likely look like. I told her it had been good to hang with her brother and his friends. And then after Ronny's second match and before Lee's third, she took me into the high school lunchroom for privacy. I knew generally what was coming... part of me had been waiting for it.

She laid into me pretty heavily and asked me some pointed questions about my workout the day before. What muscle groups did I work? Did I lift heavy? Was anyone around to spot me? I shot back that she should just go ahead and say what she wanted to say.

"What is this, Lil? This sounds a lot like last week," I said. "You pull me aside, start off talking *around* whatever it is you *really* want to talk about, and then you get to it. So *get* to it... (clearing my throat and getting into character with an over-the-top sarcastic character voice) Gee, babe, my workout was juuuust *great!* I lifted *very* heavy. There were spotters ga-*lore!* Why do you ask?"

She wasn't amused. Still without getting to the real point, she pondered aloud how I had worked out for over three hours the day before, yet I had not complained about being muscle sore even once that day.

She was right. Clever. I *always* complained when I was muscle sore; admittedly, it was part of the little bitch in me. She wondered *how* and *why* that could have been. How had I had a long, brutal workout... but had no complaints about being sore? I lost my patience more quickly than I would have liked, sarcasm thick.

"Gee, babe, I dunno. But ya know, I wonder, too, how a 40-year-old man could be fucking an 18-year-old for over three hours and not be complaining about being sore the next day? I bet *that'd* be a *real* workout."

It was said. It couldn't be unsaid. The look of indignation grew on her face, and the mounting fury inside her boiled up and over.

"God*damm*it, Liam! What the *fuck*?! Why does it have to *be* like this? I *know* what the fuck is going on, and then you turn it all around and make *me* feel like I'm crazy! *I know what's going on!*"

"*What*, then?" I asked, point blank. "*What* is going on, Lil? You're all over the map. You asked Selena to take me to a movie just last weekend so you could set up for my surprise party. Then you accused me of this bullshit *the very next day*. I get invited to a basketball game by Selena's mom the day after that, some stupid bullshit rumors start floating around, and days later, here we are again with you accusing me. What the *fuck*? Whose team are you on? You just asked me what's up, and then before I could even respond, you *tell* me what's up. What the *fuck*, Lil?"

She was crying now, and I felt truly bad about all of it. I hated this deception shit, but I was stuck. I almost wished she would just put all the puzzle pieces together, acquire the evidence to prove it, or just make a decision about what she was going to do about it based simply off of her suspicions. I didn't like any of this sneaking around shit.

I did not want to hurt her. I did not want to make her feel crazy. She was wrong about that, but I understood why she thought I wanted that. Because in her mind, *she* was at the center of all this while, in reality, it wasn't about her at all. She had disqualified herself from having a stake in this a long time ago.

And what was I to do? I couldn't call it all off with Selena at that point. No fucking way! I couldn't just say, *Yes, Babe, you're right, Babe.* I couldn't just admit to everything that had been going on. My wife and I had gotten ourselves into this very dicey situation, and there would be no good or easy way out of it.

It was at that wrestling tournament that I really began to realize the Truth. There was *never* going to be a way out of all of this. It was either going to have to morph into something new or explode. Either way, there was going to be much more turbulence, more arguing, more fighting, more crying. And the only absolute in any of it was that it would have to happen with the least amount of child involvement possible.

No matter what, those two boys would always be the two Truest loves of my life. I could sacrifice just about anything else in the world, but not my relationship with them. But I knew that living in that house with my boys might have been the biggest risk to maintaining my relationship with them. Let me say that again: living in that house with my boys might have been the biggest risk to maintaining my relationship with them.

Even if I *could* end things with Selena right at that moment, there was no road to redemption between their mom and me. There had been years of opportunity for her to even *attempt* some shred of reconciliation between us, but that time was long over. I had barely managed some semblance of Peace in that house with her until lately – and *I* had achieved that Peace! *Me!* – and it had run its course. I had nothing left to compromise. The end almost *had* to be near.

# Epilogue:
# The Dani Project, Revisited

I think that's all I've got in me right now. I know that it would be unfair of me to leave this story as it is, so I will be taking a little break, and then I'll get to work on the next installment. Admittedly, working on this project does take a significant toll on me. It wears me out. And it's not the *writing* that kicks my ass – it's the *time travel* of it. Going back and reliving all of this almost moment-by-moment, breath-by-breath... it can be extremely taxing.

It's almost as if I'm physically back there again, trying to cope with that version of my wife. Back there with those two little boys, grocery shopping for them, cooking for them, tucking them in just the right way, squeezing them with hugs, coaching, raising the little tykes.

Back there with Selena, holding her, talking with her, laughing with her. Losing her. Regaining her.

Back there in that office with Mr. Lincoln and Mr. Beckett, listening to their concerns, finding ways to manipulate the discussion, trying to keep my relationship with Selena a private matter and my job secure.

Reliving all this and so much more is just *a lot*. It's *difficult*, it is *work*, and that just seems to be part of the nature of time travel. Because we have to do all of the work ourselves, and we have to rely on memory, because there are no time machines.

SPOILER ALERT: In the novel *The Time Machine* by H.G.

Wells, the protagonist (known simply as "the Time Traveler") disappears at the end. The Narrator never finds out *where* he goes, to *when* he goes, or *why* the Time Traveler goes, but he hypothesizes that maybe the Time Traveler went here or there, to this time or that. But I wonder – was the pressure of time travel too much for him? Did he run to a Peaceful place and time to hide as a reprieve from the toll of all he had experienced across time?

And then I think of *my own* time travel being a visit not just into *the* past, but into so much of *my own* past... and it's all right there in front of me, from a dozen years ago, in my face, and I *relive* it. There are memories I'm revisiting that leave me upset (like recounting how Lily and I went wrong), or emotional (like all the memories about my little boys) or hurt (like revisiting days with my father and the loss of him). Dani is convinced this is all worth the cost, but honestly, sometimes I have to wonder.

And Dani is very pleased with my progress, of course – not just because we're publishing these accounts now, but because she and I are examining how all this relates to the issues I still carry from that time. She feels that we are building up to something very significant in my mental health journey, and she'd like me to continue this exercise until we discover it. She's even kicking around the idea of writing a paper on me and this exercise. Imagine that – Dani writing about me *writing about me*. Lol!

I don't ever mention it to Dani – and I can bitch about it all I want – but at this point, despite the toll all of this takes, I'd continue writing this out even if she told me we were finished, that we'd accomplished the goals and reached our culminating objective. That we were *done*. I know I'm not done.

I'd continue writing this even if *none* of it were *ever* to get published, even if no one *ever* read it. At this point, I'd continue writing this just for *me* because when I write, my spider-senses tingle not in warning but in *welcome*. In *invitation*. They tingle as if something in me – something unfinished and hidden – *needs* to be uncovered.

A Truth? A lesson? So yeah, I'm sure Dani is right about all this and about me. And I'm sure she's right that this is worth it. At this point, I will keep writing to discover whatever I'm supposed to learn. And, of course, Reader, you are welcome to join me when it's time to delve back into the chaos. *And* the garden.

## **<u>Note from PD McNulty</u>**

Thank you for reading *Sunsets Behind Us*, Book Two: *Somewhen*. Cal and I hope you enjoyed it! Told you the story really takes off with Book Two! Please keep an eye out for the next book in the *SBU* series, *Chaos & The Garden*.

And if you enjoyed this second book, I'd be honored if you were to leave a review on *Amazon*. Many people look to *Amazon* reviews to help guide their reading choices, and I'd just love for more people to give Cal's story a chance. Thank you!

## About The Author

Medically retired U.S. Marine P.D. McNulty wrote and illustrated his first book in second grade as a Mother's Day gift. In eighth grade, he followed that initial effort by winning the Illinois Young Author's Contest with *Love Story*, a book of poetry. He enjoys physical fitness, nutrition, and attending stand-up comedy events. He also enjoys writing character-driven, edgy fiction that explores the unique turmoil of human adversities. Probably the best interaction with a Reader would be a discussion about any of the countless religious, mythological, cultural, and/or historical allusions built into these books and the meaning or flavor each allusion adds to the stories. His first trilogy of the *Sunsets Behind Us (SBU)* series includes *The Taboo Prophecy, Somewhen,* and *Chaos and the Garden*. P.D. McNulty lives in the Chicago area where he currently enjoys writing the next trilogy of the *SBU* series.

# Author Contacts

Say Hello!

If you haven't already done so, send PD McNulty a friendly hello email to join the *Sunsets Behind Us* email group for correspondence, updates, releases, and extras at pdmcnulty.author@gmail.com.

Follow him on social media at:

*Facebook*: https://www.facebook.com/pd.mcnulty.author

*Instagram*: https://www.instagram.com/pdmcnulty_author

*TikTok*: https://tiktok.com/@pd_mcnulty_author

*Threads*: https://threads.net/@pdmcnulty_author

*Twitter/X*: https://twitter.com/pdmcnulty

**PD McNulty Website:** www.pdmcnulty.com